**Katie Groom**
Rising Moon



**Published by:** Cinnabar Moth Publishing LLC
Santa Fe, New Mexico

**Cover Design by:** Ira Geneve

**ISBN-13:** 978-1-962308-18-2
Library of Congress Control Number: 2024935797

# Rising Moon

KATIE GROOM

# HUGH

Visibly, yet quietly, annoyed, Hugh stood with his arms folded over his chest and a deep frown on his face. Still, this was his duty. Hugh held his place just off of the stage in the center of Nightbrooke.

The stage. That's all it was, in his opinion. Everyone avoided even stepping on it when it was empty. Not out of respect, but out of fear. The only performances ever held on this stage were to overflow those who traveled through the underground world, secret from all mortals, with the certainty that if they put one toe——one hair, one breath—out of line, they would be punished.

This place—Nightbrooke; Tenatoria; El Reino Mágico—whatever it was called where that particular inhabitant was originally from—was intended to be a sanctuary for supernatural beings. It was supposed to be a safe place where they could be whatever they were without having to hide it. But this stage showed that this wasn't sanctuary for everyone.

The only people who wanted to be on that stage were Hugh's fellow council leaders. He had no desire to ever step foot on those ancient wooden boards, held together by even more ancient magic.

That's why he hung off to the side. The others, however, relished these moments. Anything to see the fear in the eyes of the people they felt were a lower status than them.

Reon, King of the Abyss—the man who thought he was the King of Everything—was babbling on and on about the alleged crimes that the person before him had committed. He stood proudly on those wooden boards holding a scroll. He was nearly floating above the boards with joy. Hugh could hear Reon's flutter from where he stood.

The difference between the two of them was a constant tension on the Council. They debated on opposite sides of every decision, to the point where Reon asked if Hugh was opposing him intentionally and just for the sake of being contentious.

Hugh couldn't help but feel like their world—the secret underground world that the supernatural beings could (allegedly) go to for safety and peace, notwithstanding the occasional pub brawl—was stuck in a time so ancient that it predated his own life. He blamed a good deal of this on Reon and his reluctance to change and advance.

The entire thing would have been comical, if it hadn't been so sad.

The scroll that Reon held looked like it was made of human skin. Hugh wondered how many of these he actually had because it was something he held at every one of these *trials*. Or did he just make up the contents on the page and continue to use the same one that he had for centuries? He had done this so long and so many times, it wouldn't have surprised Hugh if Reon had the words memorized and made up the charges on the spot.

This person's crime—this time it was a vampire—was creating too many vampires in one year. The max was 12 a year per vampire, and this particular vampire had made 13. Once. This vampire had never created any vampires before or since—at least ones that were registered. Because Reon couldn't confirm that 100 percent of the vampires created had been registered properly, that was enough to charge this one with a major crime.

The vampire had successfully evaded capture for years, living in the shadows where no one could find them. Until the right bounty hunter caught up with them. The bounty hunter known to the council as the Baba Yago, since most of the criminals were found hiding in the woods and came wrapped in an enchanted vine to prevent escape.

Hugh was the only one who knew exactly who that bounty hunter was. Carefully covered from head to toe to conceal their identity, there was one thing—beyond the vine—that gave his identity away to Hugh.

His posture.

Hugh knew the man too well. In fact, he had been at his own home many times—more often in recent months. It was Silas—a warlock who drew his powers from shadows and could travel across the world in an instant. Fugitives were no match for him, because if they tried to run, he just teleported in front of them, then secured them with that magic vine, which answered only to him. They couldn't break free, no matter how hard they tried or how powerful they were. Some of the other bounty hunters felt that it was cheating; the ones that didn't care about hiding their identity would vocalize their distaste after every poor-excuse-for-a-trial. The Baba Yago was taking the financial rewards that could be theirs if he didn't have a special weapon.

Others—non-bounty hunters—would join in, of course, as if they knew anything about the job. They would back up the other bounty hunters that they had become fans of. They were armed with statistics and facts (most of the time, made up or twisted to fit their narrative) about why using the vine was manipulative of the system.

That rope didn't bother Hugh, though. It was smart to have a tool that could keep your income source where you could see it.

It was that ability to travel anywhere that really annoyed Hugh. Not because he felt it was cheating. Not because he wished he could have the power. And not even because he felt Silas, if he was working with others, could get himself to safety when everyone else was in a bind, leaving the others to fend for themselves. No. It had nothing to do with the work of the Baba Yago, and, even more than that, it just wasn't Silas's character. Silas would put himself in danger for those he cared about before he would even consider bailing. It actually pained Hugh how much of a good guy Silas was. At times, he was good to a fault.

The reason that Hugh was annoyed by this ability to travel anywhere in a moment's notice was actually pretty simple. It was because when Silas came to his home, it was typically with the plan to take Zoie on some romantic date—and that could mean anywhere in the world. She had once told him that she wanted to go to Disneyland Paris, and later that night, she came home with mouse ears and memorabilia, some of which had writing in French on it. Another time, she was in the mood for ramen, and the only complaint that Zoie had when he dropped her off at the doorstep was that she wasn't gathering stamps in her passport with the way that they traveled.

Hugh was jealous. Very jealous. He had agreed to an open relationship with Zoie, knowing that it would make her feel happy and remove some stress and pressure that she had felt in her previous relationships. And, for the most part, it was working. The part that wasn't working was his ability to separate her feelings for Silas from her feelings for him. That it didn't mean that she loved him any less, but just that she had the capacity to love very big. The phrase "She just has a huge capacity to love" was so constant at times that it had become a mantra in his head.

And even though it wasn't a competition, per se, Hugh just felt that he couldn't hold a candle to impromptu trips to Dubai, Seoul, or even Hobbiton in New Zealand. All Hugh could give Zoie was his love and his time—and he had plenty of both to give to her— but he still questioned whether it was enough. Still, that said more about Hugh's self-confidence than about Zoie's love for him.

There was no time to concentrate on that, though. Hugh had to pay attention. He had to concentrate on the spell that the three witches would use to bind the vampire to gargoyle form. This was the fourth time he would be watching this spell in as many months, and so far, all he could tell was that the Sun Witch would isolate one beam of sunlight—a feat that was seemingly impossible. Still, they knew that this was one piece, and it was one piece more than they had before.

This time, he was concentrating on the Earth Witch and the way that she would kick up the dirt. He had been trying to memorize the pattern. Due to his life as a werewolf, his sight was far superior to most, so he was able to see the dust particles move and dance, but there was so much going on in the moments leading up to imprisonment that he would get distracted and miss something.

Hugh noticed the Sun Witch holding her palm face up, which meant that the spell was about to begin. As the dirt began to kick up, something else actually caught his eye—and he couldn't believe that he hadn't noticed it before.

While the audience of peers was watching the dirt kick up,

there was some misdirection occurring. Behind the wall of dirt, the beam of sunlight was not actually being draw down from the sky but actually sent upwards—it had happened too quickly for him to notice the true direction before. Hugh made a mental note to tell Zoie of the new information; she had been trying to figure out how to draw a single beam of light from the sun for months.

Since he had already missed a good bit of the dirt pattern, he decided to concentrate on the Moon Witch. He had thought that she was drawing water from nearby sources, but when he looked more closely, he realized that she was, actually, withdrawing the water from the prisoner while simultaneously ensuring that any water that was erroneously drawn from Reon or anyone else on that stage, due to their being so close to the prisoner, was being replaced.

The dirt was mostly a misdirection. It was a curtain. But it was also something more.

As it spun around the prisoner, everything happened behind the scenes, and no one would see unless they were not only behind it but also paying close enough attention. The dirt was fusing to the body of the victim. The dirt was building the stone.

"So stupid," Hugh mumbled about himself.

The vampire, completely not ironically named Vlad, turned to him. "Hmm?"

Quickly thinking, Hugh replied, "It's just so stupid. Why didn't he just follow the rules? As if all of us don't know what to expect if we don't." He motioned his hand towards the gargoyle that was being revealed to the bystanders as the dirt and dust settled. Hugh didn't mind lying to members of the Council if it meant getting towards his final goal. The entire lot of them were deeply conservative, as far as supernatural beings go. Purists, more or less, and he barely respected any of them. Vlad was the one that he thought the most highly of, but it was a low bar.

Vlad frowned. "It is a shame. If they just did as told, followed the laws, and knew their place, we wouldn't need to do this." He clicked his tongue three times, making a *tsk tsk tsk* sound. "I really hate punishing my own kind, but what's done must be done." He shook his head sadly.

The entire Council, besides Hugh, turned to leave. Hugh, however, watched the bounty hunter walk away and dip into shadows, and then he turned his attention to the gargoyle. Figuring out what happened to the gargoyles once they were created was vital to freeing them from the solitary confinement of their dark prisons. All the magic in the world couldn't free them if they couldn't be found.

The faeries—about two dozen of them—gathered around the large block of stone. The strength of faeries always astounded him. A gargoyle, depending on the being that it was imprisoning, could weigh upwards of a ton, and these little firecrackers were usually no more than a few feet in height.

Faeries were tiny in stature, and their small bone structure meant they were never more than 35 pounds in weight. They seemed childlike to humans, but supernatural beings could see the age in their faces.

They lifted the gargoyle with ease and started off towards the dark forest on the outskirts of Nightbrooke. Their footsteps were in unison, as if they were trained to march in step, but they didn't make a sound. Faeries were notoriously sneaky—even better at staying quietly hidden than Hugh himself. In fact, the administrative assistant at the Council headquarters had scared him a few times by sneaking up on him.

The faeries continued to march forward, each of them looking miserable. They looked so tired and malnourished that it was a wonder that they were still alive. They weren't even close to reaching the 35-pound threshold of a faerie; most of them were lucky to weigh more than just their bones and skin. Not a single one of them had the sparkle in their cheeks like the faeries who worked for the Council, for example. In fact, they looked more grey than anything else. Grey like the mist that clouded the floor of the forest that day.

There were rules against going too far into the forest. In fact, the forest itself would attack any intruders. As it so happened, when Silas killed the former werewolf councilman's father, Jack, about six months prior, everyone just assumed that Jack had wandered too far into the forest, especially based upon how Silas actually killed him. He had used the trees to complete the job. It was the perfect cover.

Hugh knew what had really happened, and the other council members each had their own theories—most of which involved Hugh directly, but they couldn't prove any of it. The only thing he had been involved in was directing the coverup. Still, even more importantly to Hugh, they couldn't tie Zoie to Jack's demise, even though she had been directly involved.

As Hugh stealthily followed the faeries deeper into the forest, his theory that the gargoyle prison was the reason the forest was bewitched was all but confirmed. The further they went into the forest, the darker—and creepier—the forest got. The mist got thicker, and the branches on the trees somehow had less leaves, but they still created a canopy, blocking most of the light from getting through. It didn't matter, though, how little light there was. Hugh's werewolf vision permitted him to see during the darkest of nights.

The faeries stopped suddenly. Not a word—not a command—

was given. They all halted as if they had a hive mind. The entire lot of them turned towards where Hugh was hidden behind a tree.

"You shouldn't be here," one of them hissed. His voice was harsh, as if he was battling the worst sore throat ever diagnosed in the history of the world, and the sore throat sounded as if it was the byproduct of 300 years of smoking four packs of cigarettes a day. His stringy purple hair stuck to his face and caught in the deep lines around his mouth and in his forehead.

As Hugh prepared to step out of the shadows, a tree branch snapped, and he heard a familiar voice. "Why not?" Out of the shadows on the other side of the worn path stepped Silas, unmasked but still dressed in all black. Silas's dark hair was a mess from being pressed down, but he ran his hands through it a few times and it was then sticking out in all different directions.

Another one angrily yelled, "No one should be here!" Her sharp teeth sparkled—the only part of her that wasn't grey and brittle. One false move, and she would quickly sink her teeth into Silas, pumping deadly venom through his veins.

He held his hands out, showing that he was not a threat. "I just want to see where they go…" Silas hesitated and then cautiously stated, "I'm the bounty hunter that bought in this prisoner."

The first faerie that spoke first hissed again. "That is not the agreement. That is not the way things are done." He narrowed his eyes at Silas, and his dull purple hair rose from his face, taking the shape of spikes, ready to be launched.

"I want to know that my prisoners are treated with respect," Silas quickly added, "Section 4, subsection 3, item b: All prisoners will be humanely cared for."

The faerie laughed, a hint of wheeze in his breath. "What part of any of this is humane, Baba Yago?"

A small faerie on the other side of the gargoyle spoke as if her voice were made of chimes, "We can feel their fear when we touch them. Their pain. Their loneliness. This prisoner is terrified." Her voice had a slight shake in it, as if she was crying along with the victim inside the gargoyle. She was the only one of them who wasn't mostly grey. She had a faint sparkle to her cheeks. Her green hair still had light to it—the curls still had bounce.

"Shut it, Beagan!" The first faerie shot her a look of pure disgust. There was an order to things. Implied or explicit, the other faerie had stepped out of line.

Silas took another cautious step towards them. "Why are you tasked to carry them?"

Beagan spoke up again. "Faeries of our status are given the worst jobs. We don't have a voice…" The first faerie started to cut her off again. "No! No, Drusus! Maybe he can help."

"He's on their side," another frowned. "Otherwise, he wouldn't bring them prisoners." As Silas moved to take another step, the faerie lifted his hand and spikes made of sparkles floated in front of this fingertips; his purple hair became more sharp and took aim. "Not other step, Bounty Hunter."

Silas took a step back. "Bounty Hunter is my job; it's not who I am." Keeping his hands up, he explained, "My name is Silas. I'm a warlock, and, yes, I am a bounty hunter, but Beagan is right. I want to help." He calmly added, "I want to end this tyranny. I want change."

"Pfft." Drusus rolled his eyes. "Why? You'd lose your job." Valid point.

Silas nodded. "Yes, I would. But I don't want to do this. This isn't my calling in life."

"Then quit."

"But if I did, someone else would just do it." He explained, "If

I do this from the inside—bring this tyranny down—I can help change more than just the many who are wrongfully imprisoned."

The faerie with the spikes narrowed their eyes. "What do you mean 'from the inside'?"

Hugh took a deep breath and stepped out from behind the tree that gave him cover a few yards back. "He means that he has my help." This was a bold move, exposing that he had motives against those of the Council.

The faeries all dropped the gargoyle and bowed. The sparkly spikes fell to the ground and chimed as they knocked into one another. A few moments later, they turned to dust and the wind took the remains away.

"No." Hugh waved his hands. "You don't have to do that here." He had a strong distaste for the image that the council members were some sort of royalty. Hugh was no king, and he never wanted to be. He was uncomfortable when people bowed to him.

Beagan stood up slowly. "Do you mean that you want to stop them from creating more gargoyles? They will just find something else for us to do. Something awful."

Hugh knelt down on both of his knees in front of her, sitting on his feet. "That's part of it. I want to change the laws—repeal many of them." Beagan went to speak again, but he smiled gently at her and she closed her mouth. "And you won't have to do the jobs that you don't want to do." He added, "If I could get my ideal result, you would have someone on the council to represent your interests, as well."

The group of them huddled together, taking turns peeking out and watching Silas and Hugh to ensure that this wasn't some sort of elaborate trick to attack them.

These faeries seemed to lack trust in anyone or anything, and, seeing what they were relegated to for work and the rags they wore as clothes were just a few indications of why. The raw, red skin on their ankles and wrists indicated that when they weren't working, they were kept in bondage. No one had been watching them as they did their job, which meant that whomever held the power over their heads was feared beyond a normal prisoner and warden relationship. There was something much darker at work here.

Drusus skeptically asked, "What do you need from us?" They were considering helping the cause, and Hugh believed that if he could win their favor, it would be a great advantage.

Hugh nodded in acknowledgment of his question. "Well, sir, I don't know everything that I may need, but I know a start is seeing where these gargoyles are kept and, potentially, gaining access to them as needed."

Drusus let out a sigh. "The path to the gargoyles—we can provide that—one time only. It is too risky to show you repeatedly. Access is not our choice."

"Whose choice is it?" Silas asked.

Beagan frowned. "The Keeper of the Keys. He's a scary, scary man that is miserable because his punishment is to guard the gargoyles." She added, "For eternity." She shuddered.

"Well, I want to meet him. Can you get me an introduction?" Hugh requested.

Beagan looked at the others and then back at Hugh. "Yes. Follow us—but stay out of sight. Usually no one is down here, but if you've been able to follow us, another council member may have been able to."

Silas and Hugh fell behind a bit and walked together. Silas quietly asked him, "Why didn't the forest attack us?"

Hugh pointed to the black circle on his forearm. "I'm protected, and so are the faeries." He looked Silas up and down. "Not sure why you were protected." Silas was nothing special, so it was a mystery to Hugh as to what kept him safe. That was a mystery for another time—a time far, far, far in the future. So far in the future that Hugh would hopefully forget about it. Silas was proving useful in this situation, but Hugh still didn't like him.

Beagan turned around and quietly ordered, "Be quiet, you two. We're approaching the Gargoyle Graveyard." The fact that it was considered a graveyard, rather than a prison, was more ominous than Hugh had anticipated.

The edge of the forest appeared abruptly and then a large field of patchy, grey grass with thick fog laying over it came into view. The air was still. It felt heavy and thick with the faint stench of death hanging in the air. Hugh had been around vampires that smelled more pleasant than this.

Silas and Hugh looked at each other, and, as soon as Hugh's eyes started to glow yellow, Silas pulled some energy from the shadows. They had no idea about what they might face as they stepped out of the forest; this was farther than anyone had ever been known to venture from town—well, besides these faeries, anyone who had survived. The two of them nodded at each other and stepped into the clearing.

The faeries were gaining distance as they ran through the field, clearing the fog and leaving a brief path for a moment as they made their way through. The fog was like a zipper, coming together almost mechanically once the faeries got through that space.

Hugh and Silas slowly started to make their way through the first few yards of grey, waist-high grass. Silas had it more difficult because he was a nearly a foot shorter than Hugh. While Hugh was worried about a misstep causing him to get sucked down into marsh, Silas was using the darkness to push the grass out of his way. For Silas, there was likely no place on the planet that had more places for him to draw his power from. The warlock likely felt invincible in those moments.

Silas was able to make enough of a path in front of him. "Now isn't the time to be cautious, Hugh," he suggested. He made the path wider so they could both have a clear sight as to where they were going.

"Agreed." They both took off running to catch up with the faeries. It didn't take long with Hugh's speed and long strides. Silas was quick as well, but Hugh did question to himself why Silas didn't just teleport over. Why waste the energy to run?

The ground was rocky and spiky where the grass wasn't growing—in fact, Hugh wasn't sure that the grey grass was actually growing or alive at all. It just *was*. It was almost as if the plants would turn to ash if someone breathed on them the wrong way.

The sporadic puddles of water, if that's what it actually was, were completely black and reflected nothing. At first, Hugh thought that it was just the angle that he was looking at the puddles, but then he looked down at one as he leapt directly over it. Nothing. The black water absorbed all light, so much that absolutely nothing could escape it. This place was haunted. Evil. This place was a long, slow build of a nightmare come to life.

Ahead, Hugh saw two large, dead, black trees becoming clearer through the fog. They grew in an unnatural way—bending and curving in strange directions. Some branches even grew downwards. This was a place that no sun could reach, and any light that did was filtered through such dense fog that it was unlikely to nourish anything. The branches were bare, as if they hadn't seen a bud on them in years. Not even a single dead leaf hung on. Still, the trees reached up towards the sky, towering over everything in sight. The bark on the trunk was not dark brown; it was black, like the puddles. Dull. Hugh wondered if pulling some of the black bark off of the tree would reveal hollow insides or ash—or would it release evil into the world?

Both Hugh and Silas skidded to a halt when the gargoyle the faeries had been carrying was directly in front of them. The fog was so thick that it was almost as if they had appeared in their path out of nowhere. Even Hugh's enhanced vision seemed to be useless—or, if it wasn't, Silas probably couldn't see anything.

Drusus turned and hissed at them. "You two are like lead-footed bridge trolls." He shook his head, the six wispy dull purple hairs on his head still moving after his head stopped. "So loud." The hairs stuck back to his grey skin and took residence in his wrinkles.

This faerie was miserable. Silas and Hugh looked at each other, which made it difficult for them to hold in laughter, but somehow they managed. They knew that they had to because the success of the trip depended on continual buy-in from these faeries. Their intimate knowledge of gargoyles could make or break this mission. This Drusus seemed to be in charge, and his decision seemed to be final. They needed him.

When Hugh looked up, the fog between them and the two dead trees was starting to lift, revealing a stone wall, about ten feet tall, with a Victorian-style metal fence adding another ten feet of height. Between the two trees was a large metal gate. Hugh had expected to see something written in the curvature of the metal bars, but it was just a symmetric design on both doors.

A loud creak filled the otherwise eerily silent air. The metal gate opened in the center, and a man came through, his hands in front of him with his fingertips touching. His movements were smooth, almost as if the air moved him, rather than his body pushing the air away as the motion cut through it. His feet did not move, but rather glided over the ground as he move towards them. He was clothed entirely in black, in what appeared to be a suit that once would have been the envy of anyone. Now, it was torn and tattered, exposing grey skin, dark scars, and, in some places, bones.

"What do you want?" He angrily spat at the faeries. Beagan was right—he did seem like a horribly miserable man.

Beagan shook as she spoke; her green hair chimed lightly as the strands hit each other. The notes that came through the air sounded like a piccolo's trill during a long hold. "We have a delivery."

"Of course you do." He groaned. "There's always a delivery." The Keeper of the Keys twisted and looked through the gate, as he placed his hand on the gargoyle. Then he slowly turned back to the faeries. "Row 691. Spot Q."

"Yes, sir," all of the faeries replied—in unison, and they cautiously made their way through the gate. Their march was still in synch, just as it had been for the entire trip.

The gate slammed shut and the Keeper of the Keys's head snapped towards Hugh and Silas. "You shouldn't be here. You are neither welcome nor permitted." Half of his face was decaying, and the other half had already fallen off, exposing the bones that should have been below his skin. His eyes were clouded over, yet it was obvious that he could still see perfectly fine.

Hugh stepped forward. "We're here to help." When the Keeper of the Keys groaned and turned away, Hugh asked, "Why are you tied to this place?"

The Keeper floated so quickly towards Hugh that even though Hugh stood his ground, he didn't think the Keeper was going to be able to stop. He was ready for this ghost to fly through him.

Inches from Hugh's face, he angrily replied, "This is my retribution for a debt that I owe the Council." He reached out and put his thin, boney fingers around Hugh's wrist, yanking his forearm forward. A piece of the Keeper's skin fell from his hand, floating slowly to the ground before it disappeared, sprouting a grey piece of grass in its place. "You should know this. Your predecessor put me here, Hugh Michael Lennox Davidson." He knew Hugh's birth name—something he had not even told Zoie.

Hugh yanked his arm free, releasing another piece of the Keeper's body to the ground. "I am not Alvin. I want things to be different."

"And you?" The Keeper turned his attention to Silas, finally showing his entire face—what was left of it—to him. "Do you want things to be different?"

Silas's eyes grew wide, and he opened his mouth but nothing came out. At first, it had appeared that Silas was terrified of what he had seen, but Hugh recognized quickly that it was something different. After a few moments, he replied, "Yes. I want things to be different."

The Keeper quickly turned back to Hugh. "How different? What way?"

Hugh went on to explain how he didn't think that it was right to lock people away as gargoyles because they breathed wrong or looked at the wrong person sideways. "…and that means we could free you, too."

"No. It doesn't work like that. I cannot be freed in that manner." The Keeper scoffed. "Besides, who would guard those that truly deserve punishment? Those that kill humans for sport? That feel no remorse?"

Hugh paused for a moment. "Why do the gargoyles need to be guarded?" Everything Hugh knew about gargoyles told him that they couldn't move. They were statues, fixed into their place.

Unwilling to answer the question, the Keeper turned towards the gate. "I'm bored with this conversation." He started to walk towards the gate and raised his hand in preparation to open it again.

"Excuse me…" Hugh halted, realizing that it would be disrespectful to call him Keeper, but he didn't have a name. "You know my name. May I have yours?"

The Keeper turned slowly. "I know everyone's name, with just a simple touch. I know your entire life."

"I am not asking to know your entire life." Hugh just wanted a name, so that when he returned, it could be on friendlier, more familiar terms.

The Keeper frowned. "You already do." He turned back to the gate again, as if he was checking on the location of the faeries.

Hugh looked at Silas, and Silas shrugged and shook his head. Hugh tried again. "Sir, I want to free those that are innocent or didn't commit a violent crime. And, for those that did, I'm hoping that rehabilitation…"

The Keeper turned around quickly. He spat back, "Rows 1 through 100 have been here several centuries. There is absolutely no chance of rehabilitation for them. There are several thousands of others that have passed the point of no return. Ask your friends, the faeries. They know."

Silas interrupted them before Hugh could ask another question. "Where is Lettie Seavers located?"

The Keeper growled at him. "Row 679. Spot Z." Hugh wished that he knew the names of other prisoners, just to see if the Keeper had the coordinates of each gargoyle in his head.

"Can I see her?" Hugh was impressed that Silas would ask so plainly to enter the Graveyard.

"Absolutely not." The Keeper reached his hand in the air and closed his fist. The gates slammed shut. "Leave this place."

Hugh sighed. "We'll leave. Just promise me that you'll let the faeries out." He tried again: "And, I really would love to know your name."

The Keeper replied, "I promise they will be released from the graveyard. This place drains the life little by little of all that enter, as that is how it continues to grow to make space for the prisoners. These faeries are being unjustly punished, and while I can't reverse the curse of the gargoyle, I will not let the faeries be punished beyond what they already have to endure." When he didn't budge to say anything further, Hugh and Silas turned to leave. "Wait!"

Hugh turned. "Yes?"

Reluctantly, the Keeper decided to divulge one more bit of information. "Victor Seavers."

Hugh about choked on the thick air surrounding them at the sound of that name. "Excuse me?"

"My name." He frowned. "My name is Victor Seavers." It was obvious that he knew that Hugh was aware of who that named belonged to. Then the Keeper ordered, "Leave this place, and do not return. What it takes from you is too great." He added, "You, Hugh Davies, do not want to lose that which is dear to you."

Hugh nodded at the Keeper, thanking him silently. He turned to Silas. "Let's get out of here."

"Gladly." Silas nodded and said, "But we have to run. My teleportation isn't working here." He looked around. "This place is… it's nowhere and everywhere all at once." Hugh knew all too well what Silas was feeling in that moment—infinite and powerless at the same time.

They took off running. Silas didn't even bother to make the path for them—they just wanted to get back to the forest, where the danger that lurked there actually felt more safe and natural than the clearing and the graveyard.

Once they were beyond the clearing and deep enough into the woods, Hugh turned to Silas. "You recognized him?"

Silas nodded. "Yes. I have met him, of course." As soon as Hugh heard the Keeper's name, he knew that Silas would have recognized him.

Hugh stated the obvious. "We have to find the right moment to—."

Silas cut him off. "Don't you dare tell her."

Hugh reached his hand out and grabbed Silas's shirt, pulling him to a stop. "That's her father, she needs to know." He considered body-slamming the punk, but he held back.

Silas pushed Hugh away. "That's exactly why she doesn't need to know. What purpose does it serve?"

"She could see him again." Hugh knew that Zoie always regretted that she never got to say goodbye to her father—that she missed him desperately, and his death caused a strain on her mental health and relationship with her mother. Knowing the truth could help things to heal.

Silas laughed. "You think she needs to see her decaying father, who is tasked with guarding the very gargoyles that we want to free? His fucking—I don't know—his fucking jaw could fall off while we are there. You want that etched in her mind for the rest of her life? Her extraordinarily long life? Are you mad?"

Hugh had a different point of view about this. "Well, if we free them…"

Silas wasn't having it. "He'll die. Like DIE die. Go-to-the-afterlife kind of die, Hugh. Turn into a pile of bones and then turn to ash and blow away kind of die. He's tied to them—the gargoyles. Hugh, he even said that you were wrong about how it worked when you suggested that he could be free if we released them." Silas pinched the bridge of his nose. "If you tell her, she won't let him go. And, in the off chance that she decides to, she will have to watch him die. AGAIN."

Hugh flat-out disagreed. He had kept secrets from Zoie before, and it never went well. "Well, if we don't tell her, we'll show up at that gate and she'll be blindsided. And then what?"

Silas took in a deep breath. "Zoie was like seven when he died. She may not even remember what he looked like."

Hugh rolled his eyes. "Do you even know her at all?" Then he had it, "And you can't have it both ways. She either remembers him and being in the car with him when he died or she doesn't. Which is it?"

Silas disregarded the question and redirected the conversation. "You know, you don't always know what's best for her." He raked his hand through his hair. It started to stand in different directions than before.

Hugh really hated the arrogance of this guy. Silas had an eternal vow to take care of Zoie, but Hugh felt that it was time for him to let that go. Hugh knew that he, as Zoie's bonded mate, could take care of her better than Silas ever could. When faced with a life-or-death situation, Silas's natural instinct of self-preservation would kick in; Hugh's would be overpowered by the mating bond. Silas was of no use at this point. "And you do?"

Silas let out an annoyed laugh. "No, you fucking asshole. I don't. But Jesus fucking Christ, I do love her. You aren't the only one who loves her, you know?" Before Hugh could even make a sound—a scoff, a grunt, whatever—Silas reiterated, "Yeah, I said it, I fucking love her. And I mean it, too. Your mating bond didn't save her life before, and it won't always be able to protect her in the future." He glared at Hugh. "You think you always have the right answer, but in this case, you're wrong. Telling her that her father is the physical embodiment of death tasked eternally with guarding the very gargoyles we're trying to free would just hurt her. I definitely don't want to see her hurting." He continued, "This—this information will crush her."

"We have to tell her, Silas. I mean, *we* don't. *I* do. I can't lie to her. Our relationship is built entirely on honesty." He started walking back towards Nightbrooke.

Roots from the trees started to lift and branches reached towards each other. If Hugh was alone or with anyone else, he would have started to think of a way out of this—a way to fight the forest. But he was with Silas, and Hugh knew that Silas was using his power to block his route. He would just have to reason with him or agree with him for the moment to get out of this. Those were the only options.

Hugh let out the deepest sigh, and he felt the parts of him that were annoyed release. He had to remain calm. Silas was important to Zoie, no matter how much Hugh wanted to tear him into tiny pieces and throw him into an incinerator. She had expressed that it was important to her that they got along. Hugh had promised to try—and he was trying, but Silas was making it difficult in this moment. Silas made it difficult in most moments.

When Hugh turned to look at him, Silas was the first to speak. "I agree that she needs to know. But today isn't that day." Hugh folded his arms and glared at him, so Silas explained, "*We* haven't even processed all of the information yet. If we tell her, she's going to ask all sorts of questions, and we aren't going to have any answers at all." He added, "You know how she is. If we process the information a bit before revealing this, we may have *some* answers for her."

Hugh's jaw tightened and he let out a low growl. "Fine. Let's share what we found out—besides this little piece of information." He didn't fully agree with this decision, so Hugh just reminded himself that he could go rogue and tell Zoie later when they were alone. "I'm going to head home."

Silas released the trees and walked over to Hugh and moved to place his hand on Hugh's shoulder. Hugh grabbed his wrist. "Don't fucking touch me."

"Fine then, fucking walk it. We're far enough into the forest that my powers are working again. I'm going to teleport, but you do you, pal." Silas laughed as if he just didn't care—and, to be honest, he probably didn't.

But Silas was the only being that Hugh knew of that didn't have to take portals in and out of Nightbrooke; he just moved throughout the entire world as he pleased, and Hugh just wanted to go home and be with Zoie. "Fine." He rolled his eyes and released Silas's wrist. "In case you weren't aware, you aren't my favorite person."

Silas placed his hand on Hugh's shoulder and smirked. "That's okay. I think I'm Zoie's."

# ZOIE

There was no one in the house but Zoie. Hugh had left to handle some Council business, and, while Cade had a key, they didn't use it unless it was an emergency. She was using the time to catch up on some reading—for pleasure.

Since effectively coming back from the dead, Zoie had been reclassified as a missing person, but there was still some work to be done for her to get her life back. The legal red tape to bring a person back to life was more complicated than any of them had thought it would be. Sure, Hugh had connections that could forge documents, but bringing someone back to life who was never actually dead—nearly impossible in the eyes of the government.

Between researching that and taking action on it, Zoie was also studying magic and practicing and getting better at her skills. It was slow going because, to Zoie's understanding, because she had let her powers lay dormant for so long, she had to work much harder to get to the level that she would have been at otherwise. No amount of natural skill could make up for practice. But, sometimes, Zoie felt as if she was practicing herself to the point that it was having the opposite effect. It was beginning to feel like a job. A job she didn't want to do some days.

So between all of that and trying to figure out what she wanted to do with her life, plus balancing a life with Hugh and Silas, Zoie wasn't left with much time for fun things. So, she was taking this rare time when Hugh was out and Silas was actually with him—and she couldn't wait to hear how that went for them—to read. She had decided to go back to a simpler time in her life and read a childhood favorite: *Anne of Green Gables.*

Since Hugh had been technically working two jobs—his role as professor in the English Department and Council Member of the Supernatural World—Zoie had also settled into the role of housewife, and it was another thing that felt like a job that she hated. She had just settled down for another break from her tasks while the laundry was rolling around in the dryer.

Placing the bookmark on the table, Zoie curled up on the couch with her book and a throw blanket. She took a sip of her tea and then turned the page, engrossed in the book to the point that she didn't even hear the buzzer go off, signaling the end of the cycle.

What did take her out of the book was a loud argument from behind her. It almost made her question her own sanity because she hadn't noticed anyone entering the house.

"I'm going to fucking kill you!" Something glass fell to the floor and shattered. It sounded as if it had some weight to it.

Recognizing the deep growl of that particular voice, a completely startled Zoie jumped up from the couch, dropping her book to the floor with a thud—she would find her page again later. In the kitchen, Hugh—who had obviously and suddenly returned sooner than expected—had slammed Silas against the counter and then the wall, sending a framed picture to the floor. Glass littered the ceramic tiles of the kitchen floor, reminding Zoie that she wanted to find time to approach Hugh about doing some remodeling. She wasn't entirely sure how committed he was to the current look of the house.

Hugh was holding Silas up against the wall by his shirt collar. Their faces were inches apart. Growls and snarls were coming from Hugh, but snarky laughter and a smirk were all that she noticed from Silas. He wasn't afraid of Hugh.

He should have been.

"Guys! Guys!" She could see in the glass of a nearby window that Hugh's eyes were already glowing yellow. She needed to stop him before he went too far—a transformation into a werewolf could prove deadly, so she did the one thing that she knew, without a doubt, would make him retreat. "Hugh!"

Hugh stepped back and released Silas with a shove. He growled at him, "You are such a slimy fucking prick." Hugh turned to Zoie and smiled. His tone and entire demeanor changed the moment that she came into his view. "Hey, my love."

She laughed. "That reminds me of when my mom would be actively yelling at me when I was a kid and the phone would ring and she would answer it with the most pleasant voice in the world." Zoie got on her toes and kissed Hugh's cheek. Then she walked over to Silas. "Are you okay?"

"Yeah, I'm fine." He fixed the wrinkles in his shirt, glaring at Hugh the entire time. The jealousy and animosity between them wasn't waning with time. It was clear each time they encountered one another.

Zoie watched Silas' hand. "Are you sure?" She couldn't help but fixate on that hand. It wasn't broken or bleeding. It looked like it was changing colors or something.

Taking his focus off of Hugh, Silas looked at Zoie and smiled. "Yeah. Hugh's not that scary…"

Annoyed by the constant jabs they took at each other, she grabbed his hand. "No. Your tattoo in Latin—it's moving." She unbuttoned the cuff of his sleeve and started to roll it up. "It's moving everywhere." She moved to the front of his shirt and started to unbutton those to see the words on his chest. Zoie was engrossed in figuring this out to the point that everything around her melted away, except Silas's tattoo. Not even the other parts of Silas were visible in her tunnel vision.

Silas grabbed her hands. "Now is not the best time to undress me, no matter what the reason." He moved his eyes to motion over Zoie's shoulder. Hugh wasn't Silas's favorite person—in fact, at times, he loathed him—but that didn't mean that he was going to take an opportunity to move this beyond a point of rivalry. He did still have one teeny, tiny shred of respect for Zoie's relationship with Hugh.

Hugh cleared his throat. "Hey, Zo, remember this guy over here?" He pointed at himself, doing his best to hide that the chuckle was one of the nervous variety.

She turned around. "I'm sorry. It wasn't like that. I just…" Zoie couldn't focus on Hugh's feelings in this moment. She was truly concerned, so she turned back to Silas. "What would cause that?" The ink waved and vibrated within Silas's skin.

He shook his head. "I have no idea." He re-buttoned his shirt and sleeve. "I'm not an expert on eternal vows." Silas glanced over at Hugh.

She scoffed. "Then you shouldn't have made one." While Zoie was grateful that Silas watched over her for most of her life, she still felt conflicted about it. He'd been hired by her father to do so, and it was always in the back of her mind that perhaps that was the reason for their relationship.

Zoie started picking up the big pieces of glass and then made her way towards the closet that held the cleaning supplies. Reluctantly, and feeling as if it were her duty, she suggested, "Well, perhaps I should research eternal vows while you guys are…"

Hugh interrupted her. "Zoie, love, can you take a seat?"

She looked back and forth between the pair of them. Both Hugh and Silas looked very serious. Not angry. Not annoyed with each other. Just intensely serious about whatever was the reason for her needing to sit down. As strange as it was, Silas and Hugh were in agreement with her needing to take a seat, so Zoie slowly put the broom and dustpan down. Her stomach started to twist. If they both wanted to talk to her, it might be some big news. Was someone sick? Dying? Did one of their friends get changed into a gargoyle? She started to panic.

They each took a seat, Hugh in the chair to her left, taking her hand so that she would turn to face him, and Silas in the one to her right, behind her, due to the way she was facing in the chair. She wondered if this was strategic on Hugh's part to hold her attention. Still, that was the least of her worries. She could manage their pettiness later.

Hugh began. "Okay, so today, another gargoyle was created, and Silas and I *actually* worked together to gather some information." Zoie began to infer that the information had to be horrible, if this was the way that they were telling her.

She could feel Silas getting angry behind her. The heat from his anger radiated from his body and she could feel his skin vibrating without even touching him. There was a slight hum about it that she could sense in between her shoulders and running up her spine into her brain. Before she could intervene, Silas spat out, "Hugh, don't say it like that. We work fine together when you aren't acting like an overbearing…"

Hugh cut him off. "Shut the fuck up, Silas." He put his hand up like a stop sign. "We were fine until you decided to be a jerk and then immediately teleport us here with the intention to make me look bad."

Silas rolled his eyes. "It doesn't matter what my intention was. You make yourself look bad. If you didn't feel the need to puff out your chest any time someone knows better than you when it comes to Zoie, then there wouldn't be so many opportunities to show the world what kind of controlling…"

Hugh stood up and slammed his hand on the table, cutting Silas off again. "You…"

Zoie stood up and twisted her left wrist quickly, using her ability to manipulate time to shove Hugh back in his chair. She moved her right hand to take the rope from Silas's waist and tie it around him a couple times using magic. "Enough!"

Silas laughed, "Hey, I thought that this sort of thing was just for …"

Zoie had had enough of this. She twitched her hand and tightened the rope. "I. Said. Enough!"

Both of them just stared at her. "I care very deeply for both of you." Before Hugh could open his mouth, she turned towards him. "I *love* you, and you know that's only for you. You don't need to make a point of it so that he has to hear it. He knows."

She took a few steps back and then moved her hands to bring the two of them closer together in their chairs. "This has to stop. Every time you argue like this, it makes me sick. I couldn't bear to lose either of you, and it would be even worse if one of you were the reason for the harm to the other."

She looked at Silas and pleaded with him. "Imagine how I would feel about you if you hurt Hugh."

Hugh scoffed. "As if."

"Shut it." She glared at him, fed up with him acting as if he were truly invincible when it came to Silas, who had his own unique powers. "Hugh, if you hurt him, how do you think I would feel about you?"

"I get it." He let out a deep sigh.

She looked at them. "I have a different relationship with each of you. Neither one of you encroaches on the other's relationship with me." Zoie looked at Hugh, "and, this should go without saying, but everyone in this room knows that you, Hugh, are my primary partner." She asked, "Can this pissing contest end?"

They replied in unison. "Yes."

She smiled, not believing them for a moment, but choosing to take them at their word. She released them both with a quick flick of her hands, just as the front door opened and the screen door slammed back into place.

"You show 'em who's boss, honey." Cade snapped and pointed at Zoie.

"Dios mío, Cade." Xariella rolled her eyes. "Sorry we're late." She gave Zoie a hug as they greeted each other. "It smells yummy in here."

Cade smiled. "We were got *caught up in something.*"

Hugh rolled his eyes. "Just 'sorry we're late' was fine."

"What? We got stuck in the hammock on the deck—like twisted!" Cade grabbed an apple from the fruit basket. "What did you think I meant?" They looked back and forth between everyone else in the room. "Ohhhhh, you thought I meant that we were fuckin'?" They nodded. "I see, I see." After taking a big bite out of the apple, Cade added, "We were. I was lying about the hammock."

"Cade!" Xariella buried her face in her hands.

Cade made a dismissive motion with their hand. "Don't worry

about offending the other people in this room, Xari. Those two are men, so they make the same jokes, and Zoie gets more sex than anyone in the room because she's sleeping with both of them."

Silas very casually said, "I think you would be wise to remember that I'm the person that literally killed a man by taking tree branches and shoving them in and out of every hole in his body." He directed a shadow to grab Cade's apple, floating it in front of their face. "So I would leave me—and my gal—out of that conversation. Thanks." He dropped the apple into Cade's lap.

"Is this still safe to eat?" they asked. "Or did you poison it with the darkness?" Cade was entirely serious. They had yet to decide if Silas had earned their trust.

Silas shrugged. "You'll only know if you take a bite."

Zoie looked at Silas, silently asking if it was safe. He frowned, shocked that she would even have to ask. She looked back to Cade. "It's safe." They immediately bit into the apple with a loud crunch.

"Eeeee, I wouldn't have done that…" Silas teased.

Cade spit out the apple and threw everything in the trash. Zoie just rolled her eyes.

"Okay!" Zoie started off towards the oven—she had made individual apple crisps for everyone. She stopped as she entered the main part of the kitchen. "Hugh! Silas! Clean up the rest of this broken glass. I've decided I'm done cleaning up after the pair of you when you're acting like the testosterone has taken over your brains."

Xariella excitedly made a fist and mouthed 'Girl Power!'

Silas put his hand up. "Hugh, I got this one. I'll just…"

"Nope." Zoie cut him off. "No magic. Get on your hands and knees and clean it up." She added, "I can't safely get to the oven until it's cleaned." She then took a piece of bread from the loaf.

"Use this to clean up the little pieces that the broom just can't seem to get." She handed it to Hugh.

"Okay, Mom," Hugh teased.

"No! No!" Cade waved trying to stop him before he said anything further. "That's a bad idea."

Zoie just shot a glare at Hugh. He was already in hot water with her for threatening Silas. To her, it was one thing for them to not exactly want to be around each other every day, but they should be mature enough to behave in her presence.

This didn't mean that Silas was off the hook, either. She knew what kind of game he was playing by getting Hugh angry and then immediately transporting them to where she was. It was just an example of the ways that Silas tried to make himself look better than Hugh. Zoie was just shocked that Hugh continued to fall for it.

"You two better hurry or those desserts are going to burn." She sat down next to Xariella. "One of those men is nearly 200 years old." She poured a glass of wine. "And he's still acting like a testosterone-fueled frat boy." She shook her head.

"Done!" Silas announced.

Zoie quickly ran in and pulled the apple crisps out of the oven. "Okay! Let these cool for at least 15 minutes."

"15?!" Cade whined. "You can manipulate time. Why don't you cool them down?"

Zoie disagreed with this method. "Baking really is timing. And using magic takes the enjoyment out of it." She walked back to her seat.

"For whom?" Cade asked. "I want dessert!"

Everyone else sat down at the table, and Zoie, ignoring Cade's comment, said, "So right before you two got here, Silas and Hugh were about to tell me about some stuff they found out today. It seemed very serious."

"Hugh was being a little overdramatic. The stuff we saw, it wasn't pleasant, but there's nothing so serious that we can't just talk about it." The look that Silas gave Hugh was as if there was a secret between them. Zoie didn't want to press in that moment, but she would later, when she was alone with one or both of them.

Hugh returned the look, obviously angry. Whatever the secret was, Hugh obviously didn't agree with keeping it that way. Still, he decided to start to explain their experience that day. "So we were able to follow the faeries to—and they actually call it this—the Gargoyle Graveyard."

"It's actually the entire way through the dark forest and past this—I'm going to go ahead and say it, Hugh—really fucking creepy clearing." Silas just shook his head as if that would get the memory out of his brain. "There's a gate—it looks like the gate to a haunted mansion. I mean, could this get any more like a horror film?"

"Yes, yes it could," Hugh interjected, almost as if they had rehearsed. "So the gate opens up and there's a man that guards it—they call him the Keeper of the Keys. I saw no keys, by the way. He used magic in his hand to work the gates."

"Yeah, and he literally tells the faerie to put the gargoyle in spot-get this-691 Q. That's how many gargoyles are in there." Silas added, "and, he mentioned that there are gargoyles that have been there for centuries. Not *a century*." He stressed it: "*centuries*."

"So you got to talk to him?" Zoie asked. "Did you find anything out about Le—."

Hugh interrupted her. "Oh, Silas did ask about Lettie. She's in 679 Z. He wouldn't let us see her though. He explained that…"

Zoie didn't even give Hugh a chance to continue. "Wait a minute. Today's went into row 691 and Lettie was in 679? Are you sure about that?" The wheels in her head started to turn.

"Yes," Hugh and Silas said in unison.

Zoie pressed her lips together. "So, if each row has 26 spots, assuming that it's *only* the English alphabet, and they don't add in other alphabets, like Greek, for example—that means that nearly 70 gargoyles have been added since Lettie." Zoie stood up and started pacing. "Hugh, you've been an active member of the council for about, what, five months? Lettie wasn't taken long before that."

"You've only witnessed how many trials?" Silas asked.

"Four." He asked Silas, "How many have you turned in?"

"Three." And Silas was one of the most successful bounty hunters in their world.

Continuing to pace, Zoie asked, "Do they always do the trial right away when you bring them in?"

"Not always but usually."

Zoie looked at her friends. "They're imprisoning people without anyone else knowing."

"Lots of people." Xariella frowned.

Cade smirked at Silas and then mentioned, "And, obviously you aren't the top bounty hunter like you thought you were." They let out a little *tsk tsk tsk*. Despite their distrust in Silas, Cade was usually very nice to him, but mostly because Hugh asked them to behave. Cade's loyalty to Hugh was unlike anything Zoie had ever seen in her entire life. In fact, if Xariella would have never found her way to the group, Zoie would have believed that Cade would have given their life for Hugh without any regard for their own.

Everyone fell silent for a moment, waiting for Silas to respond. He didn't. He didn't even opt to acknowledge what Cade had said. And then it became one of those awkward silences that everyone was waiting for someone else to break. Where no one wanted to be the one to say, "…soooooooooo…"

Just as Zoie was about to stand up to get the desserts, Hugh broke the silence.

"Oh, before I forget." Hugh turned to Zoie. "Zo, the witches aren't taking light from the sun, they are taking it from the person and giving it to the sun. Same sort of thing with water. They are taking the water from the victim…"

Based on the knowledge that she had about magic—which actually exceeded Hugh's by quite a bit—Zoie had to disagree. "No, they are wetting the dirt and drying it almost at the same time so that they can sculpt it, and it's hard when the dust falls." Zoie walked directly to their bookshelf in the living room. She scanned the books for a few moments and then pulled out three of them. Carrying them back to the table, she said, "Keep talking. I'm just going to look through these." She had thought that one of the books had some spells about breaking some of these things down.

Xariella asked, "Did this keeper of the keys give you any good info?" Xariella was very good at asking the right questions, and Zoie enjoyed that about her. Zoie knew that in her absence, Xariella would still dig for information.

Silas and Hugh both replied, "Not really." In unison. Zoie found this highly suspicious.

Apparently, she wasn't the only one that did. Cade looked back and forth between them. "Did you two rehearse this or discuss your story? You are never this in synch."

Hugh laughed. "No, it's just the truth."

Almost as if they were now finishing each other's sentences, Silas added, "And we don't want to get in trouble again." Silas motioned towards Zoie with his thumb.

Without changing the expression on her face, Zoie reminded

them all, "I have good peripheral vision, Silas." Zoie turned the pages in her book furiously. "I know there's a counter spell for at least one of those in here." She whispered, "There has to be."

Xariella cautiously suggested, "No offense, Zoie, but that seems way too easy—finding a reversal to the spell in a book that anyone can read." She continued, "There has to be more to it or someone would have taken action by now."

Zoie didn't look up. "But the basic workings—the early parts of the spell—they could be in one of these books."

No one was about to argue with her. When Zoie got an idea about something, she exhausted all avenues before giving up. Besides, with what had just transpired as Xariella and Cade were walking in the door, no one was going to challenge Zoie. She was still feeling spicy about the way Hugh and Silas returned home, and everyone could feel it.

"Soooo… was this keeper just loyal to the baddies or simply unhelpful?" Cade asked, trying to get back on task. All of them wanted to free the victims stuck in gargoyle form; they were passionate about it. They just didn't know where to truly begin.

Silas and Hugh looked at each other. Hugh decided to respond. "I don't think he's loyal to Reon and friends. I think he's just stuck there. It seemed like punishment."

"You agree, Silas?" Cade asked. The suspicion in their voice gave away the expression on their face, and Zoie didn't even have to look up. Cade's eyebrow had to be raised so high that it could be starting to lift off into the air above their head, like a cartoon character.

Silas nodded. "Yes. I think he would choose to help us if he felt that there was a way out."

"Anything else useful?" Xariella asked. She didn't trust this sudden alliance either.

Hugh sighed and shook his head. He decided to take the focus off of this Keeper of the Keys. "I didn't know this about them, but the faeries can sense how the prisoners feel in the gargoyle form with just a touch. Makes me wonder if all of them can do that with anyone."

"That could be very useful, actually," Xariella replied. "I wonder if they can do the reverse, too, and make someone feel an emotion just by a touch."

"Oooooh, that's good." Cade interjected, impressed yet again with their mate. "Where do you come up with this stuff?"

Still reading, Zoie replied, "She's intelligent and creative, and she has the confidence to speak up when she has an idea." These were all things that Zoie had told Xariella before, especially early in their friendship. She could tell right away that Xariella was, beyond a good friend and Cade's mate, a valuable asset to have around in a pinch. She had earned Zoie's respect, which was something that was difficult to do. The only thing more difficult would be to try to regain that respect once it was lost.

"How are you doing that?" Cade asked. When Zoie didn't respond, they asked again. "How are you reading and holding a conversation at the same time?"

Zoie shrugged, still flipping through the books. "I think it comes from years of being on the sidelines and wishing I could be part of something bigger. I would read my books and simultaneously listen to what was going on around me." It didn't matter how much money Zoie's family had; the other students at school still made fun of her mercilessly, and her mother had no time for her. Regardless of whether she was at home or school—she was in the background, and her only friends were within the pages of the books she had read. Her dear Auntie Lettie was the only person she felt comfortable around. Safe.

Getting the topic back on what was important, Silas suggested to Hugh, "We need to find that Beagan. I get the impression that she really wanted to help us."

"I think so too," Hugh agreed. He pointed out, "She looked so much younger than the others. Do you think that one just replaces another when they've had…"

"All the life drained from them? Yeah. I think that's how it goes." Silas frowned.

Xariella asked, "Okay wait. Who exactly is Beagan?"

"One of the faeries. She gave us the most information, and she seemed the most passionate about fighting the obvious classism in our world." Hugh reached his hand over the table and put it over the page the Zoie was reading. "Can we eat these desserts yet? Because, um, they smell really good, and I feel like it's a human rights violation to make us smell them and not let us eat them."

Zoie looked up. "Not one person in this room is actually human." She placed her hand over Hugh's and then they twisted their hands together, interlocking their fingers. They looked in each other's eyes and smiled, each of them feeling their bond strengthen—for him, the gentle buzz of electricity traveling through his body; for her, the fire that manifested in her stomach.

Clearing his throat, Silas interjected, "We are." He motioned back and forth between Zoie and himself.

"Okay, Mr. I-was-born-in-1962-but-look-26." She stood up to get the desserts. She quickly checked to see if any glass was missed when the two man-children were cleaning up, but didn't see anything. Hugh's enhanced vision probably helped with the cleanup. Still, she was glad to be wearing socks.

"I have really good genes." His eyes followed her the entire way into the kitchen. "I have this young girl that I'm dating, and she keeps me on my toes."

Hugh cleared his throat. "Yeah, I'm still here."

Silas put his hands up in surrender. "I'm sorry. It's usually just me and her when we're together." It was the most genuine he ever sounded with an apology to Hugh.

Perhaps making them clean up the mess they had made was bringing them together. Zoie doubted it. She still was hoping to figure out what was causing this strange, new alliance.

Zoie handed out the desserts—and Cade inhaled theirs, as Zoie was making her way back towards the refrigerator.

"Do you have any extra?" Cade wiped their mouth with their sleeve.

Zoie laughed. "Cade! I was headed back to the freezer to get ice cream to put on them. Did you eat it already?"

"…Noooo…" Their cheeks flushed with embarrassment.

She shook her head and chuckled lightly. "Just take mine."

"But then you won't get any." They were already reaching for hers and slowly moving it across the table.

"I'll have a couple bites of Hugh's or something. Plus, I made them and have had them before." She brought over the vanilla bean ice cream and put a scoop on top of each of the remaining apple crisps. "Does anyone want any caramel?" She presented some homemade caramel.

As they all finished eating, Silas stood up. "I'm going to go home." He grabbed Zoie's hand. "Will you walk out with me?" He ran his thumb over her knuckles.

She nodded. "I'll be right back," Zoie stated as she looked back at Hugh, and he nodded at her. She hadn't been asking for permission to walk Silas out, but she did care about Hugh's feelings and would take them into consideration if he didn't want her to go.

As soon as the door shut behind them, Silas had his arms

around Zoie and his forehead to hers. "I'm sorry about earlier."

She put her hands in the hair on the back of his head. "You really need to stop instigating with him." She quietly reminded him, "I gave him the option to tell me that he's not comfortable with this, remember?" Zoie knew that it would take a lot for Hugh to tell her that he needed her to end things with Silas, but that didn't mean that he wouldn't make the request if Silas pushed him just a little bit too far.

"I know." He pulled back a little. "I almost forgot." He reached into the air and pulled something out of nowhere. "This is for you." One of the most interesting things about Silas's power was how not only could he make himself travel through the shadows, he could also make objects do it. His power seemed limitless, since darkness was everywhere. The darkness is what would make the light shine the brightest.

The small object, about the size of a cell phone, could have possibly been sitting in a dark cupboard at his home. As long as he knew where it was, he could reach into the shadows and will it to himself.

He held it out in front of her—it was a cassette tape from the late 80s or early 90s. The label read "Zoie's Mix Vol. 1."

As Silas placed the cassette in her hand, Zoie couldn't help but laugh. "Is this…?"

"A mix tape? Hell, yes." He laughed. "All songs that remind me of you." He reached into the air again and snapped. "Here's an old-school number 2 pencil so if you need to wind it, you can."

The yellow octagon shaped pencil smelled like it had been freshly sharpened. It took her back to school and standardized testing in an instant. She could almost hear the winding of the pencil sharpener affixed to the walls. Her height—or lack thereof—made it difficult for her to reach, even though they were lower on the walls than the ones in high school or at university.

The feel of the pencil as she rolled it back and forth between her index finger and thumb took her back to another memory— one of her with her father. They were sitting in the basement next to his sound system. She remembered that he had built the wooden stand so that it would work for everything—and he would add on more pieces when a new form of technology came out. In her memory, she could picture the record player and the CD player, but the main focus was on that cassette player.

She had been crying because the tape had gotten caught on something and had pulled out. Her father had reassured her that it was okay, and then slid a number 2 pencil into the holes of the rollers and turned, showing her how to fix such a tragedy.

She recalled that it played nearly perfectly, with a small stretch and distortion over just a few seconds of one song. She had waited by the radio for days that summer to record the song she had been waiting for, so she was sad that it had the imperfection. Still, decades later, she could only hear the song with that unique sound at that point when it played.

That was when she realized that she didn't have anything to play this mix tape on. "But…"

Silas put a finger to her lips. Reaching out to nowhere again, he materialized a Walkman, complete with headphones. "I took care of everything."

She out everything on a nearby chair and pulled him in for a hug and a kiss. "This is perfect."

He pushed some of her curly, red hair behind her ear. "I am in love with you, Zoie."

"Silas…" She hated hurting him, but there were some conditions that she agreed to with Hugh. Hugh had always been, and would remain, her primary partner. Some things with him just took precedence.

He shook his head. "I know that you've promised to reserve that word for him." The disappointment in his heart was so strong that his face couldn't hide it.

She let out a deep breath that she hadn't known she was holding. "I care very deeply for you."

Silas sighed. "That sounds like you're letting down a really good friend." He frowned.

She had to come up with something to make him feel special. Something that was just theirs. "How about this?" She took his face in her hands. "I *adore* you."

He smiled. "I adore you, too."

As their lips met for a kiss, Zoie felt like she was floating on a cloud. She felt his warm hand touch the skin on her back, under her shirt. She pulled away from their kiss, gently. "Silas."

"Come home with me." He kissed her quickly and admitted, "I want you desperately."

She kissed him. "When the time is right."

"Do you not want to…?" He swallowed hard. "Do you not want to be with me like that? Is sex not going to part of our relationship? Did you promise him that you wouldn't?"

The questions were fair, but, at the same time, Zoie and Silas had gone over everything at the start of their relationship. However, she knew that relationships changed and developed over time. New questions would come up that they hadn't thought of before. She didn't mind answering anything that he asked, even if it was something that he had inquired about before.

She laughed quietly. "It will be part of our relationship, Silas. I'm just… I'm not ready for that yet."

He pushed another piece of hair behind her ear. "We used to live together. You've been in my head. You know me, Zoie." They had lived in close quarters—a one-bedroom cabin that Silas had built with his own hands, without the use of magic—in the forest of Northern Canada. The pair of them had a cozy little life, tending to their chickens and gardening, when they weren't deep into her magical training.

Then words came out of her mouth that she never meant to say and that she didn't mean the way that she said them. "Yeah, and you stalked me for a year before actually meeting me and are paid to watch over me."

He let out an annoyed sigh and stepped back, breaking any touch between them. "You're never going to let that go, are you?"

"No, I didn't mean it. I just meant…" She knew exactly what it sounded like she meant, and, once she had found out that it was the truth behind how he was able to save her in Romania, she believed that he was dealing with her just because he was being funded to do so.

"What did you mean, Zoie?" He paced and turned around. "How did you mean it, Zoie?"

"I just meant that you've had a longer time to fall in love with me." And that was the truth of the matter at hand.

"Okay," he said. "That's fair. But what about the part where I am paid to do it?"

She shook her head. "I shouldn't have said that, and I didn't mean anything by it." That was mostly true. A small part in Zoie's mind would always wonder if he was just spending so much time with her because her father had set him up for life.

He took her hands in his. "Don't say it again. It hurts." Silas added, "When I made the contract with your dad, I had no idea I would fall in love with you." He corrected himself, "I mean, that I would end up *adoring* you the way that I do." He sighed. "You were a child then. I didn't even think I was going to like you."

"I know." She felt horrible.

"But, for real, I am going to go. You need to get back inside." He put his arms around her and pulled her close again. No matter how many of their enemies that they eliminated, there were always more. And, while Zoie was safe with Hugh, Silas would always feel as if he was leaving her vulnerable any time that he parted from her.

Their lips met again, and she felt like she was on that cloud again. But it was over much sooner than she had wanted. Part of her did want to go home with him, but she belonged at home with Hugh. No matter what the arrangement was, Zoie knew that Hugh was her primary partner, not only by title but also in her heart.

"Good night, Zoie." He blew her a kiss and then disappeared into the darkness—literally. The strangest thing about his ability to transport wasn't that he could actually do it. It was that he did it without a sound. He didn't disturb a thing-not the grass or any leaves or even the dust. It was just as if he was never there.

Traveling with him was different. She would get sucked into the nothingness and always felt as if her body was zipping through the air and being rearranged.

It was then that she realized she didn't get to ask Silas about the apparent secret that he and Hugh were harboring. "Damn it." She let out a sigh and then resolved to ask about it later. Besides, it was probably better to try and dig the information out of Hugh. He was more likely to give into her requests because of the mating bond. She would just have to wait for the right time.

She gathered her gift and took it inside with her. As she placed it on a side table, Xariella and Cade stood up. Disappointed, she asked, "Are you leaving?"

Xariella nodded. "Yeah. I have to… feed. It's not safe for me to stay much longer. Cade and I are going to head out of town for a few days."

Zoie nodded in understanding. Being friends with Xariella had opened up all kinds of knowledge about vampires for Zoie—in fact, it had shed the light on vampires for everyone.

Silas, who never really trusted vampires before, found out that they didn't actually turn to ash in the sunlight. He had previously believed that they had to have some sort of spell, potion, or ointment to keep it from happening, but, as it turns out, it was just a myth. Xariella explained that for the first several weeks, however, the new chemical makeup that was running through her veins did make it difficult to go out into the daylight without getting a massive, throbbing migraine. She figured that this is why many vampires stayed away from the light. But, after some exposure, the pain eased. And, while ibuprofen or aspirin didn't touch the headache, Xariella had found that a little bit of Vicks VapoRub actually would ease the headache if she sniffed it. So, she carried a little bottle of it with her everywhere that she went.

For Cade, they found that the moment that the mating bond was activated by their touch, the scent of vampire that they had found so offensive completely disappeared. Apparently, the mating bond took over every cell in a werewolf's body and transformed something within it to solidify the bond.

Hugh actually found this fascinating, and he theorized that it had something to do with the mitochondrion and vowed that his next bit of scientific research would be on this. In the meantime, he was pleasantly surprised to find out that he could eventually get used to the smell of a vampire to the point that he didn't have to stand twenty feet from Xariella when she was in the room.

And Zoie had no idea that they had to drink the blood of a human being once a year. She had hoped that this was just a myth, but it wasn't. They needed human blood—just not as often has Hollywood had led her to believe.

Many vampires had tried to get by with drinking animal blood or visiting a blood bank. It just didn't work. It had to be fresh, human blood. And, it had to be truly human—not activated supernatural.

Zoie had found in her research and through some gentle experiments that vampires—or at least Xariella—could smell the difference between human blood and supernatural blood. She could even tell when the blood was from a human who didn't yet know that they were a witch, warlock, or werebeast. She explained that there was a certain sound to the way that it flowed through the body.

Xariella once explained that Hugh and Cade's blood flow had a low hum to it as it passed by pulse-points or changed chambers in the heart. She said that Zoie's had a chime to it and that when she closed her eyes, she could even see light where it flowed. For those with genes that would let them in the pack, she could faintly smell campfire, if she concentrated. Xariella wanted to expand on this skill but knew that it would take some training for it to develop over time.

Still, blood that wasn't pure human wouldn't revive her health to where it needed to be. It would drive her thirst further and further into the forefront of her mind and cause her to go on a hunting rampage.

More annoying than that, she needed to consume at least five pints, and even through their extensive research, no one in the group was able to confirm if it had to be all of the same blood type, too. It was just a better idea to try and drain one human.

Besides, at the present time, none of them knew enough

humans that would let Xariella suck one pint out of them and then just move onto the next one.

And, worse than that, Xariella didn't know that she had the strength to stop after one pint, either. She was a relatively young vampire. She had enough trouble suppressing her thirst when an ambulance would come buzzing down the street with a bloody passenger to get to the emergency department downtown. She didn't want to risk taking things too far if someone was brave enough to volunteer.

So, Xariella and Cade needed to go somewhere. Somewhere far away from Birmingham. Somewhere that there were people, but not a lot of people. Maybe somewhere that there was a higher concentration of bad people. She didn't want to kill a good person. If she was going to have to be a monster, Xariella wanted to take out another monster.

They had a plan—well, the makings of one—and they were running out of time to make it better. If they waited too long, Xariella's thirst would take over and, well, that would not be good. Birmingham had seen enough tragedy to last many lifetimes, and it wasn't ready to experience what would happen when a vampire decided to feast on its citizens.

So, Cade and Xariella were off for a few days to a week (they weren't truly sure), and they weren't even telling Hugh and Zoie where they were going. Something about plausible deniability if things went awry.

Once their friends left, Hugh put his arms around Zoie from behind. "I'm not ready to sleep yet." He moved her hair and kissed her neck.

"Me either," she confirmed. "Let me clean up…" She started to move towards the table. While she was partly teasing about cleaning up, a part of her was also serious.

Hugh playfully pulled on her arm. "Leave it for tomorrow."

She let him pull her back into his arms—this time facing him, and she looked up at him. "As long as you're sure about it." Both she and Hugh were very tidy, and Zoie was surprised that he would even suggest leaving the mess for the next day. She was worried that leaving it would be distracting, no matter what they were going to do for the rest of the evening.

He slid his hands down her body to her waist. Hugh looked her in the eyes and said, "I'm certain." Then, he quickly picked her up and put her over his shoulder. "No more stalling."

She shrieked with laughter. "Hugh! Put me down!" Zoie always loved playful Hugh. Whatever he had gone through earlier in the day, it had been serious, and she knew that he needed to forget about that for a while. So, instead of pressing the matter about the secret that he was guarding, she decided to let this play out.

As requested, the moment he was close enough to the bed to put her on it, he put her down. "Gladly." He smiled and immediately pulled his shirt over his head.

"Oh, you really meant it when you said 'no more stalling'." She stood up so that they could both tear each other's clothes off expeditiously.

"Definitely meant it." His kiss ignited a fire in her body that she couldn't fight if she wanted to.

# HUGH

The sun had barely started to rise, but Hugh was already wide awake. It was a side effect of his brain being in overdrive due to a lie via omission. He had known that he wasn't going to get a full night's sleep the previous night. The anxiety of lying to Zoie kept his brain doing the "what ifs" all night long. He would have loved to be able to say that he tossed and turned, but he really lay on his back and stared at the ceiling. He hated keeping secrets from Zoie.

For starters, he knew that she could find them on her own—all she had to do was invade his thoughts. She could find anything that he remembered, and, sometimes, things that he didn't know that he remembered. She could insert herself in the memories, as if they were simply dreams that she was invading. Zoie could discover emotions and manipulate them by pulling on the metaphorical strings that controlled them.

She had promised that she would never do it without permission, but, over the past several months, she had become so skilled at telepathy, that she could do it without the victim knowing. On days that she planned to practice, she always warned Hugh that she would be reading his mind at random points in the day, and her training notes journal would always have several thoughts that he didn't even know that she had invaded.

Thankfully, Zoie was trustworthy, so he believed that she wasn't sneaking in sessions behind the scenes. Still, he worried that he might have inadvertently revealed a secret. A big one. Something that could change their relationship and future.

But the secret that he was nervous about—it wasn't about the knowledge of her father. Though he truly believed that she needed to know that information, he wasn't sure when the right time to tell her was. Telling her the wrong way or at the wrong time could alter the way that she processed the news.

However, this secret—while it was a doozy—was a different one. Something that he had been hiding for several weeks. This was another thing that needed to be the right place and time. Hugh felt that this was something that he needed to share one-on-one with Zoie, and someone was always there, so he had not found the right opportunity.

He was choosing this day to be the right opportunity.

He quietly got out of bed, careful to not move so much that it woke Zoie. She had more than once told him that he was as subtle as a rhinoceros when getting out of bed. The very first thing that he did was go to his office to grab a couple boxes from his closet, careful to not let the door creak as he opened it—Zoie insisted that door was haunted, based on the loud noise it made.

Zoie rarely went into his office, let alone the closet, but still, he had placed these presents up on a shelf that he knew she could have never reached, even with the little stepladder that he had gotten for her. As he placed his hand on the items, he casually thought about why he bothered getting her the stepladder when she could just use magic to move the items—*it's because she likes to do things independent from magic, just to prove she could do it anyways,* he reminded himself.

After making sure that he was quiet up to this point, he accidentally disregarded his efforts by not being cautious as he closed the door. It creaked so loudly that it nearly echoed throughout the nearly silent house—the electric buzz from the refrigerator was ever-present (and ever-annoying).

Hugh rolled his eyes at his blunder and sighed. He considered checking whether or not this woke Zoie and decided against it. If she woke up, then he would just have to deal with it. Checking on her would create an additional opportunity to mess up his entire plan.

He quietly made his way out to the kitchen. He placed the larger of the two gifts on the table and, for the small one, he actually took it out of the packaging and put it in the pocket of his pajama pants. He took the packaging and put it in the trash, actually going to the extra effort to put other things on top to hide the evidence.

Zoie particularly enjoyed waffles, but she never went to the effort to make them. She never had a particular reason as to why, but she often claimed that it was because cleaning the waffle iron was such a pain in the ass.

Hugh was still on a mission to keep things quiet, but he must have made too much noise because Zoie came walking out, in his shirt—the buttons totally done wrong—and her hair in a messy bun. In Hugh's opinion, she looked adorable. Perfect.

"Good morning." He smiled and immediately got back to work.

"Whatcha doin'?" She started encroaching on his space in the kitchen as if she was investigating. He could even hear her making sniffing noises as she took in the scent of the waffles cooking in the iron.

He looked up. "Making breakfast. Your favorites." He pointed towards the table. "Go sit down."

"Did you do something that I should know about?" She eyed

him suspiciously as she did as he told. The kettle and the tea—her three favorite flavors only—were already at the table. "Just my tea?"

Hugh nodded. "Yes."

"And waffles?"

"Yes."

"And raspberries?" Those were on the table too.

He chuckled. "Yes."

He heard Zoie make a "hmmm" sound, and once he turned around, she was examining the large box on the table. She was trying to peek while not actually opening—or even touching—the gift.

Trying to not make a big deal about it, he said, "Oh, that's just a gift for you."

"Why?" She was really starting to get suspicious. She even squinted a little in his direction.

He replied, "No reason."

She was still mildly suspicious. "It's not my birthday." She shrugged. Then she smiled widely. "But I like when you get me gifts. They are always so good." She sat down and started opening the box. She was always someone who tried to open the wrapping paper very gently, as if she was going to use it again, to present the illusion that she was an adult and beyond childish excitement. But Hugh knew otherwise. She was aching to just tear into it.

He refused to interfere. Especially since he needed a few extra moments to ensure that he was truly prepared. His initial plan had involved breakfast in bed, but this was going to have to do.

As he pulled the last waffle out of the iron, Hugh turned to see her pulling the gift out of the box.

"A book?"

He nodded. "Read it." Of course he was going to make a book part of her surprise. He loved books. She loved books. They loved to read books together, and now that they had eternity together, their goal as a couple was to read as many books as possible. It had started as "a million books each", but Zoie had started to feel like that wasn't enough. After picking two or three more large numbers, she just suggested "as many as possible" and that's what stuck.

She opened the first page. "Oh! It's a pop-up book!" Looking at it very closely, she asked, "Is this the first time we met? Look at the apple on the floor. It even has a bite out of it!" She looked up at him. "How did you do this?" She was impressed and excited—this was going exactly how he had hoped.

He revealed honestly, "I'm not even going to pretend that I put it together. I had it made." He sat down next to her. "Keep going. I want to know what you think."

He watched as she went from page to page, each with a pop-up of memories from their relationship, like their first date or the day they moved in together. As she got to the second to last page he got up and moved the chair. She was so engrossed in looking at the pictures, she didn't even look up when it scratched across the floor.

When she turned to the last page, the pop-up was a likeness of them, with him proposing to her. There was a banner that read "Will you marry me?"

"Hugh…" She turned towards him, finding him on one knee next to her.

This was the most nervous that he had ever been. In his entire life. This topic of marriage had come up several times over the course of their relationship, and only recently had she indicated that it was a possibility. A few weeks ago, he had decided to take the chance and ask her.

Hugh took a deep breath and then said, "Please, let me ask before you…" he wasn't certain that she was going to say yes—

which was no bearing on how she felt. He knew that she loved him, no matter how she answered. But he also didn't want to give her the idea of saying no. "Just let me ask before you respond, okay?"

She smiled at him. "Go on."

"It's really simple, Zoie." He pulled the ring out of his pocket. "I've waited nearly 200 years to find someone that I want to spend my forever with. It's you, Zoie. I'm asking you to spend your eternity with me. Will you marry me?"

Zoie nodded and then, quickly and quietly, replied, "Yes."

Hugh looked up at her, more surprised by her answer than he thought he would be. "Yes?"

She stood up. "Yes, Hugh. Yes, I will marry you."

As he stood up, he put his arms around her, picking her up and spinning around. When he put her down, he kissed her. "You sure?"

She laughed. "Are you?"

"Yes." He kissed her again.

"I'm sure." She looked up at him. "Do I get to wear the ring or is it just a prop?"

At that moment, he realized how badly his hands were shaking. The werewolf who could effortlessly rip someone limb for limb was completely at Zoie's mercy at any given moment. "Oh, it's yours." He took her hand, gently sliding it on her finger.

She looked at it and smiled. "You did a really good job." She added, "I wish you would have waited for a moment where I was better dressed, but…"

He disagreed. "No. This is exactly how I wanted it. Us, how we are when no one else is around."

He watched as she moved the ring to see how it looked when the light hit it different ways. Then she sat down and looked at the book again. "This was just so clever." She smiled and started to touch the pages and the pictures, feeling how it worked when the pages opened.

"I'm glad you like it." He could see Zoie trying to not look at the ring—and he knew it was because she was trying to not make a big deal about the actual engagement ring. It had come up in conversation before how she really felt it was tacky when people were obsessed with the ring more than the commitment they'd just made.

"Can we keep it to ourselves for now? Tell our friends when we see them next, instead of calling?" She took a bite of her waffles and flipped back to the first page of the book again.

He sat down next to her. "You can choose who we tell and when. We can do whatever you want. At your speed." He actually was in favor of this, anyways. He loved their friends, but sometimes, he wanted things that were just for them for a while.

She moved her chair closer to his. "I want to find a way to free nearly 18,000 innocent people. I don't think I could concentrate on planning a wedding until we've completed that task or I feel confident that we, well, at least exhausted all possible attempts at doing so."

He put his arm around her. "We have eternity to figure out both." Hugh really didn't care how long it took them to get married. He actually just wanted to be engaged for a while—so that they could enjoy each stage of their relationship. This was the first relationship that he was truly in. The only time he had ever been in love. Besides, this was definitely a big step for Zoie, especially since she didn't think she would ever agree to it again after her previous broken engagement. He was happy taking these steps at a pace that worked for her.

She continued to flip through the popup book, smiling. Each time she visited a page, she found something new and was excited about it. Hugh knew that the novelty of it would wear off eventually, but, for a while, she was really going to be giddy about it.

This was a major tick in the win column for Hugh and his gift-giving skills. He did his best not to think about—not to compare—but while Silas could whisk Zoie away to anywhere in the world, Hugh felt as if his bond with Zoie gave him the opportunity to take a different route. One with a deeper connection or meaning.

Zoie eventually stood up and placed the book on the coffee table, in the front of the basket of books that were displayed there. "I really love this. Where did you come up with that?"

"It kind of just came to me." Hugh chuckled. "It was either that or I was getting a mug and writing 'Say Yes' in the bottom so that you would see it when you finished your tea."

She pretended to be shocked. "And poison me with permanent marker? Hugh Davies, I thought you were smarter than that. You kill off your partner after you're married and have confirmed that the life insurance policy has you named as the sole beneficiary." She walked back over and sat on his lap. "Tsk tsk tsk."

He shrugged. Then he reminded her, "You're already dead, remember?" He had meant it in a joking manner, but when she frowned, it was apparent that he had missed the mark. "What's wrong?"

"Well…" she sighed. "Well, it's just never made sense to me. Why did my mom move so quickly to have me marked as deceased? There was never a body—obviously." She motioned towards herself. "I was a missing person, not dead."

Hugh felt the electricity that radiated through him when he and Zoie touched start to vibrate so slowly that it was feeling sluggish. She was truly upset about this, and it pained his heart.

"I didn't know it bothered you so much. I mean, the last time you saw her…" He didn't exactly know how to express how badly he felt that it had gone. The entire thing had culminated with Zoie—rightfully—blowing up on her mother.

Zoie's frown wasn't going away. "I think I just understand some things…" She clarified, "SOME things, not all." Continuing, she explained, "I was angry about how I felt that she dishonored the memory of my father. I think a lot of it was not being able to handle grief."

Surprisingly, Hugh agreed with that assessment. He hated giving Carol the benefit of the doubt in any situation, but the inability to handle grief was likely the culprit. "I know a little something about not being able to handle grief, and I think that it's definitely part of it." He suggested, "Maybe she wanted to get everything over with so quickly because she couldn't bear to face that she lost you too." None of these statements meant that he thought that Carol had a free pass, though. She was a grown adult and should have handled some situations with much more grace than she did.

Still, Hugh was grateful that Carol did completely off-the-wall things—such as sleeping with her daughter's fiancé—because they had led Zoie to him. And while he would have liked to believe that they would have found each other eventually no matter what, he couldn't guarantee it.

Surprisingly, Zoie admitted, "I want to see her." Hugh's face must have given away how bad of an idea this was because she added, "I don't need to talk to her. Just see. Watch for a bit. I just want to know that she's okay. That maybe she's found a way to make her life full."

"Zoie, if she sees you, she'll think she's gone completely mad," he cautioned.

She stood up. "Why? I was never dead. There was never a body."

"Zo…" He had to think of a good reason to keep her from doing this.

Shaking her head, she interjected, "No. I was a missing person.

I mean, what the fuck was even in the casket?"

He sighed. "Zoie, listen." He reached out and took her hand. "You're actively using your magic now. You aren't going to age. How are you going to explain that to her in, I don't know, ten years?"

Zoie laughed. "I'll say it's her wonderful genes and thank her. She'd love that."

He pinched the bridge of his nose. "How are you going to explain where you were for all this time?"

"She won't ask that."

Hugh looked her directly in the eyes. "You fucking kidding? *Your* mother? Not ask? She asks almost as many questions as you do."

Finally, Zoie revealed what was likely the core of what brought this up. "It's bad enough that Daddy won't be there to walk me down the aisle when I marry you. I want her there." She twisted the ring on her finger.

Deep in Hugh's brain, he started to think of ways that Victor could be there—especially now that he knew where to find him. Perhaps Silas was incorrect. Perhaps her father wasn't tied to the gargoyles in the way that his life depended on their continual existence. Maybe he could walk Zoie down the aisle like she wanted. Everything was so uncertain—Hugh decided to stay the course with what he and Silas had sort-of-agreed upon.

"Come here." He waved her over and took her hands in his. "Are you sure that you want your mother telling everyone what to do on your wedding day? Telling the person doing your hair exactly how many spritzes of hair spray on each strand? Telling the caterer that he has the cake angled one degree too far? Directing the professional photographer what they need to take pics of?" To put a point on it, he reiterated, "You know that is exactly how it will be, Zoie."

He wasn't trying to change her mind. Not exactly. Hugh wanted to make sure that she knew exactly what she was going to get herself into if she went down this road.

When she didn't answer right away, Hugh requested, "Promise me that you'll think about it before taking action. And, for Christ's sake, please don't call her. She'll think it's some sort of deep-fake-conspiracy-theory and will end up on the news."

Zoie started to clean up the dishes, and, after she placed them in the sink, she paused. "Wait." She turned around to Hugh. "She knew what Lettie and Daddy were."

"Yeah?"

"She sent Lettie away because she wanted to put a stop to all the magic stuff." She smiled. He was surprised that she was happy about Lettie being sent away, since they had been so close.

Then it hit him.

*Ugh.* Hugh knew that people joked about their in-laws hating them, but Hugh knew that Carol really did hate him. Loathed him. "And?" He knew, though, that he had to go along with this line of thinking because Zoie wasn't going to let up.

"She knows about our world already. We don't have to worry about hiding this stuff." She stood in front of him, and quietly said one word, pleading. "Please."

Pretending like there was a chance that he would say no, he took in a deep breath. "Well… Zoie, you know…" He looked up at her, and she was standing there, pouting. Zoie was an expert pouter; she had different ones depending on the situation. If she was faking a pout this time, he couldn't tell. Her eyes looked genuinely disappointed that he hadn't agreed yet, and her chin was moments from shaking as if it was assisting her tear ducts in holding back the waterworks. His heart crumbled. "Fine." He wished that he could pretend to be tough—and in everyday life he was, but when it came to Zoie, she had complete control over him.

"Really?" She smiled and quickly made her way to his lap. Her hands twisted in his hair as she kissed him.

He interrupted their kiss by laughing. "I'm agreeing to this, Zoie, because I feel like if you see Carol once a year, that will be too much for you."

She started to pull his hair. Repeatedly. Sure, she probably thought his answer was unnecessary, but it wasn't like Zoie to resort to any sort of unnecessary violence—especially to Hugh's hair, which she loved so much.

Then panic filled her eyes.

"Zo? What's going on?" When she pulled again, he grabbed her arm. "Okaaaaayyyy… Stop yanking on my hair," he laughed. It didn't hurt, but he didn't understand why she was doing it.

She tried one more time, but his hold made it impossible for her to move more than her hand. "The ring. It's stuck in your hair." She looked terrified.

He laughed loudly. "Well, I guess I didn't brush it thoroughly enough." Hugh reached his hand to where Zoie's was. "Okay. I have the ring. Slide your hand out."

"I don't want to take it off." She blushed.

"My love, we'll still be engaged if you take it off." He touched his chest over his heart with his free hand. "The commitment is in here."

She slid her hand out so carefully that he could feel the reluctance racing from her brain to her hand. As soon as it was free, she held her hands, palms up, ready for him to give the ring back.

It only took him a few seconds to get it free. "…aaaaaand that is what I get for getting you a really big diamond in a really high setting." He made the gimme-gimme motion with his hand. She placed her left hand in his and he slid the ring back on her finger. "Please don't hit me with that. I've got enough scars." Hugh kissed her hand. Immediately, he pulled his hair up into a messy bun. Before she could say anything, he quickly said, "No, I'm not angry at you, and there's no danger or battle."

She laughed. "I have absolutely no fear that you would ever be *that* angry at me."

Over-dramatically pretending to be offended, he stood in disbelief. "You don't *fear* me?"

She shook her head and smiled. "You may claim to be a werewolf, but you're just a *giant teddy bear*." Zoie's lips met his, and all that electricity shot through his body. "I promise I won't tell anyone," she whispered.

"You'd better not."

# ZOIE

Hugh pressed his lips to hers very gently. "You'd better get ready. We're going to go to Pittsburgh later today. See your mom like you wanted."

"Get ready?" Zoie asked. They were very likely to just walk through Nightbrooke, and it would look ridiculous if they were carting luggage through the cobblestone streets. Hugh attracted enough attention at this point, since he was a member of the council. Plus, Zoie was the witch who came back from the dead. No one wanted to interact with her—some newer members of the community actually feared her due to her alleged ability to cheat death. Add that to being a council member's bonded mate. It was like high school all over again, and she was the biggest outcast. The clicking of the wheels against the stones would just exemplify what was already a target on them.

Hugh pushed a piece of hair behind her ear. "Yeah. Prepare. Mentally." He kissed her forehead. "Emotionally." Bringing her hand to his mouth, he kissed it. "If you think she's going to lose her mind about your being alive, you know that she will be unreasonably unhinged about our engagement." He chuckled. "She really hates me."

Zoie wished that she could tell him that he was misreading her mother's signals, but the truth was that he wasn't. Carol didn't mince words. She disliked Hugh and, despite her distaste for many of her daughter's decisions—and sometimes her daughter herself—she didn't think Hugh was good enough for Zoie.

More excited than she expected to be, Zoie quickly ran to the bathroom to begin preparing for the trip. She turned on the water for the shower, but before stepping in, she paused. "Oh, I can't wear this in there."

Looking down at her hand she finally really took a look at the ring: a black, square cut diamond in a platinum setting. Zoie loved that it was simple, yet unique, and she had meant it when she told him that he did well.

Smiling, she slid it off of her hand and put it securely on the tiny dish she had for her other jewelry when she was in the shower. "You'll be safe there."

Zoie liked to believe that she did some of her best thinking while in the shower, which she used as an excuse if she took an extra-long one. This one was going to be an extra-long one, as she tried to practice explaining to her mother what took her so long to come visit.

After thinking of several, she started saying some of the options out loud, so she could test them out. "…I wasn't sure if you would be safe…" she shook her head. "No, no. She'll never believe that." She rinsed her hair out. "Maybe I should just go with the truth: I didn't want to see you after the last time we were together." So far, that was her favorite.

She ultimately decided to say whatever came to her mind when the time came. With that, she was able to concentrate on the rest of her shower and getting ready.

The getting ready part only took a long time when she was nervous. And this time, she was actually nervous. She wanted to make sure that whatever she chose complemented the beautiful ring that Hugh had given her, but she also didn't want her mother to be able to make some negative comment about how she chose to dress herself.

After four different outfits and staring at herself in the mirror, pretending to be the critical mind of her mother, Zoie finally decided that there wasn't an outfit on the planet that she could choose that her mother wouldn't find something wrong with.

She opted for dark jeans and a black sweater with three large, silver buttons up the sleeves. She pulled her hair into a messy bun and threw on her favorite pair of earrings—long, black triangles. Zoie then changed from her tortoise-shell-colored glasses to her black frames. She was ready to go.

"I'm ready," she announced as she walked out to the living room, where Hugh had been relaxing and reading a book while he waited for her.

When he looked up, he chuckled, and immediately, Zoie knew why—he too had dressed in dark jeans and a black shirt. He asked, "Do you want me to change my shirt or are we going as twins?"

"Twins." She grinned. She didn't care that they wore the same thing, but rather, she thought that it was kind of cute.

"We're just spending the day there, right?" He asked, nearly begging.

Zoie chuckled. "Correct. Why do you ask?"

"I just wanted to know if we could leave our car parked in downtown or if we should get a Lyft." That was, most certainly, a lie. Zoie knew that he wanted to minimize the time that he had to spend with Carol. Still, she let it go. It didn't matter in the big scheme of things. Hugh grabbed the keys to the car from the little bowl next to the door. "Ready to do this?"

Zoie nodded, and it wasn't long before they were on their way to the Storyteller Fountain in the 5 Points South area in Birmingham.

This fountain—The Storyteller—was one of her favorite places in Birmingham. It was the first place that she experienced real magic, and beside this fountain was where she stood when she first consciously decided to allow herself to trust Hugh.

Hugh held her hand as they walked towards the side where the portal was. He put his hand on the top of the wall, and Zoie tossed a coin in the water, even though it wasn't truly necessary. Hugh's magic alone could get the portal opened, but she liked doing it. Besides, even though the coin represented the magic that it took for her to open the portal, Zoie secretly always made a wish, too.

This time, she wished for a good, healthy visit with her mother. She knew it was a long shot, so she wouldn't give up on coin-wishes when it didn't come true, but she honestly did hope that it would.

Stepping into the magic and walking down the damp stairs that appeared within the fountain, Zoie still held Hugh's hand, tightly. Just in case the magic didn't want to work for her that day. Most days, she had to pinch herself to make sure that she was awake— she couldn't believe that magic or a supernatural underground world really existed and that she was someone who actually had supernatural powers.

Hugh reached forward and opened the old wooden door and then guided Zoie through. The moment that her foot touched the cobblestones, she felt a sense of peace and belonging, and then in the next moment, she rolled her ankle.

Her fiancé quickly caught her, but the damage was done. No, not her ankle—her ankle was fine. Her ego was bruised, and her cheeks were red.

She tried to laugh it off. "I'm such an embarrassment."

Hugh smiled at her. "Well, I don't think anyone saw, and, if they did, fuck 'em." He added, "Besides, I don't think they would dare say anything about a council member's partner. Y'know, the gargoyle life doesn't seem too appealing."

Walking off the embarrassment, Zoie turned to him, shocked by what he had just said. "You wouldn't!"

Leaning in closely, he whispered in her ear. "No, I wouldn't, but others might." As they started walking again, he admitted, "I don't like that sometimes I do have to act like a total dick."

Zoie was conflicted about this. Both of them firmly believed that being your true self was always the best way to go. However, when politics get involved, sometimes there's a game to be played. She knew why he had to do this—he had to play the part so that they could get the info they needed. At first they had considered if he should just be himself, but, together, they determined that the other members of the council would never truly let him in if he didn't give in a bit.

On the other hand, she hated seeing—and feeling—his anguish from going against his personal beliefs. Their mating bond created an empathetic connection between them, and the amount of times that he wished he could have made a difference totaled far, far more than either of them had expected.

She constantly wished there was something that she could do to ease his mind or make things better, but, in the end, Zoie convinced herself that freeing these gargoyles would be a start. With that, she made it her personal mission to try and find the spell that would release these victims from their prisons. That was why she purchased and read every spell book she could find— even those ones online that were obviously made up as a modern version of self-care. So, while she was soaking in the bathtub in the "potion" she made from ground up rose petals and essential oils, she was reading another book about the power of the sea or the moon. Protection spells. Green witch theory. *Solar Flares and Mercury Retrograde: How to Combat the Chaos.* Literally any book on magic she could find.

She was coming up empty. Knowing more about how the witches created the gargoyles didn't really lead her anywhere near how to reverse it. The ideas she had all fell through.

As the pair of them walked through the center of town, her thoughts were interrupted by the sighting of a figure in the shadows near the entrance to the forest. For a second, the trauma of her experience with Miles came back to her. But only for a second. After reminding herself that his presence in the world was impossible, she recognized the figure pretty quickly.

Turning to Hugh, she went to open her mouth, but he interrupted her. "Go. I'll be at the tavern."

When he released her hand, she didn't want to seem too eager, so she waited for him to take the first steps away from her. Then, taking her quick, small steps, her little legs carried her to the man who was leaning against the building, waiting for her.

The moment she was close enough, she felt a hand around her wrist, pulling her close, further into the shadows behind the building. As soon as they were out of sight, his lips were on hers.

"Silas," she stated the obvious, as their mouths parted. "How did you…"

He cut her off. "I can always feel where you are. I told you— there's nowhere you can go that I wouldn't find you." Silas ran his hand down her arm and went to take her hand, but stopped. "What's this?" He lifted her left hand to look, and the smile that had been on his face evaporated from existence. "Oh."

"Silas…"

He stepped back. "No. No need to explain." He ran his hand through his hair. "I mean—Congratulations." The sentiment seemed little more than half-hearted, but Zoie knew he was trying his best to be supportive. Silas and Zoie had talked at great length about the dynamic of their relationship and how it would fit into the relationship she had with Hugh—and among that, potential future plans with Hugh and how that could change the dynamic.

"Silas, it's okay if you aren't overly excited about this news." Zoie reached out for his hand, but he moved away.

Silas turned around and paced, and then returned. "Zoie, I expected this someday. I expected you to agree to marry him. He's your primary partner, and you love him. I get it. But… but… and I know that we've talked about it, but how will this affect our relationship? Have you and Hugh discussed this? Now that this is a real thing that's happened and the next logical steps will happen, have you really discussed how this changes things?"

Zoie shook her head. "This just happened this morning, and we've not had time to."

Silas let out a deep breath that he was holding, and Zoie knew that there was nothing that she could say to ease the hurt that he was feeling. She reached out, again, and took his hand—his hand that *used to* have a tattoo in Latin that led all the way up his arm. "Silas… your tattoo… the one that was moving last night. It's gone."

He seemed disappointed. "I'm no longer bound to the contract I made with your father."

"That's strange. Like, what could have changed? My father has been dead for nearly twenty years." In all of her research, she had never found anything that could release an eternal vow besides the party that initiated it releasing the other party—not even death.

Silas shrugged. "Maybe there was a time limit or something that I missed. Or maybe once you make a binding commitment to someone that can protect you, it expires." He didn't seem convinced of any of those ideas. He frowned and then added, "At least now you know for sure that I'm with you because I want to be."

Zoie frowned as he referenced their conversation the previous night. "I deserved that, I suppose." She pressed her lips together. "Look, maybe I should go. It seems like we're having an off day, and we're hurting each other. I don't want one of us to say something we will regret."

Then Silas went one sentence too far. "Go ahead. Run back to your *fiancé.*"

Zoie wanted to fight back, but she held back every instinct that she had. She reminded herself that he was hurting, and she did her best to give him a pass in her heart. Instead of saying something harsh or hurtful or anything that could be misconstrued, she chose a bit of honesty. "We're going to visit my mother. I'll reach out once we're done with our visit, okay?"

He pressed a gentle kiss on her cheek. "Talk soon." Silas turned and walked into the forest, disappearing behind a tree. Sometimes she hated how he could just disappear into the shadows.

She stood there for a few moments, wondering if she should have left the ring in her pocket or at home. Should she have told Silas in another way? Should she have not taken the detour to come to speak with him? The one thing she wasn't questioning was her response to Hugh's proposal. That resolve, even though she was hurting Silas, just reinforced how she had made the right decision for herself.

Zoie took a deep breath and headed towards the tavern, where

Hugh was waiting for her. The moment she walked thought the door, she found him, sitting at the corner of the bar. He wasn't alone, though. He was engaged in a conversation—that he actually seemed excited about. He was smiling. Smiling with his eyes. While talking to a woman. A woman that Zoie didn't know. She searched her memories of women that Hugh had mentioned—and this woman didn't fit any of the descriptions.

There had been very few times in their relationship that Zoie was jealous, and this moment just happened to become one of them, possibly pushing the count into the "several" category.

This woman looked flawless. Tall. Probably zero percent body fat. Not a wrinkle or blemish on her face. Her hair was long, straight, and without a single flyaway. It was a bold red—obviously her natural color, and it didn't appear as if she had a single white or grey hair in it. Zoie could see the sparkle in her blue eyes from the doorway. This woman was hitting on Hugh, and if there was any uncertainty on Zoie's part, it was completely confirmed when this woman playfully reached her hand over and placed it on top of Hugh's hand that was on the bar.

Zoie didn't wait to see his reaction, but if he hadn't moved his hand by the time that Zoie got to him, there would be hell to pay. Simultaneously gathering her courage and centering herself, she walked through the loud crowd and, when she reached Hugh, she reached up with her left hand and touched his forearm. His other hand—the one in question—was on his drink.

He turned to her and smiled. Immediately her turned to the woman he had been talking to. "Vivienne, this is my fiancée, Zoie." He stood up to give his seat to Zoie, kissing her hand once she was seated. "Vivienne and I were just catching up after not seeing each other for quite some time."

Vivienne smiled, "Oh, she's *adorable*." The word was spoken so patronizingly that even Hugh picked up on something being wrong.

His facial expression was of concern for himself more than anything else, as he looked back and forth between the two of them before motioning to the bartender.

Zoie knew that she should have just been mature and said thank you for the backhanded compliment, but she couldn't. "So, Violet, how long have you known Hugh? Were you someone that he met when he had first become a werewolf or…?"

Vivienne interrupted her. "It's Vivienne." She continued, "Hugh and I were friends when he studied in Spain. I was there for a year, visiting a friend, but spent most of my time with Hugh. I'm honestly shocked he had any time for his studies."

"Hmm." Zoie pretended to be thinking. "Hugh's never mentioned you." She added, waving absentmindedly, "but, you know how men are, Victoria. If they don't think that something's important, they just forget about it." The bartender slid a drink over to Zoie—her usual: unsweetened iced tea—and Zoie took a sip through the straw. The bartender smiled at Zoie, knowing exactly what her intentions were with her side of the conversation.

Hugh must have felt the tension because, just as Vivienne was about to correct Zoie again, he interjected. "My love, when you are done with your drink, we should probably get going. I know you're eager to get to our destination."

Vivienne stood up and grabbed her bag. "Actually, I best be going as well. I have someone I'm meeting. Wouldn't want to keep *him* waiting." She looked Zoie up and down. "It was lovely meeting the *girl* that has finally managed to make an honest man of Hugh Davies."

Zoie waved at her. "It's always lovely meeting an *old* friend of Hugh's. Don't be a stranger, Vivica."

Vivienne rolled her eyes before turning towards the exit, not even bothering to correct her. Zoie watched her leave with a critical eye. She took another sip of her drink.

It took just a moment for Zoie to realize how hypocritical she was being. She quickly apologized to Hugh. "Were you on a date with that woman? Did I just crash a date?"

Hugh laughed loudly. "Vivienne? No. Absolutely not."

"What do you mean '*absolutely not*?'" Zoie asked. "You seemed into the conversation before I made my way over here…"

Hugh let her trail off, smiling at her the entire time. "Wait—are you *jealous*?" He poked her side a little bit, tickling her.

"No…" She blushed. "Maybe a little." She was insanely jealous, even though it wasn't right of her to feel that way. But agreeing to an open relationship didn't create some contract with her emotions that would keep them locked away.

"Zo…" He took her hand in his. "You know it's only you for me." Hugh wiggled her ring a little bit. "It'll always be only you."

Zoie knew of one time after they met that it wasn't *only* her—but it was a time that she forgave him for, since he was grieving due to her supposed death. Besides, the woman was a witch and had enchanted him. Still, Zoie reminded him, "You can date, Hugh." Placing her arms around his waist, she looked up at him.

Hugh touched her chin gently and then placed a kiss on her cheek. "I don't want to." His mouth lingering next to her ear, he repeated in a whisper, "It's only you for me." He looked her in the eyes so intently that it nearly bore a hole into her soul. "Forever."

He touched her nose with his finger, actually vocalizing "Boop", and then kissed her cheek quickly, once again. Zoie couldn't help but laugh. She bunched some of his shirt in her hands and pulled him closer.

As he held her with one arm, he reached in his pocket for his wallet with the other and settled the bill with the bartender. Zoie was impressed that he signed the receipt with his left hand—and that the scribble looked pretty much like his actual signature.

Hugh held the door for Zoie as they exited the tavern, but as soon as they both were beyond the threshold, a young girl—appearing to be maybe in her late teens or early twenties—was in front of them.

"Mr. Councilman." She held an envelope in her shaky hands.

He smiled at her, gently. "You can call me Hugh. What's your name?" Hugh motioned for her to walk with him so that they were out of the way.

She followed him, and her small stature made her look like a child next to him. "I'm Penny." She glanced at Zoie, uncertain if she could speak freely.

"Penny, this is my partner, Zoie." He motioned towards his mate. "She can be trusted with whatever you need to speak with me about, but if you would feel more comfortable, she can step away."

She looked cautiously back and forth between them, and then nodded. "She can stay." Her shaky hands presented him with the envelop. "This contains a petition signed by me and about 100 other vampires to request that the limit on vampire creation be reviewed and punishment for those that would no longer be in violation to have their punishment ended and records expunged."

Hugh smiled and took the envelope. "Penny, I would be happy to take a look at this and bring it to the rest of the council for review."

"The vampire that recently was imprisoned," she admitted, "is my brother. He has been a model citizen for many, many years. Decades. There must be a statute of limitations."

Trying his best to remain neutral and not make any promises, Hugh nodded in understanding. "I will request that the council review his case. You are welcome to ask for an update at any time." He grabbed a business card from his wallet. "My contact information is on this card."

She took it and smiled as best as she could. "I appreciate this, Mr. Hugh."

"I hope I can be of some help." As she walked away, Hugh's face fell into a frown. He turned to Zoie. "Please, put this in your purse. When we get somewhere more… private… I want to take a look at it and see what they are proposing." He ran his hands down his face. "I agree with her, but I feel like I'm powerless to make a change, even though I should be able to."

She knew that being stuck between a rock and a hard place was killing him. It was painful for her to watch. "Hugh…" Zoie placed her hand on his forearm. "I think it says something that she chose to come to you with it instead of the vampire on the council." She reassured him, "Penny thinks you *can* make that change. I'm sure others believe in you, too." She added, "I know I do."

He sighed and looked at her. "They believe I can—you do, but can I actually do it?" Hugh shook his head. "I don't know. I don't want to let her down. I don't want to let those innocent victims locked in gargoyle form down. The faeries that are stuck in forced labor…" He took in a deep breath. "Let's talk about this later."

Zoie could feel that he was hurting—the fire inside of her that was lit by him was waning. She didn't want to talk about this later. She wanted to fix this now. But Hugh had voiced what he wanted to do, and she wasn't going to push. At least not right in the moment. There would be plenty of negative emotions for both of them once they got done visiting her mother.

# HUGH

The gravel under the tires crunched as the car slowly made its way closer to Carol's house. Hugh couldn't understand why she didn't pave the driveway—she certainly had the money to do so—but Zoie had once insisted it was because if the driveway was paved, she would have to commit to it always being in that location, and Carol couldn't commit to anything.

Once the car was in park, Hugh turned to Zoie. "Are you sure you want to do this?" He sure as hell wasn't.

"I have to know that she's okay." That's what Zoie kept saying, but Hugh felt like she was trying to convince herself more than she was trying to convince anyone else.

He reminded her, "You could do that from afar." It would be easy—check in on her time to time; check in on Bradshaw. Send her random care packages. Get her a dog. Install a secret security system. Anything but visit her.

Zoie shook her head. "I have to talk to her." She sucked in a deep breath, held it for about five seconds and then released it. Quickly opening the car door, Zoie stepped out and made her way towards the front door. Hugh knew that Zoie needed to do

79

that breathing thing about six more times before she was actually calmer, but, alas, there she went, briskly power-walking to Carol's front door.

She went to turn the doorknob. Her hand was actually on the doorknob, and before Hugh could stop her—this wasn't her home anymore; not after she *died* and Carol claimed all of her inheritance—she actually hesitated.

As Zoie pressed the doorbell, she turned to Hugh, "I suppose just walking in would have been terrifying, if combined with being back from the dead." She chuckled nervously.

He put his hand on her back. "Correct." For Hugh, though, visiting Carol at all was terrifying. Yeah, he had no problem standing up to her, but she really was brutal. The woman's tactics were no-holds-barred. He didn't want to fight with Zoie's mother and be miserable when he should have been celebrating his engagement to Zoie earlier that day.

Moments later, the door opened slowly at first, and then Carol swung it open quickly, with a flourish. She stood there, as healthy and happy as ever. No sign of mourning for her daughter. She looked at Hugh once and scowled, and then at her daughter. "What took you so long to come visit?" Swinging open the glass door, she motioned for them both to come in.

Zoie, who had assumed that her mother would have to take some time to come around to the idea of her daughter being a witch and some kind of immortal, was shocked by Carol's reaction. As she stepped into the house, she asked, "You expected me? You knew I was alive?"

"I expected you months ago." Carol didn't hold the door open for Hugh—in fact, she let go so that it would hit him in the back. "Well, I know what your father was, and Lettie. She had told me what you were when you were very young. And," she continued, "shortly after you went missing, she came to visit and told me that you were alive and safe, hidden somewhere until things got better."

"You spoke with Auntie Lettie?" Zoie asked.

Leading them to the kitchen, Carol replied, "Yes. She came to visit me a few times after you disappeared. First to explain to me what happened. The second time it was to give me some things to keep for you, and the third was to warn me to be careful. That some things had been set in motion and she didn't think that she would be able to return again for a while."

Zoie and Hugh looked at each other. Hugh asked, "These items she had you…"

Carol cut him off. "You! You knew what she was. You knew she was in trouble. You didn't protect her, and she nearly died." She put her finger in his face. "You knew my daughter was in danger and you left her alone! To die!" Carol shook her head. "Victor told me— never trust a werewolf. He would say to never trust those temper fueled dogs. He always said that there was something… something unpredictable about you!" She let out a loud, annoyed, "Ugh!"

Hugh backed up. "You knew what I was? The entire time?" She had never let on; he had just assumed that Carol hated him because he was Zoie's boyfriend. Or because he looked too old for her. Or maybe it was the scar on his face. He never considered that she knew what he was.

She started rummaging through some drawers. "I knew what you were the moment that I laid eyes on you. Lettie had told me years ago about you, when I was pregnant with Zoie. She had a vision. She was able to describe what my daughter would look like as an adult. She told me what year you would meet. She described you, and the moment I saw you—that scar—I knew you were *that* werewolf." She shook her head. "*That* werewolf that would take her into that world that I despised. The world that took my husband from me." She even admitted, "That's why I tried to push you to keep your engagement. I knew that you wouldn't be unfaithful if you made it to the altar."

Zoie rolled her eyes and shook her head. She disregarded the most recent statement and went back to something that shocked her more than anything. "Mom, you knew about him? You knew what Hugh was?" Zoie asked. "Why did you treat him with such disrespect when you met him? That's a risky move, knowing the temper of werewolves."

She turned to Zoie and smirked. "No matter how much you believed that you hated me, I knew that you didn't. It's a thing that children go through. One day, you would realize that everything I ever did was for you. So, in the end, I knew he wouldn't hurt me. If not because he loves you so much, then because you would just say his name and stop him." She glared at Hugh. "I knew I could push you as far as I wanted because your bond with her wouldn't let you hurt her in any way. Physically or emotionally." She looked back at Zoie and frowned. "I guess I was wrong. He abandoned you and let that warlock drown you. He left you to die."

Carol continued to rummage through drawers and cupboards in the kitchen like a thief and then snapped her fingers. "I'll be right back. The items Lettie left for you—I've remembered where I hid them." She headed off towards part of the house where most of the bedrooms were located. Hugh could hear her heels clicking the entire way and was actually able to pinpoint that she had entered Zoie's childhood bedroom.

As soon as she was out of earshot, Hugh turned to Zoie. Before he could speak, Zoie smiled and said, "So Lettie did actually have a vision that we were destined for each other."

He took her left hand in his and brought it to his mouth for a kiss. "Doesn't matter. I would choose you anyways." He spun her engagement ring back and forth and then smiled, "Mrs. Davies."

Slamming a leather-bound journal on the counter, Carol announced her return. She glared at Hugh and then looked at Zoie. "You've agreed to marry him? The werewolf? That let you die?" She shook her head. "I thought, at the very least, you had given up on the institution of marriage after your broken engagement?" She grumbled, "Your first fiancé was a good match. He's made partner at the firm, you know. Webster, however, is a lowly professor."

Ignoring her mother's tone and negative comments, no matter how much she wanted to remind her mother that she—her promiscuity—was actually the reason for the failed engagement, Zoie responded, "Yes, Mom. Hugh just asked today, and you are the first person I've told." She looked over at Hugh and smiled.

"Hmmm." Carol asked, with a disapproving tone, "You haven't told your friend Stevie yet?" It was almost as if she already knew the happenings of the supernatural world.

Zoie frowned. "No. Stevie and I had a falling out." He could nearly feel that she was still sad about how things ended up with Stevie. He wanted to fill that void in her heart, but how could he? No matter how hard he tried, he could never fully take off the partner hat and just be the best friend. And, even if he wanted to—which he didn't—he couldn't go back and undo the damage he had, quite literally, done.

Still, despite his best intentions, if Hugh didn't see the glare Carol was giving him with his own eyes, he certainly would have felt it. She never stopped looking at him as she asked, "What caused that?"

Oh, well, you know, Stevie just was the person that fed information to the person who nearly succeeded in killing Zoie, and when Hugh found out, he tore Stevie's skin apart so that it would never heal properly. He cut her where it counted—the one thing that truly mattered to her: her beauty.

"It's not important," Zoie replied. She changed the subject. "Tell me about this book."

"It appears to be some sort of journal." Carol slid it across the counter. "Lettie left it for you. I tried to open it, but never could. She had said that you would know how to open it. I wanted to see if I would know how too, but, since I'm just a *regular* person, I guess it's beyond me." She shrugged absentmindedly and then reached into the wine fridge and pulled out a rosé; then she turned and grabbed three wine glasses. They were surprisingly plain—no ornate designs or interesting stems. She must have been saving the good drinkware for more important guests.

Zoie was busy trying to pry open the locking mechanism. She pressed on it, tried to twist, slide, wave her hands over it. Each attempt was met with a failure. She shook her head and then looked at Hugh. "Did she give you any indication about how to open this?" She was desperate to get inside that book.

He ran his hand down her back. "No. I didn't know about this at all."

Carol, twisting the corkscrew, reiterated, "She said that you would instinctively know how to open it." She flippantly added, "I guess she was wrong." She smirked as she poured the wine into each of the glasses.

A low growl vibrated in Hugh's chest. He glared at Carol, but said to Zoie, "Sometimes, if we think about these things too much, they are more difficult." He turned to Zoie. "Leave it for later."

Carol then reached around to the back of her neck and unhooked a necklace. "This, I did open, because I recognized this item immediately." She handed it to Zoie, along with a little purple pouch, and admitted, "I wanted to keep this. It was your father's. But Lettie insisted that you would need it." She continued, "Maybe it's to protect you. So I just kept it safe. And, yes, I wore it." She sadly admitted, "It made me feel close to your father while I had it." For a single moment, Hugh felt some semblance of sympathy for Carol. He knew what it felt like to lose Zoie, and if it was a single percent of that for Carol when she lost Victor, he wouldn't wish it on his worst enemy.

Zoie opened the locket mechanism on the gold pendant to find nothing inside. The front did have a sun etched into it. "Daddy always wore this. How did Lettie get it after he died? There was nothing left…"

Carol said, "She told me that a young man—the one who had helped you get out of the car before it exploded—had found it and turned it over to her. That's all I know." She added, "She just told me, after she let me know that you were alive and safe, that one day, you would return and that I needed to give it to you." She reluctantly said, "So I am giving it to you."

Even though she had this huge house with all these belongings and money that Victor had left for her, plus all of Zoie's worldly belongings after her death, this one simple item seemed to be the most important.

Hugh took the necklace from Zoie and put it on her. "You should keep this close." She held the pendant in her hand and closed her eyes. A tear fell down her cheek. Hugh wiped it away with his thumb and started to regret, once again, that he was keeping her father's location—the fact that he was still some sort of alive—from her. It was becoming increasingly difficult for him.

Carol looked back and forth between Hugh and Zoie. "Look, I know that you can't tell me. I know that I shouldn't know about you and your world and what you are at all. But I know that if Lettie is leaving things that you will *need*, either for protection or a spell or whatever, then something big is about to happen." She stared at Hugh—right in the eyes. "Protect my daughter. Protect her with your life. Because, if anything should happen to her, I will kill you. And, if you die protecting her and she still gets injured or dies, I will bring you back to life and kill you again. It won't be pretty." She reiterated, "Not a strand of that beautiful red hair will be harmed. Do you understand me?"

Hugh wanted to laugh. The odds of Carol actually being able to give him a paper cut, let along kill him, were slim to none. However, he knew what she meant by the threat. Instead, he nodded. "Carol, every decision I make, even the unconscious ones, are in the best interest of Zoie."

She didn't believe him. "Then you should have shielded her from your world. You should have never spoken to her. You should have let her lead a normal life. Without you." She shook her head and looked at the floor. "Victor was killed because of his power and knowledge, and I just wanted my daughter to stay out of that shit. You should have kept her out of it, if you had any sense." She took a seat at the nearby table, alone except for her drink.

Zoie went to speak, but Hugh knew that it would be in his defense, and he didn't want any further strain in their relationship on account of him. He put his hand up and mouthed, "No". Stepping closer to Carol, Hugh took a seat beside her. "Carol, you're right. I failed Zoie. I have yet to really forgive myself for that. I thought I lost her, and… it was my fault. I trusted someone

I shouldn't have, and I let Zoie out of my sight for a matter of minutes, and someone took her from me. From us."

He reached out to her hand that was resting on the table. "And I wish I could say that I'll never let Zoie out of my sight again. Or that I could keep her locked away from everyone else. From anything that could hurt her. I really do." He continued, "and, I promise you, I will try to protect her. I will lay down my life for hers. In a heartbeat. I love her endlessly."

He glanced at Zoie and then continued, "But there are times when your daughter—your *difficult* daughter—makes the most bizarre decisions, and the one thing I can't protect her from is herself."

Carol shook her head. "I know you are right. I know." She actually squeezed his hand and then added, "Maybe you aren't all bad, Webster."

"Jesus fucking Christ," Zoie mumbled under her breath.

"I heard that, missy!" Carol laughed. She reached towards her daughter. "Let me check out that ring!"

Hugh excused himself for a moment, heading out to the greenhouse in the backyard, to allow Carol and Zoie to begin to rebuild their relationship. The greenhouse was secluded, and he could pace around in there and think—especially about how maybe Zoie could get that book open. It had to have some vital information about freeing the gargoyles in it. That necklace had to have some sort of use as well. Lettie wouldn't have left those items with explicit instructions to get them to Zoie if they weren't important.

In between ideas, he was admiring some of the vegetables when he heard some rustling behind him. Ready to attack, Hugh turned quickly to see what was causing the ruckus—knowing full well that it could simply be a squirrel.

To his surprise, it was Beagan, the faerie from the Gargoyle Graveyard. "What are you doing here? How? When?"

Beagan smiled brightly. "Faeries don't have to use the portals. We just think about where we want to go and we snap and, voila! We arrive!"

Hugh set aside that this was the first time he had heard of anyone—besides Silas—who didn't have to use portals to travel. He had a bigger question. "How did you know where I was?"

Beagan shook her head. "We don't have time for that." Apparently, it was an even bigger question than Hugh had thought. "I came to report some findings to you." Hugh nodded for her to continue. "The spell to create a gargoyle—it was actually created out of love."

Hugh didn't believe her. "Who would lock their love in solitary confinement?" That just didn't make sense.

Beagan shrugged. "I don't know. But I wanted to check on some of the…prisoners. Y'know, see if there was a cutoff point to where everyone had just gone mad or something. So that we knew if maybe it would be a kindness to… destroy… them."

Looking at Beagan a little more closely, he noticed that she was starting to age more rapidly than he had ever anticipated. The corners of her eyes had begun to wrinkle, and her hands were starting to look as if they had done decades of work. Faeries were supposed to have unnaturally long lives just like the rest of the supernatural beings.

She must have been spending a good deal of time in the graveyard to find him this information. She was risking her life, and he was concerned that she would go too far. "Beagan, I don't know…"

"Listen!" She hissed at him, almost as ferociously as Drusus, but her greying hair still chimed like a song, whereas his was barely there. "I went back to the very first of the gargoyles. He was crying, lovesick for someone named Mitzi. A witch. He told me of how he is stuck, decaying at the same moment in time forever—he's sick. Dying, but unable to. His lover locked him in Gargoyle form to save him, until a cure was found for his ailment."

"And a cure hasn't been found in multiple centuries?"

"Well…" Beagan frowned. "The problem is—and I corroborated this with the Keeper of the Keys, since he has all knowledge of life—once a being has been confined for 100 years, if they are freed, they will become the wind."

"Become the wind?" Hugh asked.

Beagan nodded. "Turn to ash and dust and float away. Maybe become the grass. The trees."

"So we can't save anyone who's been in there for more than a century…" He pressed his lips together and let out an angry breath. "They are suffering needlessly."

She squinted her eyes and spat at him, "All are suffering…"

Hugh interrupted her sharply, "I know that, Beagan."

"The woodland realm faeries are also…"

"I know." He shook his head.

The door to the Greenhouse opened with a creak and Zoie entered. "Who is this?"

The little faerie turned to her and curtseyed. "Beagan, ma'am. You must be Zoie. Hugh belongs to you, correct?"

Zoie looked over at Hugh and smiled. "Yes. Yes, he does." The idea of Hugh belonging to Zoie had her amused, but, for Hugh, it was just the truth.

"Well, I mustn't stay long. If other members of the council find that I have found a way to free myself, then I will be punished." She moved her hand to prepare to snap.

"Wait!" Hugh quickly called out. When she paused, he asked, "If you have the power to get out of their bonds, why do you stay?"

Beagan replied seriously, "Because I want to free all of the others, and I must do that from the inside."

"Can the others escape?" Zoie asked.

Beagan shook her head. "And, no, I do not know why I can." She was quick to make sure she didn't have to answer more questions than she wanted. Beagan hurriedly stated, "I really must be going. I will try to bring more information later." She snapped her fingers and all that was left in her place were a few sparkles that disappeared into the air with the light sound of chimes.

Hugh pulled out his phone and sent a quick message to Cade, knowing that they and Xariella were not likely to answer for a few days. He turned to Zoie. "She just told me that anyone that's been in gargoyle form for more than 100 years will be reduced to ash and dust once freed."

"Then why are they keeping them?"

Hugh shrugged. "Willful ignorance for most of them, I suspect. But all I can think is that there are some innocent people that have less than one year left of actual survival if we don't act." He said, "Beagan actually just gave me a good bit of information, and I think that we should all discuss it together. Including Silas."

"But Cade and Xariella…"

Hugh's phone started to buzz. "They are calling me right now." He answered. "Hey, you okay? I thought you wouldn't—"

Cade interrupted him. "Xari and I discovered something about her powers yesterday, so we left early. We'll be home by this evening."

"Is she… still hungry?" Hugh asked cautiously. He looked at Zoie while he was talking, worrying that if Xariella wasn't fed well enough that Zoie could become an accidental victim.

"She's good. I promise." They never took making a promise to Hugh lightly, so he was convinced well enough. Then Cade said,

"We discovered something very… interesting… while on this trip. Can we come over when we get home?"

Hugh looked at the engagement ring on Zoie's hand and smiled to himself. "Yes, but that depends on when. We've got some traveling to do before we can get home." Zoie was watering some of the plants, but Hugh wasn't convinced that she wasn't listening.

"Call her side piece and have him take you," Cade laughed.

Hugh shook his head, even though Cade couldn't see it. Lowering his voice a bit, he stated, "I don't think he's likely to assist me with anything right now."

"Did you kick his ass, finally?"

Hugh chuckled lightly. "No. But I'll tell you when I see you next." They both immediately said their goodbyes and, as Hugh was shoving his phone back in his pocket, he was reminded of the petition he had received earlier in the day. But he couldn't think about that at that moment.

Getting back on track, he told Zoie, "Apparently Cade and Xariella have something to tell us about Xariella's power. I hope that it's useful. They should arrive home tonight. How do you feel about telling them our good news as well?"

Zoie's face looked enthused, but there was a sadness behind her eyes. "Sure! That will be wonderful."

Hugh put his arms around her. "Something is off. Tell me."

She placed her hands on his chest and, despite not physically stepping back, she was mentally pulling away from him, despite trying not to. He could feel the electricity of his bond with her surge very gently and fade.

"You've been slightly off most of the day. Is this about Silas? Did he not react well when you saw him earlier?" He searched her eyes for a response. "If you want, I can talk to him about how this step forward for us doesn't mean that anything has to change for you and him."

"No." She replied. "I mean, yes, he reacted poorly—and why wouldn't he? But, no it's not about Silas, and, most certainly, no, I don't want you to talk to him about it." Still in his arms, there was space between them. Dropping her hands from his chest, she kneaded her left palm with her right thumb. "I just…"

Her hesitation was killing Hugh. "Zoie, it's not like us to keep secrets from one another." Oh, the hypocrisy because he was certainly keeping a cosmic secret from her. "Tell me."

A tear that she had been trying to force back into her tear ducts escaped. "I just kind of thought, ever since we met, that when this time came… I just thought…"

He wiped another tear from her cheek. "Zoie, whatever it is, you can tell me." Even if it was that she felt that she made the wrong decision saying yes to him.

She finally blurted it out—rapidly, without a breath and almost as if it was one long, run-on sentence. "I just thought that Stevie would be here with me, right beside me. My best friend. And, and, and… And I really like Xariella, and she's much better for Cade. And she's great, but Stevie was the one who *really* put us together in the first place, after I thought you were trying to make up an elaborate story to break up with me. She was my first ever best friend." She buried her head in Hugh's chest and sobbed.

"It makes sense that you would want to include Stevie in this big moment in your life." He continued, "Sometimes people come into our life for a reason and once that mission is completed, they exit." Hugh knew that telling her that wasn't really helping. He just didn't know what else to say at the time.

Hugh wanted to be angry. He wanted to tell Zoie that she

was being foolish to even think about *considering* the possibility of *entertaining* the idea of Stevie being a part of her life. But he couldn't be angry. She was still, in a way, grieving the loss of her friend. Sure, Stevie wasn't dead. But the Stevie that Zoie knew was long, long gone. It was possible that the Stevie that Zoie had known never even really existed.

The best thing that he could do, Hugh figured, was hold her while she cried. He didn't say anything. Just held her tightly. Before, he simply thought that there was a slim chance that he could forgive Stevie for what she did, but in this moment, seeing Zoie hurt and vulnerable because she lost a friend—not simply because this person was an agent of her death—due to Stevie's choices, Hugh felt that slim chance become smaller and smaller until it was less than dust in a beam of sunlight.

In this moment, he regretted not ending Stevie when he'd had the chance.

# ZOIE

It took Zoie far too long, in her opinion, to gather her composure in that greenhouse, and, once she did, her mother asked her what could have possibly been making her cry. Zoie claimed that she hadn't been crying, that it was allergies from the plants. Carol didn't buy it, but she didn't push—for once.

Something had changed in Carol, and Zoie didn't know what it was—but she also wasn't going to question it. Maybe it was that she was glad to have not lost her daughter forever. Maybe it was the idea of wedding planning. Maybe it was a facade just for the day. Whatever it was, it was good enough for Zoie.

By the time that Hugh and Zoie were on the road back to the nearest portal, Zoie felt as if she had made real progress with her mother. She was starting to feel like there was a possibility of some sort of relationship, especially since her mother knew what she was—she knew about their world, and she was an agent of delivering them some vital tools for their mission, even if she didn't know what the actual mission was. Zoie recognized that Carol could have easily neglected to give her the book and the necklace; or, she could have destroyed them; or refused to hold them for Lettie, but she'd gone with the plan. She wasn't going to ask her mother what caused the change. Zoie was just going to appreciate it.

Still, as she sat there in the passenger seat, absentmindedly slipping through her phone, the one feeling she couldn't shake was that she was missing a piece of her life without Stevie—the first real friend she had ever had. Well, Zoie had thought that she was a real friend. Apparently, in the end, though, she wasn't. Another example of how Zoie struggled to read people for what they really were.

Hugh and Cade had both told her that Stevie allegedly made that choice to get back in with her family, as her father had threatened to cast her out if she didn't. Perhaps that was a lie to save face, but if it was the truth, it could have been Hugh's scarring her for eternity that took it into the territory of no return. The final nail in the coffin may have been Cade's finding their mate and brushing Stevie aside.

But what if there was a way to salvage it? Zoie didn't want to live for eternity with regret, and if she didn't reach out to Stevie, she would have regrets. On the flip side, if she reached out to Stevie, she might not have long to live.

Seemingly involuntarily, Zoie found herself drafting a text message.

*Stevie-it's Zoie. I am not even sure if this is your number anymore, but I just had to try to reach out. Some exciting things have been happening lately, and ever since the day I met you, I had always thought you would be here with me during these moments. I am not sure if you're open to reconciliation… TLDR: I miss you.*

She glanced over at Hugh, just to make sure that he wasn't paying attention. His eyes were fixed on the road and the excess traffic in Pittsburgh, so Zoie pressed send. She turned her phone over on her leg so that she wasn't watching it like a pot of water waiting to boil.

Before she knew it, her phone was vibrating. Trying not to be overly excited, Zoie flipped her phone back over. The banner notification on her lock screen stated that she received a text message.

She opened the app and read the message: *Message sent to invalid destination. Please check your number and try again.*

Disappointed, Zoie slid her phone into her purse. Then she pulled out the book from Lettie and started to examine it. She sighed. "How in the French toast am I supposed to instinctively know how to open this?"

Her forearm warmed from the touch of Hugh's hand. "You'll figure it out."

She turned the book over in her hands, stopping to admire the spine. The cover was leather and all of the designs were obviously hand-created. Hearts with daggers through them. Trees with defined roots. Crescent moons over waves. And then she saw it in the center of the spine: A sun shaped exactly like the design on her pendant.

"Hmmm." Refusing to unlatch the chain, Zoie tried to line the design up to the etching in her pendant while still wearing it. The navigation of Pennsylvania roads made it difficult for Zoie. Hugh had to evade potholes as if it was a challenge in a video game, so they were swerving all over the road. She made the conscious decision to wait to try again until they were at home, as she didn't want to lose the last thing that she had of her father's into the abyss of the rental car—never to be seen again.

Failure.

She let out a deep, annoyed sigh. "I'm just going to give up for now."

Still focused on the road, Hugh replied, "Good." When Zoie shot him an angry glance, he continued. "Zoie, if you concentrate on it too much, you'll just never get it. If you are supposed to know *instinctively*, then it will just come to you." He cautiously added, "I love you dearly, but sometimes, honestly, you get in your own way."

Zoie rolled her eyes. "I wish Lettie or my dad were around to just tell me what the fuck I need to do." A lightbulb went off in her head and she excitedly suggested, "Maybe you could take me to that Gargoyle Graveyard and your friend Beagan can help me communicate with Lettie."

"Eh, Zoie." Hugh shook his head. "That's not a good idea."

"Why?"

Answering too quickly—as if he had a prepared answer—Hugh replied, "The Keeper told me that that place draws the life out of you."

For a second, Zoie thought it was a reasonable thing to worry about, then she stated, "But we're immortal. We have eternal life."

Hugh actually let out a quiet growl. "Zoie, you of all people know that we're not truly immortal. Just because we're kind of immortal, it doesn't mean that we can't die. We age. It's extremely slowly when we use our powers regularly, but if we stop, we'll age like normal." He looked over at her, only to be met with furrowed eyebrows.

Her arms were folded across her chest. "Did you just growl at me?" He opened his mouth to reply, but she cut him off. "Don't deny it. You just growled at me."

"You're too cavalier with your own life," he explained. Almost as a plea, he told her, "I don't want to lose you again."

Zoie shook her head very slightly. "There's something more going on here." Despite her best efforts, an angry breath escaped her nose. She stared straight out the front window, not even wanting to look at her fiancé at that moment. "You're hiding something from me, Hugh. Hiding something or lying."

He wouldn't look at her. He didn't respond. He just kept driving.

If he did anything besides concentrate on the road in front of him, he wouldn't be able to hide the information any longer.

"That's fine," she announced, passive aggressively. Zoie shrugged and then added, "You know that I can just go in your mind and find the truth."

His head snapped towards her. "We've not even been engaged 24 hours, and you want to go the route of violating my privacy? Really?"

Not backing down, Zoie didn't miss a beat. "And you are going to go the route of lying to me? Even if it's a lie by omission?"

With a sigh, Hugh flicked on his turn signal, pulling into an empty parking lot that belonged to a restaurant that looked like it had been vacant for decades. He angrily put the car in park and then turned towards Zoie. "I feel like you going to the Gargoyle Graveyard is going to cause you more pain than you could ever imagine."

"Hugh, you constantly underestimate—."

He cut her off. "No, this isn't a physical pain sort of thing. I'm not worried about your getting hurt—I mean I am, of course, but that's not what I'm focused on here."

"What other kind of pain is there?"

He looked down and shook his head. "Look, I'm not sure how to tell you this, and I've been wrestling with having this information since I got it…"

She slammed her hand on the armrest. "Damnit, Hugh. You asked me to marry you when you had a huge secret hanging in the air between us?"

As if a dam broke, Hugh revealed what he had been holding back. "I don't want you to go to the Graveyard because your father is there."

"Well, Hugh, if he's a gargoyle instead of actually dead, then that's even more reason for me to want to free them all." She quickly added, "and if you're afraid that I would just sit in there and talk to him and waste my life—."

"No, Zoie." He put his hand on hers. "He's the person that guards the graveyard."

She yanked her hand out from under his. "You knew that my father was alive and you hid that from me?"

Pre-emptive sympathetic tears actually welled up in his eyes. "Zoie, he's not alive."

"You just said that he was the Keeper of—."

"I did, and it's the truth, but you haven't seen what it's done to him. He's… he's just… he's decaying, like the weather corrodes the stone of the gargoyles." He cautiously admitted, "We have reason to believe that if we free the gargoyles, he will no longer have anything tying him to our world."

Zoie started to let that sink in, but after a few moments, she paused. "We?" That one word hung in her brain. "We." She slowly looked up until she made eye contact with Hugh. "Who is the rest of 'we'?"

Hugh pressed his lips together and shook his head. "I think you know."

She did.

He would never have to say who it was. Zoie let out a frustrated breath. *Maddening.* "And the two you together decided that it was best for me to not know this information?"

"Not until we knew some more things for certain…"

Zoie was furious. "Well, I'm glad that you two could finally agree on something." She turned her body so that she was seated correctly and stared out the passenger side window. "Take me home."

# HUGH

Well, there it was. Not even one day into being engaged, and he'd already fucked it up by withholding information. Zoie had told him, time and time again, that she felt like secrets were lies by omission.

He put the car in drive and pulled the car back onto the highway. Even after being alive nearly 200 years, ten minutes of silence—heavy silence—between him and Zoie felt like an eternity.

Slowly he said, "Sooooo…"

Still staring out the passenger window, she simply replied, "No."

"So you're just never going to talk to me again?" Well, that was a mistake.

She slowly turned her head towards him. "I was giving myself time to take in the news of my father and to try to understand why you would keep that from me." She admitted, "I'm not there yet."

He tapped his fingertips on the steering wheel. "Are you… are you reconsidering marrying me?"

She shook her head. "No. I am, however, trying to figure out why you keep things from me? We're supposed to be partners, Hugh." She immediately added, "This isn't even the first time you've done this."

"Hey! If you're talking about not telling you about what I am at first—."

She cut him off. "Piss off. You know I'm not talking about that." Zoie rolled her eyes. "How about knowing that I was witchy? Hmm? How about not telling me that my life was in danger with that price on our heads? Hmm?"

Hugh slammed his hand on the steering wheel. "'Piss off?' Really Zo? What is happening to us right now?" He added, "I did all of those things to protect you."

"Hugh, I love you. I do. I love you endlessly, but I'm furious." Hugh moved to apologize but Zoie cut him off again. "I'm, surprisingly, not angry about the specific information that you withheld. It's that you withheld it in the first place."

"Zo, I swear I wanted to tell you."

*Pfft.* She pressed her lips together into a thin line and then asked, "So, you're telling me that Silas convinced you to lie to me?"

Hugh knew that there was no way that he could win this argument. It was time to stop trying to justify what he did. "Look, Zoie, I'm sorry."

Zoie's smile had a veil of anger over it. "Hugh, you can apologize until the end of time, but unless your behavior changes, it means nothing." She looked directly at him. "Do you hear me? An apology means nothing without action."

Hugh took that in. In his nearly 200 years, he'd never cared enough about anyone that he had wronged to do anything beyond apologize, usually because those that he wronged would be out of his life shortly thereafter. This lesson, while it made sense, had been one that he never taken the opportunity to learn. He needed to soak it up like a sponge now. Immediately.

"I won't hide anything from you ever again," he promised.

Hugh reached his hand out to Zoie, with his pinky extended.

She linked her pinky with his. "You can keep presents secret." The smile on Zoie's face indicated that not only that this distinction was very important to her, but also that she was going to work towards not being angry at Hugh.

With their pinkies still linked, Zoie firmly stated, "I want to see him."

Hugh didn't think that this was a good idea. Plus, he wasn't entirely sure if the forest would permit her to travel beyond a certain point, assuming that he could even remember how to get there.

Still, he knew that if he didn't agree to this, she would just go on her own. "If that's what you truly want to do, then I will do what I can to help you. But—" Just as her mouth opened to interrupt him, he put a finger in the air. She held her thought so that he could finish. "But, Zoie, I think that we need to have some sort of plan to make sure that we aren't just wandering lost in the forest."

"Okay." She looked out the window, falling silent for the rest of the drive. Zoie was still working on that not-being-angry thing.

It wasn't until they were home—with Cade and Xariella—that Zoie actually spoke again.

"How was the trip?" Zoie asked cautiously.

Xariella looked the most physically refreshed that she had in weeks—months even. The dark, purple bags that had hung heavy under her eyes had vanished, with no evidence that they had ever even been there, and her honey-toned skin had regained all of the elasticity that had vacated it previously. Even her dark hair had regained its shine.

Still, she looked emotionally exhausted. Xariella responded to Zoie's friendly inquiry, still looking down at the table. "I chose a man from the town I had lived in as a child. He had assaulted my best friend, and I was the only person that had ever believed her." She looked up. "I was right to do so."

Cade supplemented her response. "Xariella found that she sees and feels the regrets of the individuals that she drinks." They cautiously reached out to offer a comforting touch on her back. When Xariella flinched, they retreated momentarily, but then continued the course. "The first time that she had fed, upon newly becoming a vampire, she hadn't really thought about it. It could have been that person's life flashing before their eyes or whatever."

"I had seen a wedding that time. But it wasn't until now that I realized that I was feeling my victim's regret that they hadn't spoken their feelings to the bride prior to that day." She sobbed. "I saw my friend. I saw the fear in her eyes." She turned and buried her face into Cade's shirt.

Cade held her, running their hand through her hair, gently. "Her friend ended her life because no one in a position of power believed her. Her reputation had been ruined, and she had never had the means to get out of that town. That man had continued to walk around."

Zoie, attempting to comfort Xariella suggested, "Well, you were able to get justice."

"It doesn't bring her back." Xariella's fists grabbed more of Cade's shirt, nearly tearing it away in her hands.

Cade waved their hand, silently requesting that they drop the conversation.

There was a gentle knock at the door and each one of them looked at the rest, counting, because all four of them were there, and they couldn't imagine who it could be.

Hugh motioned for everyone to be quiet while he walked towards the door. His body started to heat up and he could see the yellow color of his glowing eyes reflecting off of the glass of a clear vase.

Zoie began to say Hugh's name, but Cade reached over and covered her mouth. They whispered, angrily, "You'll keep him from shifting if he needs to."

She pushed his hand away. "It's fine. It's just Silas." She showed her phone to Cade. "Hugh, I checked the camera. It's Silas."

Hugh felt himself relax, and he opened the door. "Since when do you not just teleport to wherever you please?"

Silas ignored the question, shoving past Hugh, hitting him with his shoulder to try to move him. Trying—he hadn't been successful. In fact, he likely had bruised himself rather than done anything else.

He approached Zoie and when he reached out for her hand, she stepped back and folded her arms across her chest.

Silas didn't even ask her what was wrong; he immediately turned around and glared at Hugh. "You told her?"

Hugh refused to be provoked. "I did." It was the decision that he had wanted to make since the moment that he found out that the Gatekeeper was Zoie's father. His only regret, so far, was that he had waited to tell her in the first place. He could have avoided an argument.

Zoie cleared her throat aggressively. "And why didn't you?" Zoie's glare never faltered. Her eyelids didn't even begin to move to blink—Doctor Who's Weeping Angels would meet their match with her.

He turned around and met her glare with his own ferocity. "Because I believed that it wasn't necessary for you to know at that point. End of discussion."

Cade's eyes met with Hugh's, fearing that Zoie was going to set the entire house on fire in response to Silas.

Xariella said what everyone else was thinking. "You're going to let him talk to you like that?"

Zoie shook her head. "There's no point in arguing with him right now. He's not in the space to hear that there was another choice he could have made."

Without missing a beat, Silas replied, "You mean like you could have made another decision before just deciding to weigh your hand down with all of the responsibility that goes with that ridiculous ring?" He turned to Hugh. "You could have given me the slightest courtesy to tell me that you were planning that."

"Why?"

"Because it's the right thing to do. I'm her partner, too, and we," he pointed back and forth between Hugh and himself, "are on the same team here."

Hugh scoffed. "You mean like how you had the courtesy to pursue Zoie, knowing her commitment to me? You mean like how you showed me so much courtesy when you kissed her during a vulnerable moment and then brought her back here?" He threw his hand up like a stop sign. "No, Silas, you don't get to lecture me on the dynamic of my relationship with Zoie." He stepped towards him. "I don't tell her how to manage this pointless, temporary fling between the two of you. You certainly have less than a zero percent say in my relationship with her."

The front door slammed shut and then the car started. Hugh was knocked out of his tunnel vision of hatred towards Silas and saw Cade sitting alone at the table, eating an apple.

"Yeah, so, while you two were arguing over who knows what's best for Zoie, she and Xariella decided that they didn't care and left." They threw the apple core into the sink. "Three-point shot!"

"Where are they going?" Hugh asked, frustrated. "Also, you're putting that in the compost."

Cade stood up. "They didn't say."

Silas closed his eyes for a moment and took a deep breath. "They are headed towards Storyteller Fountain." He opened his eyes. "They are not quite to downtown, but she plans to turn onto 18th then the 20th—but she's considering going a different way to confuse us." He motioned for both of them to come closer. "We can beat them there."

"How do you know that?" Cade asked, as they stepped closer to Silas, waiting for him to put his hand on their shoulder.

He shrugged. "Sometimes when I close my eyes, I can see what she sees and feel what she feels." Silas added, "It's easier when I know that she's feeling a really strong emotion." He placed his hand on Cade's shoulder and then felt Hugh squeeze his shoulder with an unnecessary amount of force.

# ZOIE

Releasing her arms from the tight fold across her chest, Zoie reached over to Xariella and tapped her softly. When Xariella looked over, Zoie motioned with her eyes toward the front door. Xariella nodded just enough to be noticed.

The two of them got up and headed towards the exit while Hugh and Silas continued with their pissing contest, leaving Cade as the only witness to find out who would be the winner.

Grabbing the keys from bowl on the small table next to the door, Zoie intentionally let the screen door swing hard as she exited. "I have somewhere I want to go, but it may be dangerous."

Opening the passenger door, Xariella smiled. "No matter what it is, I'm in." Zoie was appreciative of her friend's willingness to just be on board, without condition.

After driving a few minutes down the road in silence, Zoie finally spoke up. "I'm going to see my father."

"Okay." Xariella smiled.

Zoie glanced over at her. "You realize that this means that we are going to have to try and navigate the forest, right? And, remember, it attacks those that aren't supposed to be there." She was trying to actually convince her friend to not put herself at risk.

Xariella shrugged. "I will go with you as far as I can."

"I may not be able to go any farther myself." She concentrated on the road, taking the most out-of-the-way route to the Storyteller Fountain, hoping to throw Silas off the trail. She knew it was only a matter of time before he figured out where she was.

She even parked a few blocks away, but as soon as they walked past the Chick-fil-a and the Fountain came into view, Zoie let out a growl. "Ugh."

Silas was sitting on the top of the wall of the fountain, swinging his legs like a child. He hopped down and walked up to Zoie, placing his hand on her forearm. "Zoie, I'm telling you that you don't want to do this."

Zoie yanked her arm free. "And I am telling you that I do."

"Zoie, we agreed to make a plan." Hugh reminded her.

She shook her head. "No, you said that we should make a plan, and I replied with 'okay' to end the conversation."

Hugh gently took her hands and guided Zoie a couple of steps away. Quietly, he asked, "What purpose do you see in doing this? What is the result that you want?" He ran his thumb over the back of her hand.

She looked up at him, realizing that the emotion behind the gaze of his green eyes wasn't angry or annoyed, but truly concerned. She sighed softly. "I just want to see him once." She admitted, "I have a feeling that our mission doesn't give him a happy ending, and I want to see him once before…"

He pulled her into a gentle hug. "Let me help you."

Zoie felt the warmth of his body against hers, and she let herself melt into him. She had focused so hard on being angry that he had kept this from her that she hadn't realized how much any decision he made was just to help her in one way or another, whether she agreed with his methods or not. She had failed to realize that he was hurting by withholding the information from her.

She then, courageously and vulnerably at the same time, admitted, "I *need* your help."

His hand slid up and down her back. "Then you have it." He held her tightly. "You have whatever you need, if I can provide it to you."

She didn't even need to say anything more. Hugh waved everyone over. "Listen, we're going to try and visit the gargoyles, but I don't know if everyone can make it the entire way." He looked Cade directly in the eyes but spoke to everyone. "If it gets too difficult or dangerous, you leave. You don't try to keep going. You will be killed—the forest won't stop."

They each entered the fountain—except Silas, who teleported and was waiting for them on the other side of the hidden wooden door. Taking all of them would have been too much of a spectacle for a public location.

They made their way through the small village center, the stage being avoided by everyone who walked passed it. Someday, Zoie hoped that she could walk right over it just before it was removed and destroyed.

There were plenty of places to enter the forest, but for some reason they chose to follow the stone path between the tavern and a shop. This was the very same path that she had used to follow Jack into what would become the last place he was ever seen alive.

The forest was in a perpetual night. At the edge, it was just after dusk, but looking into the forest it appeared as if little to no light entered or escaped.

As they continued to walk, the stones below their feet became dirt and dead leaves. The little amount of light that was guiding their way down the path was seemingly disappearing, and Zoie's heart started to pound. Her anxiety was bubbling up from her stomach and into her throat. The sound of their feet crunching the leaves was starting to become further and further away. A strange buzzing started to take over her ears. The path stretched out, and the trees got taller, and then it started to twist and spiral. Her knees and thighs felt weak.

Breathing was becoming difficult. She was back in the scene when she was in the forest last time. Jack was circling her—the trees were circling her. The vines were growing from the ground, and they were starting to wrap around her.

A hand touched hers, and everything went back into shape. The trees and path shrunk; the buzzing stopped; and the vines disappeared. Everyone was staring at her.

"Zoie? I said your name like five times. Are you okay?"

She looked down at the hand that held hers. The mustache tattoo that crossed paths with hers brought her back to reality. Zoie had been stuck in the scene from the last time that she had ventured in this area—when she was following Jack and Silas ended up saving her. As they walked past the scene of that crime, Zoie stopped. "The branches—they remain as they were, except where they cut him down?"

Silas put his arm around her and turned her away. "I haven't released the magic, so, unless someone cuts them down, the branches will remain in that formation until I do,—and I never will."

Zoie buried her head in his chest. "I think I was having a panic attack—I was back there. I was in the moment. I was me and then I was him…"

Silas held her tightly. "Tell me five things you can see, Zoie."

"Your black shirt. Hugh's yellow eyes. Dark brown bark on the tree trunks. Cade's mismatched socks. Your mustache tattoo." Zoie felt his arms drop from around her and they started to walk, hand-in-hand.

"Four things you can hear." He was bringing her back to reality. Silas was centering her.

"Leaves crunching under our shoes. A light wind moving the leaves on the branches." She paused to listen. "Cade just cracked their jaw, and Xariella is struggling…"

There was a definite sound of Xariella gasping, and everyone slowed and turned.

"The air…" Xariella stopped walking and put her hands on her thighs as she leaned over. "The air is so thick."

Cade turned around to her. "What do you mean?"

She tried to take a deep breath. "It just feels so heavy. Humid, but not." Her hand rubbed her collarbones nervously and then she put her hand just to her throat. "I can't get enough air." Xariella's brown eyes filled with panic. "Cade…"

They ran to her side. "Xari?" Cade reached her just as she collapsed, catching her before her head hit the forest floor. Without a word to the rest of them, Cade carried Xariella back towards the village, never thinking of looking back. Zoie wanted to check on her, but she also wanted to keep going. She needed to keep going—seeing her father just this once meant too much to her.

Hugh turned to Zoie. "Are you okay? Do you want to turn around, as well?"

She shook her head. "I'm fine." Before he could pose another question, she replied, "I had a moment back there, but it was just getting through where I encountered Jack—where he died. If it was something more—something like what Xariella was going through—I would tell you. I'm not looking to die."

A natural fork in the path appeared in front of them. Staring forward, Hugh asked, "Which way?" He didn't want to truly acknowledge that he was asking if Silas remembered.

Silas shrugged. "I don't know," he admitted.

To the left, the path seemed more clear. Leaves danced over the dirt, getting caught momentarily on a jagged rock or lifted root. Still, they could easily take that path.

On the right, though, there was no wind. The path was covered heavily with leaves that had dried up and fallen from the trees. The branches were nearly empty, and that part of the forest looked more dead.

Pulled towards the right because of the Robert Frost poem, Zoie almost instinctively wanted to go against her gut and choose to go left. Hugh could potentially see just fine, due to his werewolf sight abilities, but she could see a twisted ankle in her future.

She decided to try another method.

Zoie tightly clutched onto her pendant and closed her eyes. Hoping that her father would direct her through the pendant, she came up empty. But just as she opened her eyes, she saw a light glimmer in the distance farther down the right path. "Do you see that?" She squinted.

The fire in her core ignited—a small flame, so without even thinking, Zoie started down the path, trusting her gut, but halted when she felt a warm hand on her bicep. "Zoie, it could be a trap."

Snapping back into reality, she nodded. "Right." She stepped back in line with Silas and Hugh. Rubbing her hands together to awaken her magic, just like Auntie Lettie had taught her as a child, Zoie started to truly draw on the energy at her core. It was, of course, more difficult in the darkness, where no sunlight could reach them. But she did know of one source of light—even if it was a trick—so she drew from the light in the distance.

"It is a cabin." Her eyes started to dart around as if she was searching for something. "It's one bedroom—there's a cauldron on the fire…" She smiled and turned to Silas. "It's much like your little home."

"Don't diss the cabin," he replied, annoyed that she always referred to it as little, small, or even, at times, tiny. He had built it himself, without magic, and took pride in that. Beyond that, it was where they fell in love, whether or not either of them had realized it in the moment.

Zoie released the magic. "I want to see who lives there." She nodded with certainty.

"The witch from Hansel and Gretel. That's who lives there." Hugh suggested, "Let's go down the other path."

Zoie refused. "No, I want to see about this."

Hugh and Silas looked at each other, wordlessly trying to determine the next move together. Hugh took a step forward, and Silas guided Zoie to follow. They knew that there was no stopping her if she was determined, so they just needed to protect her.

The moment that the trees started to slide along the ground—their roots kicking up the dirt and moss and dead leaves, nearly tripping her—Zoie realized that she shouldn't have let that magical connection to the cabin subside.

She turned to ask Silas if he could hold the trees in place for a moment, but he was nowhere to be found. She turned towards Hugh, who also was gone, and that's when she realized that the trees were forming a circle around her. Other trees were gathering and then moving in on her.

Branches and bark began to crack and splinter, flying in every direction. Claws pushed through the trees, causing the trunks to bend and creek, and that's when she saw a pair of glowing eyes that she recognized.

For a moment, her fear took over and she nearly called out Hugh's name, but she needed him to stay in his wolf form in order to help her. So instead, she made eye contact with him. Determined, she drew from the glowing light of his eyes and let out a roar from the depths of her lungs, lighting up the entire forest and blowing the trees—roots included—back the distance of a football field.

Hugh and Silas both landed on their asses among the debris but were no worse for wear.

Brushing himself off as he walked his way back into his human form, Hugh ordered, "We're going back."

"No."

Motioning to the path behind them, Hugh said, "You had a panic attack back here, and," Hugh pointed at the uprooted forest around them. "It looks like a fucking tornado blew through here. The forest is trying to kill you, and you said that you aren't looking to die."

"I'm not, but that wasn't the forest."

"Sure as fuck looked like the forest," Hugh replied, motioning again towards the pile of soon-to-be firewood.

Silas approached, brushing the dirt off of his pants. "No, she's right. It's not the forest." He slowly motioned behind Hugh and, despite trying to hide it, nervously pointed out, "It's her."

Zoie looked up to see a cloaked figure with long, wild, frizzy lavender-grey hair acting as curtains to her 300-year-old looking face. The woman approached, carrying a basket of fruit, but Zoie knew the story of Snow White. She wouldn't be accepting any of those poisoned apples if offered.

The woman's eyes were glowing white, so brightly that even though they were sunken into her skull, her black eyebrows were still visible. Her nose was long and crooked in multiple places, and a beauty mark was situated just below it, nearly touching her dry, blue lips. Her shaky voice was angry. "You have just lit up this forest like the sun. You must hide, before the wolves find you." She reached out for Zoie.

Hugh stood between them. "The only wolf you need to fear is this one standing in front of you."

The woman swatted at Hugh. "Get out of my way, dog. There are other wolves in this forest. Feral ones. There are other evils that lurk here in the dark." She took Zoie by the wrist. "To my cabin." The woman quickly glanced at the two men. "All of you. Now. Don't dillydally."

Zoie felt as if she was being dragged by this woman. The path they had been traveling was long gone, and Zoie worried that she was going to trip over an elevated tree root or a bush or anything else that she couldn't see outside of what the woman's eyes illuminated.

"Quickly!" she ordered as she opened the door to her cabin, watching at alert while the three of them piled in.

Zoie's mouth dropped once she was inside. "This—this isn't what I saw at all. Your cabin—it's bigger on the inside."

The woman took off her cloak and hung it on the back of the door. As she turned to face the three of them, all of the old age and wickedness melted away to reveal a woman who couldn't have been more than 40 years old.

Her wild hair became smooth and brown, falling at her shoulders, with fringe that just brushed her eyebrows. Her brown eyes were doe-like, with perfect long lashes. Her long, evil-looking nose faded away into a perfectly petite, albeit slightly upturned nose over her small mouth that appeared to be covered in pink lip gloss.

She placed her basket of fruit on a table and then reached up to cut down some herbs for the soup in the cauldron over the fire—

which made Zoie feel much better about her own skills as a witch. Zoie had it in her mind that witches did everything with magic, rather than do it the human way, and she was happy to be proven wrong.

The wind whipped around the cabin, howling in a chorus with the other—wild—wolves that were circling around them.

The woman looked over at her guests. "Please, each of you, take a seat. As you have noticed, there is much more room than you could have ever imagined. Isn't magic just grand?" Her voice sounded like starlight bouncing off of a prism. Then she called out, "Sister! We have company." She snapped her fingers and a piece of a rug lifted, revealing a trap door.

The trap door lifted open, and out climbed a woman just a few years younger. Her straight black hair was so long that it followed her out of the basement, and she had to lift it out of the way before shutting the door. Her blue eyes sparkled as she looked over at the three of them. "It's gotten caught in there before." Just as pale as the other woman, with the same small, lip-gloss-covered smile and petite nose, she didn't use magic to move the rug. Instead, from under her pink dress with a black lace overlay popped out a small pink Mary Jane, and she kicked the rug back into place. Her voice was a little less singsong than their host's. "My name is Meadow."

"Hello, Meadow." Zoie smiled at her. "I'm Zoie, and this is Hugh, and that's Silas."

Meadow nodded hello towards each of the guys, but Zoie did not like the way that her eyes lingered on Hugh for a moment too long.

"Mitzi," Meadow asked. "Will our guests be staying for supper?"

Mitzi smoothed out her apron and then spun her index finger in a circle, casting a spell on the spoon that was mixing whatever was in the large yellow bowl in front of her. "Our guests will be staying for the entire night. It will not be safe for them to continue their journey for several hours."

Meadow clapped excitedly. "We haven't had guests in centuries! This is thrilling." She began to set the table, placing what appeared to be hand-thrown plates, bowls, and cups—nothing matched— on the long wooden table. "It's been Mitzi and me for so long…"

Mitzi smacked a rolling pin on the counter. "It makes me wonder—how did you find us? My spells have kept everyone away for thousands of years." She looked back and forth between each of her guests. "Who are you?"

Hugh stood up. "I'm—."

She cut him off. "I know who you are. You're Hugh Davies and you're on that council. That horrible awful group of power hungry beasts…"

"Mitzi!" Meadow hushed her sister. "You don't know if he's like the others."

Mitzi rolled her eyes. "They are all the same." She didn't even give Hugh a chance to respond. "You—boy! Tell me who you are and what you did to get past my spells."

Silas put his hands in the air. "First of all, ma'am, I'm not a boy. I'm nearly 70 years old." She scoffed, 70 years being mere moments to her. "Secondly, I don't know what we did to get past your spells. The three of us were headed to the Gargoyle Graveyard—."

Her brown eyes turned red. "Stay away from that place! You are not supposed to go there. No one is supposed to even know that place exists." Her hair turned into Venus fly traps and started snapping in their direction. Her magical voice became deep and angry. "But you and your evil council have taken advantage of the essence of that spell. You have gone much, much too far. I will not let you torture those prisoners any more than they already have been!"

Zoie shook her head. "No, no. We aren't looking to harm them. We are looking to free them."

"Impossible. There's no way you have the skills nor the materials necessary." Her hair snapped more frequently at Zoie.

Meadow got in between Mitzi and their guests. "Sister. Sister! Sister, please!" She reached forward for her hands. "Sister, if they have gotten through our defenses, perhaps they could be of some assistance."

Her hair fell back into place and her eyes returned to their chocolate brown. "Why do you want to free them? What's it to you?" When Hugh went to speak, she cut him off, back to her pleasantly, nearly annoying, sounding voice. "No. I want to hear from the one who wields the power of the sun." Her eyes fixed on Zoie's pendant.

Zoie quickly tucked it underneath her shirt. "There are people who have been unjustly imprisoned as gargoyles—some for thousands of years. We want to release them."

"What will you get out of this?" Mitzi snapped her fingers and the spoon finally stopped mixing.

"Honestly?" Zoie asked. "Not much personally. My Auntie Lettie will be released, and my father will finally get to rest, but mostly, it's about seeing others gaining the freedom that they deserve."

Mitzi shook her head. "No. I won't allow it." She turned around and went back to cooking.

Meadow offered them each a cup of tea, but they all refused. "It's not poisoned or drugged. It's just some lavender and chamomile." She presented the cup to Zoie again, as she explained, sweetly, "You see, Mitzi stands to lose a lot if the Gargoyles are freed."

"How so?" Hugh took a cup and smelled it, hoping that his werewolf senses would detect any nefarious intentions. When he took a sip, Meadow smiled sweetly.

Meadow sat down next to him on the couch. "Mitzi created the spell to lock beings in gargoyle form."

"Why?!" Hugh growled.

Meadow turned to look at her sister to make sure that she was so involved in cooking that she wasn't paying attention. Narrowing her eyes at Hugh, Meadow replied, "It's not like that."

She leaned in to tell the group the story.

"In the year 1705, Mitzi met a man named Thomas, and they fell in love." She continued, "They quickly decided to marry. His parents were never a fan of Mitzi. They loved how well preserved she was and believed that she would create beautiful heirs—but she was a tad strange." She explained, "Mitzi could be found at any given time with wild flowers in her hair, and she had been caught a few times chanting incantations. Dancing in stone circles under the stars. Things like that."

She glanced back at her sister again. "She had waited hundreds of years to find her match." She smiled at Hugh and batted her long black eyelashes. "You must know how that feels, no?"

Zoie felt Hugh's hand cover hers. He must have been clueless to Meadow's not-so-subtle advances because he looked at Zoie and smiled. "I do."

Feeling validated, Zoie smiled, though trying to keep it under the radar. She wasn't sure how much she wanted to reveal to these two women just yet.

Not even noticing, Meadow immediately got back to telling her story. "Thomas and Mitzi enjoyed a few years together, but he fell ill. The doctors tried everything, but they couldn't fix him. Leeches, blood-letting, nothing worked." She let out a sad sigh. "Mitzi decided that she was going to find someone that could cure him, and she didn't care how long it took."

Silas leaned forward. "So she created the Gargoyle spell to freeze him in time while she found that person."

"Exactly." Meadow smiled. "So, she came to me, and we found two friends we could trust—or so we thought."

Suddenly, Mitzi spoke up. "My friend Victor…" she looked at Zoie, directly in her eyes. "You must be one of his descendants to have that pendant." Zoie held the pendant tightly in her hand but didn't respond any further. Mitzi continued, "Victor has remained true to me for hundreds of years—he remains loyal to this day."

Zoie reasoned that Victor may have made the choice to guard these gargoyles for Mitzi. Why was Mitzi so important to him?

"Your other friend?" Hugh asked.

Mitzi frowned deeply. "I didn't know that my other friend, a werewolf…" She narrowed her eyes at Hugh. "He was not so true." Shaking her head, she sadly continued, "The four of us worked together to bring the spell to life, and my sister and I enchanted four pendants that could only be used together to undo the spell. We separated the four pendants so that I didn't release Thomas before a cure was found."

Hugh cleared his throat. "Your werewolf friend…"

"Please let me finish." She nodded at Hugh—they both knew who that werewolf was. "After we froze Thomas in gargoyle form, the werewolf friend, Alvin, stole Meadow's pendant and my grimoire. He married a witch…"

"Edie." Hugh said at the same time as Mitzi.

Mitzi nodded sadly. "He taught her the spell and they used it for nearly two centuries to eliminate the werewolves to gain and maintain power, until Edie's sudden death."

Meadow interjected, "She was killed when they tried to eliminate…"

"Me." Hugh admitted. "I killed Edie." No matter what he

found out, he still always felt awful about ending Edie's life and the aftermath that followed him for more than 150 years.

Mitzi's eyes widened. "The pendant—did you happen to pick up the pendant?"

"I'm sorry." Hugh shook his head. "I never even noticed a pendant, Mitzi."

Her excitement evaporated. "In addition to the pendants, there is another book—a smaller grimoire—that has the antidote spell."

"That was smart," Silas complimented. "Keeping them separate."

She nodded gratefully. "Yes, I had even had the foresight to keep that book in a separate location from my usual spell book. Alvin never knew of that book; I never knew where it was because Meadow hid it for me."

"And I'll never tell," Meadow sing-songed.

Zoie looked over at Hugh and Silas, knowing at her core that the book she had received from Lettie by proxy of her mother was that very grimoire. She wasn't sure if she wanted to reveal that information just yet. Still, she needed to know how to get that book open.

Mitzi sadly added, "And I never want you to because releasing the Gargoyles will take any chance of my Thomas returning to me." She shook her head. "The cure for his ailment has been found, but he's been in gargoyle form for so long that he cannot be revived. You are wrong about the thousands of years—it's only 100—and removing his prison will end his life. It's been too long for him."

Zoie leaned towards Mitzi. "So you leave him there, alone? In solitary confinement?"

Meadow answered for her sister. "She visits him at times to speak to him, and he is guarded by Victor—your ancestor." She smiled gently. "The faeries communicate on their behalf, at times."

Before anything more could be said, Mitzi declared, "Supper

is served," as she placed the final dish on the table, just as the howling chorus of the wind and wolves was joined by maniacal cackles and heavy rain fell, leaving rainbow sparkles splashing as it hit the forest floor.

# HUGH

Meadow led the three of them to rooms far in the back of the magical cabin. "All three of your rooms have their own bathrooms…"

Hugh went to explain that he and Zoie would be sharing a room, but Zoie elbowed him and mouthed, "No." He couldn't hide his disappointment from her.

Once they each went into their rooms, Zoie snuck quietly to Hugh's. As soon as he heard her soft knock, he pulled her in the room and kissed her. "I thought you weren't going to visit me tonight."

She giggled but pushed away from him a little. "Of course I want to spend tonight with you, but that wasn't my purpose for visiting."

Hugh was confused. What other purpose could she have for sneaking into his room?

"I think you need to appeal to Meadow about getting her on our side about freeing the gargoyles." She continued, "Right now, she doesn't want to see her sister hurting by losing all chance of her getting Thomas back. But Mitzi doesn't see that she's unnecessarily punishing the person that she loves."

"Okay, I see that, but why me?"

Zoie laughed. "She has the hots for you, so I think you can flirt your way into getting her on your side." She poked him playfully in the side.

"I think you are mistaken." Hugh shook his head and laughed. "And, in the off chance that you aren't, I don't think my skill—or lack thereof—in flirting is going to make this happen."

"I am most definitely not mistaken," she replied, nudging him. "And you say you don't have skills. But if I'm, yet again, not mistaken, you won my heart, didn't you?" Zoie reminded him, "We also need to figure out more about that spell book. That journal from Lettie—I believe that's the grimoire, and we need to confirm that and how to get into it."

He nodded, and reluctantly replied, "Okay." He kissed her cheek.

"Oh! And we need to see if she will lead us to the Graveyard."

Hugh chuckled. "Anything else? Winning lottery numbers? Door to Narnia? Partridge in a pear tree?"

Zoie pretended to think. "Hmmmm… Nah, I think that will do." She got on her toes and reached up to kiss his cheek. "I think you should do this sooner rather than later." Quickly, she made her way back to the door.

As soon as the door clicked shut, she heard Zoie gasp and let out a little shriek. "Meadow!" Hugh let himself relax, as he listened through the door.

"Is your room satisfactory?" Meadow asked sweetly.

Zoie replied, "Of course."

"Hmmm." Meadow asked, "Then why were you in Hugh's room?"

Hugh opened the door before Zoie could come up with a response. He noticed that Meadow had a tray with some tea and cakes in her hands. "Are those treats for me?" He smiled.

Her pale skin flushed—she blushed so hard that it didn't stop at her cheeks but warmed her entire face and neck. "Well, I was planning to bring some to everyone, but yes, this specifically is for you.”

Hugh frowned. “I see there’s only one cup. You won’t join me?”

Her blushing deepened. “Well, that would be improper. I couldn’t go into a man’s room. What would everyone say?”

Hugh didn’t believe for a moment that Meadow cared about what was proper. His experience with witches—besides Zoie—was that they would use their powers to get anything that they wanted—societal norms be damned. No matter how much she pretended to be the perfect hostess with top skills in manners, he had little faith in Meadow’s intention to be proper. Still, he suggested, “Then perhaps out in the main room?”

She politely agreed and as soon as she turned around, Zoie winked at Hugh and then headed into her room. He followed Meadow, but immediately his eyes were fixed on what was going on outside.

The large front room window was filled with light from outside. Light that shouldn’t have been there in the middle of the night. Moving with the wind was thick dust colored an electric lilac—but it wasn’t random dust. Each line was a part of a bigger picture. A figure.

These figures didn’t make sense to Hugh. He didn’t know what kind of creatures they were. They were nothing that he had learned about in his nearly 200 years, and they were never mentioned in the Council meetings.

He stepped closer to the window. “Are these… Are these ghosts?” he asked aloud—maybe to Meadow, but more to himself. Despite his own existence in the supernatural world, Hugh had never believed in ghosts or spirits. It just felt like it was something too far for him. Something just too unnatural. Besides, he never encountered one in his life.

A sad howl from one of the ghosts shaped like a werewolf filled the air.

The serving tray clanged a little as it hit the coffee table. "Not exactly." Meadow sighed. "These are the spirits of the gargoyles."

Hugh still didn't turn towards her. He was watching out the window as these spirits ran through the forest, as if they were finally free. "Does this happen every night?"

Sadly, Meadow replied, "Only when Pluto is changing signs. So, on average every 20 years, but it could be 12 or 40 or whatever. It's a generational planet, but with its orbit being the path that it is, well, it sometimes varies." She added, "Mitzi just has to pay attention to the charts and then she will know when to start planning and…" She abruptly stopped talking and walked quickly to the window, her heels clicking with a sense of urgency. "No…"

Hugh tried to find what she was looking for, but the electric lilac light outside and the light behind him was messing with his vision. "What is it?"

"He's not arrived yet. Thomas usually rushes to be at Mitzi's side." She pointed to a dark figure out in the forest amongst all of the bright creatures.

The werewolves didn't bother her—they dodged her as they ran, playing with each other as if they were all members of the same pack. The merpeople swam in the air around her, dancing in the wind. A long line of vampires walked slowly, shoulder to shoulder, splitting apart to avoid her.

Her shoulders slumped as she began to feel defeat. As more creatures ran back and forth through the forest, Meadow got closer to the window, placing her hand on the glass.

"Do all of them always come?"

Meadow, still watching her sister, replied, "They all have the option, but they can choose to stay in their gargoyle prison. We don't know why some choose to stay behind…"

"Because they have given up hope." Hugh had been so engrossed in what was going on outside that he hadn't heard Zoie walk into the room.

Zoie continued for Hugh, "They've lost all hope of freedom and the hours they would have out here is just a tease—a sick reminder of what they could have."

Hugh and Meadow both turned around. Zoie had the spell book clutched tightly in her arms, Silas standing behind her right shoulder. "Help us end their torture, Meadow." She took a few steps closer. "You have a kind heart, and I know that you want to help your sister and Thomas. But I think you know, deep down inside, that you need to help free him so that he can rest."

A large thunder rumbled as some of that electric lilac light struck the ground. All of them ran to the window to see whatever they could.

Mitzi was still standing amongst the trees, alone, as the spirit creatures turned and quickly ran back towards the graveyard. She fell to her knees and placed her face in her hands.

Meadow ran quickly to the door and turned the knob, then stopped. Turning to her guests, she politely requested, "Excuse me for a moment." She fiercely opened the door and bolted out towards her sister, her hair, dress, and petticoats flowing in the wind. She ran flawlessly, even in heels, never taking a misstep.

Comforted by her sister, Mitzi was sobbing. "He didn't come. Why didn't he come to visit? It's our one time for decades…"

Meadow continued to rub her sister's shoulders. "Maybe he got caught up at the exit…" She looked up at Hugh and mouthed, *Just a moment.* She led her sister into her bedroom and, for the first time that they saw, used magic—to start brewing a tea.

After steeping some tea leaves and other herbs, the mug lifted off of the counter and a little saucer slid underneath it. A small spoon hobbled its way to the saucer and lay down. Then, two sugar cubes and a biscuit danced their way over. Once everything was in place, the saucer lifted them all into the air and took a path to Mitzi's room in the back of the house.

Silas turned to Hugh and Zoie. "Now is our chance. I think that this will convince Meadow to help."

Hugh nodded. "I agree. There's nothing keeping them tied to these gargoyles and their fate anymore."

"I know you are both correct." Zoie frowned. "It just seems so evil to take advantage of someone's heartbreak."

Hugh reached his hand out for Zoie's and when she took it, he kissed it gently. "My darling, I don't know if you've noticed this over the past, I don't know, couple of years," he chuckled, "But we are the bad guys."

Zoie's hand slid out of his faster than a greased pig at a rodeo. "Excuse me?"

He chuckled. "C'mon, Zoie, we were going to kill Alvin to save your life. We couldn't come up with anything else. Straight to murder." Hugh smiled and added, "And you did kill him…"

She cut him off, "For you. Because he begged for it!"

Hugh laughed again, "You still killed him." Then he added, "I ripped his son limb from limb and burnt the remains. Silas killed his father—for your safety, yes, but it was part of our plan, remember?" Then he added, "and I maimed Stevie." Running his hands through his hair, he smiled, "And, now, we're just going to go ahead and release all of these gargoyles, not knowing what the real results could be."

"Yeah, we're shitty people," Silas chuckled. "None of us follow the laws." Hugh and Silas laughed together.

Then Hugh added, "All of this was set into motion because I fell in love with someone and my alleged moral compass felt that she needed to know everything before she entered into a relationship with me."

Zoie was taken aback. "This is my fault that you're bad people?"

Hugh, still laughing, put his hands up, and he and Silas both replied, "No!"

Hugh explained, "I've always been a problem. I mean, remember how I became a werewolf? I started a fight in a pub."

"…Over a woman being assaulted…" Zoie added.

Hugh motioned for her to come closer. "Yes, all of the things we do are with the best of intentions, but we aren't pure." He took her in his arms. "And I won't pretend that I wouldn't do every single one of them over again, especially if it leads me to having the honor of being loved by you."

Silas cleared his throat, and when Zoie and Hugh looked over at him, he was indicating that Meadow had returned to the room.

Meadow slowly walked to the couch, her long black hair dragging on the floor behind her. She motioned for everyone else to take a seat around the room, and then she snapped, bringing a few more mugs and saucers over to the tray. She gently poured the tea and handed it out. Politely clearing her throat, she looked up at Zoie, directly into her eyes. "If Hugh was caught in the form of a gargoyle and his time to be brought back to life—real life-had passed, what would you do?"

Zoie didn't hesitate. She didn't have to think. "Let him rest."

"Most of my life," Meadow stated, "Has been in this cabin. I have never had the pleasure of falling in love, and, until today," she glanced at Hugh, "I had never wanted to find out what it would be like."

"Meadow…" Hugh started to speak.

She put her hand in the air and pushed it forward, snapping his mouth shut. "I know that you two are in love, and I can sense it also between Silas and Zoie. My strongest power is sensing emotions and connections." She gently stirred her tea. "My attraction to you isn't because I actually want to be with you. It's because I can feel how much you love her, and how much she loves you, and I want that." Meadow glanced at Silas, "Please, don't worry. She loves you, too. It's just very different." She smiled gently.

Placing the spoon on the saucer, she continued. "My sister's love for Thomas has always just been very… I don't know. It feels very desperate and selfish, and it has never felt pure." She reached out. "The grimoire, please."

Zoie held it to her chest. "I'm sorry, but we want to free the gargoyles, and we need this book. My dearest aunt gave it to me."

"You do not have to fear that I will take it or destroy it." She explained, "I just watched my sister more or less disintegrate into nothing—a shell of what she is—because her love didn't show up for her." She continued, "Then I heard you speak of how you would break any laws, any rules—hell, you would fight nature—to be together. And that you would do it over and over again." She explained, "I believe that the reason that you want to free these gargoyles is right. And that you are doing it out of love and respect for everyone." She looked directly at Zoie, "and I recognize that you feel like you have a lot to lose but are planning to go through with it anyways."

Zoie cautiously handed over the book. "We just think that it's unfair to hold people in confinement like this."

Meadow nodded. "That was not the intention of the spell." Placing the book in her lap, she looked up at Zoie. "You will need all of the pendants." She continued, "If you do get all of them, they each have certain powers and only certain people will be able to wield them…"

Zoie's shoulders slumped. "We'll never…"

Meadow still smiled. "You don't need the right people to complete the spell. In fact, the pendants don't much in the spell except for transfer energy." She stated, "But this would still be important to know."

Zoie nodded for her to continue, and Hugh felt her hand squeeze his a little. She had some hope.

She pointed at Zoie. "You have the light pendant. As a Sun Witch, you should have no problem mastering its use." She then said, "At one time, Alvin had both the Earth and the Water pendants. At some point—likely after Edie's death, the Water pendant passed to Reon, King of the Abyss. Only a Moon Witch or a Merperson could properly control the Water pendant."

"Fuck," Hugh groaned. "Alvin was buried—I believe, in the earth outside of the walls of the Abyss—most certainly with the fucking pendant on."

Meadow, completely serious, responded, "Well, then you had best get some shovels and start digging." She stated, "You, Hugh, are powerful enough to control that pendant, if you release your stubbornness and allow others to teach you."

"The fourth pendant?" Silas asked, likely to cover up the laughter in his chest about Meadow's constructive feedback for Hugh.

"My sister, Mitzi, until tonight, held the Love Pendant close." She reached into her pocket and held it out to Silas. "This is for you. You wield the power of the shadow-realm faeries. That combined with your ability to love, even when you think it is hopeless, will make you dangerously powerful with this." She placed it in his hand, surrounding it and the bottom of his hand with hers. "You—and others—may think that your huge capacity to love is a weakness, but it's not." She stated, "You placed yourself in isolation for decades under the veil that you didn't want to be bothered with other people, but that was not the case." She softened and her the pain in her eyes was real. "You loved someone very much, but she broke your heart. Badly." She frowned. "You never thought it would repair itself."

Hugh actually felt sorry for Silas in this moment, but, at the same time, he thought, *Who's laughing now?*

Meadow's frown turned into a smile. "Then you met Zoie. She mended your heart. Her loneliness; her grief from being separated from Hugh—you both connected over those feelings." Her hands were still on his. She leaned forward and looked into his dark eyes—into his soul. "You will survive your next heartbreak as well."

Silas took a deep breath in and sat up, removing his hand from hers. "Oooohhhh kaaaayyyy."

Hugh felt Zoie's energy skip a few pulses. Was she planning on ending things with Silas? Or was it shock that she was going to get the news that she would break his heart? Or—and this was the worst in Hugh's opinion—was she upset that someone else would enter Silas's romantic life and break his heart?

To keep things moving, Hugh asked, "The water pendant…"

Meadow nodded. She explained, "You will need someone to take on the power of the water pendant. Like I said, Moon Witch or Merfolk."

Zoie looked over at Hugh. "Stevie is the only person I know."

Placing the pendant around his neck and tucking it under his shirt, Silas replied, "Then Cade is going to have to convince her to help us."

"They aren't going to be able to do that. Not with the way that…"

Meadow cut Hugh off. "You will need to figure that out on your own time. However, I don't have long before Mitzi finds out that her pendant is missing." She held the book out towards

Zoie. "The latch. Hold your hand over it and say the following incantation: *Revelare Mysteria.*"

Placing the book on her lap, Zoie closed her eyes and repeated as instructed. The book flew open, causing her to jump. "How would have I ever known how to instinctively say that?"

Smiling gently, Meadow said, "You instinctively knew you needed to come here to find answers. Instinct isn't always a direct line to an answer." She poked Zoie playfully in the stomach. "Trust your gut, Sister Sun."

Zoie's pendant began to glow, and Silas's was showing through his shirt. "What is going on?"

Quickly, Meadow explained, "Reon's pendant will be glowing as well. That happens when the book is opened. You will need to secure the pendants and then study the book. Then you will need a plan to get to the gargoyles and free them." She reached over to Zoie's lap and quickly slammed the book shut, all the while sliding another grimoire on top of it. The pendants faded back to their usual state. "The pendants will not glow when you open that book. It contains all of Mitzi's other spells, and some of mine."

Desperate for some secret passageway or spell that Meadow could just throw into the air and make happen, Hugh begged, "Meadow, we will need our friends to complete this mission, but they cannot make it through the forest."

"Mitzi created the spell to enchant the forest. I, of course, know how to take it down, but only for a short period of time." She looked at Hugh. "The three of you can make it through unharmed. You and Zoie are protected by the Council, and Silas, you are protected because you are part of the shadow-realm faeries. Faeries are immune to this kind of magic. Your friends, however, will need me to bring down the spells to get them through."

She went to continue, but Silas interrupted her. "I have never heard from anyone else that I've encountered that I'm a descendent of the faeries. I've been always told that I'm a Warlock."

Meadow took his hand. "Your grandfather—the one that gave you a compass—Zoie has it now. That grandfather's grandfather was a shadow-realm faerie. They are usually very, very evil creatures, which is why they take their power from the darkness. However, when he left the darkness and fell in love with a human, he decided to leave magic behind." She heard some rustling from Mitzi's room and her words became more urgent. "Look, we have no time, but it's just a part of you. You're a Warlock, but there's this other part of you. Tap into it." She looked at the three of them. "The forest is safe for you right now. You must go." She quickly grabbed some parchment from her secretary desk in the corner. "Write to me on this. Burn it outside in a light breeze and the ashes will travel to my desk and a letter will appear." She ushered them to the front door. "Best of luck to you."

# ZOIE

Stepping off the porch, Hugh turned to Zoie. "I promised you that I would take you to your father, but…"

She nodded at him. "I understand. We need to do this first." Zoie added, "I feel like it may be better to get all of this information and *then* go see him."

The warmth of Hugh's hand enveloped her left hand, and then she felt the roughness of Silas's hand slide against her right hand. Then she felt her entire world suck inward.

It didn't matter how many times Silas transported her somewhere; Zoie still felt dizzy for a moment when they came out on the other side. Even in cases where she knew where they were going—and had been there before—it still was difficult for her to find her bearings.

She fully expected Silas to transport her and Hugh directly to their home, but instead, she found herself a familiar location, though she wasn't quite sure where it was. It was when she saw all of the wax and wicks strewn about on the table that she recognized where they were: Xariella's art studio at Cade's house. Xariella had been trying to build a little candle-making business before she had been turned into a vampire, and Cade wanted to give her the space to pursue that dream again. They had remodeled their shed so that she could have privacy while she worked on her art.

"Why are we here?"

Silas replied, "I assumed you would want to see your friend after she almost died."

"Of course I do. What I meant was, why her studio?"

Silas shrugged. "Sometimes Xariella and I come out here when you three are deep into your super-close-best-friends mode and we're feeling ignored." He admitted, "It's the place on their property that I know the best."

Silas opened the door and start walking towards the house.

"Silas," Zoie called out. When he didn't respond, she hurried to reach him and grabbed his wrist. "Silas."

"Hm?" He turned around.

"You feel ignored sometimes?"

Shrugging again—Zoie hated that—he replied, "It's no big deal. It's natural that the three of you would be closer than Xariella and I are to the group as a whole. You have been through some stuff before either of us came into the picture." He asked, "Don't you sometimes feel left out when Hugh and Cade start talking about something pre-Zoie?"

In truth, she never really thought about Hugh's life pre-Zoie. Sometimes certain people or comments would make her jealous of his previous life, but they were few and far between. Hugh always made it a point to make her feel like his life didn't begin until she was a part of it. She wondered if she was too self-centered to ever be like that. Perhaps, she thought, she was too self-centered to actually be in a polyamorous relationship dynamic. If Silas was feeling ignored, should she consider letting him go?

Her thoughts were interrupted by Cade's arms wrapping around her. "You all made it back safely!" They even gave Hugh a big hug—and shook Silas' hand. "Did you accomplish everything?"

Silas cut Cade off. "How's Xariella?"

"I'm fine," she called out from the living room. She was wrapped up in some blankets and watching a movie, listening to music, and reading all at once. "That forest can be brutal, but I was fine almost instantly when we left. But this goofball has been making sure that I'm waited on hand and foot since we got out of there. They don't want me to strain myself."

Cade bought over a mug of tea. "Here's a muffin, too. The kind you like. Cranberry-orange."

Xariella shook her head. "Cade, sweetie, I can get my own tea." She then told the smart speaker to stop and clicked pause on the remote. She placed her book face down on the table. Hugh immediately went over and slid a bookmark between the pages and shut the book, placing it back where it had been. Xariella looked at the book and then at Zoie, and mouthed, *what the heck?*

Hugh replied for Zoie, "You were going to break the book's spine. How would you like it if someone used you and then broke your spine? Hm?" He then added, "Just because you're mouthing the words doesn't mean that I can't hear the breath coming through your throat and mouth." He pointed to his ear. "It's a wolf thing."

Cade's mouth dropped. "Hugh!"

Xariella sat up straight and looked at Cade. "That's how you always know when I've said something to Zoie and no one else! I had been considering that Zoie wasn't a good secret keeper!"

Zoie gasped a little. "I'm an excellent secret keeper." Mostly because she didn't have anyone to tell secrets too. She became even better at keeping secrets once she found out that she could invade other people's memories. In her mind, if she could do that, someone else out there could do it to her. Once she realized that, Zoie started to visualize secrets being locked away in deep parts of her brain.

Xariella felt horribly about misreading the situation. She got up and hugged her friend. "I know that now. I thought you were telling things to Hugh and he was telling Cade." She shook her head. "Unbelievable. And you let me believe it, too, Cade."

Cade changed the subject. "So did you get to see the gargoyles? Zoie, did you see your father?"

"We actually didn't make it much further beyond where you two were," Zoie explained. "But we did meet these two witches that live in a cabin in those woods, and one of them actually created the spell!"

Each of them took turns recapping what happened while they were at the cabin and how they needed to get possession of the two remaining pendants.

"…and that's where you come in, Cade," Hugh explained. "We're pretty sure that you are the only one that can convince Stevie to join us."

Cade stood up and started pacing aimlessly. "No. No! Nope. Not a chance! I don't think so!"

"Why not?" Silas asked.

Cade glared at Silas, as if he didn't even have a right to be there. "Because we would be using our romantic history as a weapon, and I'm not okay with that. If Xari wasn't here, maybe-MAYBE—I would consider the idea, but I'm not going to even remotely be convincing if I tried."

"No, Cade," Zoie interjected. "But you could appeal to your friendship."

Cade sat down across from Zoie. "No, Zoie, *you* could appeal to your friendship." They continued, "You're actually the only one that has the power to let her back into the fold. She was an agent in basically killing you."

"Cade has a point," Xariella added.

Hugh let an angry sigh out of his nose. "I really don't want you anywhere near that Judas."

Silas pointed out, "There's no reason to worry. Zoie is protected by you and the Council. A move against her would be asking for death." He continued, "Stevie knows that she couldn't get back into your little group without Zoie's okay."

Hugh leaned back in the chair. "I don't like this." He repeated himself, "I don't like this. And I know, Zoie, you're going to do what you want to do—whatever you think is best. But I, speaking as your fiancé, don't fucking like this at all."

Zoie looked straight at him. "Then don't speak as my fiancé. Speak as the leader of this group of rebels."

He took in a deep breath. "Zoie, I can't just turn off our bond and what that means for me and my decision-making." She raised an eyebrow at him, so he did his best. After thinking about it for a few moments, he finally responded. "If it was anyone else that I was in the place of making the decision about, yes, I agree that it's probably the only way to really get what we want without cutting some throats."

"Plus, we need her power," Xariella responded. "None of us are Moon Witches or Merpeople, so we need her."

Folding his arms across his chest, Hugh reiterated, "I don't like this."

Zoie walked over to him and grabbed his hand, yanking on his arm to get him to stand. She knew that she had absolutely no power to force him, so she just did it playfully until he stood up. Once he was in front of her, with his arms around her, she looked up at him. "Hugh, do you really think that I am enamored with this idea? This decision?"

"Zo, you never got to really experience a goodbye with her. You sometimes miss her. I think you *want* to be the one to speak with her." His eyes were full of concern.

She shook her head. "Hugh, you forget that for the entire time that you didn't know that she betrayed us, I did. I witnessed what she did like a goddamned out-of-body experience." Zoie explained, "Yes, I wish the Stevie that I knew was a part of my life, but, no, I'm not thrilled about the idea of being in a room alone with her and trying to convince her to, yet again, betray her family. Especially since we know how that turned out the last time."

He looked in her eyes. "You aren't making this easy for me to get on board with. In fact, I'm about to rescind my statement."

"Trust that even if none of us are thrilled with the idea— including me—I have the strength to do this. Mentally, emotionally, physically, and magically." She looked up at him. "Trust that I can do this." She pleaded, gently, "Trust me."

His chest raised as he took in a deep breath. "All five of us are going, and I'm going to come up with some excuse to make it a political visit." He kissed Zoie's forehead and then released her from his arms. "You're all going to want some formal wear because these people are abso-fucking-lutely ridiculous about formal dinners." Hugh looked at Silas. "Do we need to go the old-fashioned way or can you teleport us?" Then he asked, "Wait- before I assume that you can take all of us at once—Are you even comfortable going, with your job as a bounty hunter and all? I know you like to keep it anonymous."

Silas smiled, "As long as everyone holds on, I think I can take everyone, and yes, I'm good with going. I want to see this place. But, yes, I do like to stay anonymous. Let's, please, just tell him that

I'm a cynical, grumpy farmer or something and I like to keep to myself. Thank you for thinking about that."

"Then why would you be on this trip with us?" Xariella asked.

Hugh paced for a moment and then agreed. "No, you're not going to be able to walk in there like that." He admitted, "But we need you there. We need you in case we have to sneak into somewhere—plus, Zoie's magic will be weak without the sun. You draw from the shadows." He sadly admitted, "You balance each other and can channel power from each other." Hugh looked down towards the floor, trying to hide his jealousy. "I've seen it."

Cade suggested, "Why can't he be the political reason?" They continued, "Reon knows that you feel that the court needs more representation."

"Warlocks are represented by the Shrews," Hugh reminded them. "Reon will never go for that. And he definitely won't go for the faeries having representation. That would mean he'd lose his servants."

Zoie suggested, "I think we should play it that Silas has kept to himself for much of his life, and perhaps he's never fully harnessed his powers. So we thought that we should make double use of the trip and bring him to meet Zhenga, who is part of the reason that I found my powers."

Cade smiled. "Zhenga would love that. She loves learning about new magic and helping others find their abilities."

Xariella tried to not allow her face show too much sadness or feeling of betrayal. While it seemed to be universal that everyone hated Reon, everyone also loved Zhenga—especially Cade. Cade's relationship with Stevie allowed him to really get to know Zhenga—and Xariella hoped that his fondness for her didn't lead to a rekindling of the feelings he once had for Stevie.

Changing the subject to hopefully change Xariella's focus, Zoie asked, "What's your political reason for visiting?"

Hugh smiled at Zoie and then playfully tapped his finger on the tip of her nose. "Council business. Need to know."

Cade chuckled. "In other words, he hasn't come up with the reason yet."

# HUGH

The end of a teleportation was always smooth, but the actual travel part was one of the worst things Hugh would ever experience. He always felt like his insides were being flipped around and twisted—even worse than the pain that he would feel as he transitioned into a werewolf. That, he had gotten used to over the years, but he didn't see himself ever getting used to teleportation.

The air at the Abyss was always slightly damp, but the temperature was perfect, so the humidity was never overpowering. The bioluminescent lights were just as bright and perfectly placed as ever. Nothing had changed since the last time that he had visited this place.

He would have loved to say that his trust in Reon was more limited than the last time he had visited; however, he'd always had slim to no faith in Reon, even prior to his part in Zoie's death or disappearance—whatever they were calling it on that day. Being on the Council with Reon didn't restore, rebuild, or create any trust either. It just reinforced everything Hugh believed prior to taking his seat at the table.

But, while physically, nothing had changed since Hugh had

brought Zoie to the Abyss to really share the magical world, there was one relationship that had. His relationship with Stevie was completely destroyed, and he had no desire to repair it, but he would use whatever he could to accomplish the mission that he and his friends had. And he would push past that disgust at her mere existence if it meant making Zoie happy.

Hugh took Zoie's hand as they began to walk towards the ridiculous castle that Reon, Zhenga, and Stevie lived in with their hired help. He brought her hand to his mouth and kissed it. "Are you okay with being here?"

Zoie smiled—at least half fake. "Yep." She swung their hands in an overdramatic way. "I'm not overjoyed by it, but I'm fine." She reminded him, "I told you that I didn't want to do this but I need to—and I can." Then she added, "and, maybe, it will force Stevie to speak with me. Maybe we can fix things."

Hugh stopped walking. "Fix things? She helped Miles kill you. She can never take that back." He added, "And I am not sorry that I took my revenge, and I never will be." He meant it. One hundred, one thousand, or one billion years from now, he would never regret taking Miles's life or scarring Stevie for eternity.

As they approached the oversized palace, Xariella stopped walking. "What if I'm not welcome here?"

Cade placed their hand on her back. "None of us are actually welcome here." Somehow, they felt that this statement would be calming. To Hugh, it was funny, but to anyone else, it had the possibility of making things worse.

"Yeah, but she…I used to work for her and…" She pointed back and forth between her and Cade. "Then there's us."

Cade turned and took her hands in theirs. "Xari, there's nothing that she can do that will ever come between us." Xariella opened her mouth to reply, but Cade put their finger to her lips. "And if she even thinks about *thinking about* doing anything to you, I will end her."

Xariella shook her head. "That doesn't change the fact that I'm not welcome here."

Hugh interjected, "Xariella, I have never once been welcome in the Abyss, and it's never stopped me. The trick," he said as he and Zoie continued passed them, "is appearing as if you don't give a fuck that you aren't welcome." He smiled and looked at Zoie. "Ready?"

Before they could even reach the giant front door, it was slowly opening, and the five of them were being ushered in, and Zhenga was there to greet them.

She immediately approached Zoie. "I'm so glad you decided to come with Hugh for his visit. You've been missed." She added, "Stevie is here, and I hope that you both take this opportunity to mend things."

"That really is the purpose of my part of the visit," Zoie admitted. She then motioned for the others to join her. "Of course, you know Cade, and perhaps you remember Xariella, their mate. And this is Silas. He's recently joined our little group, and he has powers he's still looking to explore."

Zhenga's face lit up. "That's one of my favorite things to do in this magical world." She turned to him and said, "I've researched hundreds of different powers and all of the types of beings that we know of." She added, "I helped Zoie find her powers—well, I'd like to think that—so maybe I can help you."

Out of nowhere, Xariella requested, "Could you help me with mine, too? It's… broken." She frowned. Cade looked over at Hugh, confused. Everyone in their group was shocked with this revelation. It could have been a ruse to try and get on someone's good side, but the vibe coming from her energy just seemed too real.

Zhenga reached her arms out, pulling Xariella into a hug. "Of course, honey, I can do my best." She started to walk with Xariella and Zoie and then motioned for Silas to follow. "I can work with both of you."

Cade started to follow, but Hugh grabbed their bicep. "No. Let them do their thing."

"But…"

Hugh looked them directly in the eyes. "Silas will protect her."

Cade let out a low growl. "I can protect her better."

The loud clicking of heels filled the room, drawing their attention away from the conversation. "You certainly don't think you're *actually* welcome here, do you?" Stevie stopped in front of them, arms folded across her chest.

Hugh was about to respond but was interrupted. "He's here on diplomatic business, so yes, he is." Reon took command of the situation. "Hugh, I expected you to bring Zoie. But," he then glared at Cade. "Not sure why *it* is here."

Stevie snapped her head towards her father. "They. Cade's pronouns are they and their, not *it!* They aren't an inanimate object. They are a person; a fantastic, kind, brave, fiercely loyal…"

Reon cut her off. "Not loyal to you…"

She snapped back. "I deserved their complete dismissal! I was wrong. I was disloyal to Cade." She held back tears and then turned and walked away, heels clicking more angrily than when she had arrived. Wiping some tears from her left cheek, she said just loudly enough, "I hate this place."

Hugh would have been lying to himself if he said that he even wanted to feel sorry for Stevie. He had no regrets about how he reacted upon finding out about her betrayal. He knew with absolute certainty, his reaction would be the same, no matter how many times he relived that moment. Zoie's turning out alive didn't change anything for him. She still betrayed them.

Additionally, Hugh would be naive if he didn't notice that she wasn't admitting any wrongdoing towards Hugh and Zoie. Even if she did, he would be hard-pressed to forgive her.

Reon shook his head as the echo of Stevie's shoes faded away. "Now, Hugh, let's get you and everyone settled before we start in on our business." He motioned to someone to help with the luggage. "Perhaps after supper?" Glancing at Cade, Reon continued, "Of course, not even Zoie can join us."

Hugh nodded. "Obviously."

# ZOIE

Taking a seat on the bench in front of the pond, Zoie took in a deep breath and closed her eyes.

An involuntary smile took up residence on her face, as she remembered her first magic lesson from Zhenga in this very same spot. The story of the Earth and her two Moons was etched in her mind as if it was a book she had read dozens of times.

She had wanted to be able to wield magic for her entire life, but her first trip to the Abyss was what solidified it as more of a need. As part of the very core of who she was. Some people were meant to be doctors, lawyers, leaders, musicians, artists… Zoie was meant to be a witch. A Sun Witch. Every day, she knew that more and more. She just wished she was a little better at the magic she had.

Zhenga took Xariella's hands in hers. She closed her eyes and breathed deeply. "You have the power of influence, but it's not functioning…"

Xariella explained that ever since she found the group, she'd not been able to make her power work. "…I used to sing little songs. I'd make them up really, and, even as a child, I would make these things occur." She shook her head.

Zhenga started on a series of questions with Xariella, just as Silas sat down next to Zoie. He whispered, "I'm starting to wonder if my alleged reason for being here is a wise one."

Sighing heavily, Zoie nodded. "I forgot how intuitive Zhenga is. She knew I was a witch before I did. She blurted it out at supper." She chuckled, "Looking back, now I know why Hugh nearly choked to death in that moment."

Rolling his eyes and letting out a little angry breath, Silas stated, "I know you think it's funny or cute or whatever, but he lies to you—withholds shit—so often. It's neither cute nor funny." He added, "And he underestimates you like it's his job to do so."

Knowing that she had to keep her composure, Zoie turned towards him. "Let's not do this here." When he opened his mouth to reply, Zoie cut him off. "Okay, you want to do this here?" She looked him directly in the eyes. "Silas, it isn't a competition between the two of you, and this shit just has to stop. And, if it can't," she frowned, "I am going to choose him."

His mouth dropped open. She discreetly slid her hand on top of his. "He is my primary partner, and that does come with certain—I don't know—privileges or perks. Those are not the right words."

"Zoie." His free hand went to his chest. "Zoie, you are the love of my life. I just want… I just want what's best for you…"

She squeezed his hand gently. "Silas, I know this. And…" she paused and got quieter. "And I'm only going to say this once—I love you, too." The betrayal to Hugh and their promise to only use the word "love" with each other weighed heavy on her. "But, Silas, the only way that this works…" She pointed back and forth between the two of them, "…is if it's healthy for both of us."

He looked at the ground. "And you aren't sure that this is healthy for you?"

"Sometimes, I wonder if it's healthy for you. But I can't make that decision for you." She continued, "But for me, this relationship isn't healthy if you are going to continually disrespect my primary partner."

His hands raked through his hair and then down his face. "Zoie, I can't stand by and watch him disrespect *you*."

Zoie took a sharp breath in. "Hugh isn't perfect, and our relationship isn't perfect." She added, "I'm not perfect." Continuing gently, she said, "But we love each other, and we are going to spend our version of eternity together."

Silas asked, "Do you see a version of eternity for you and me?"

Zoie paused. She desperately wanted to say yes, but if the animosity between Silas and Hugh didn't subside, she couldn't see her relationship with Silas lasting. "Silas…"

He stood up. "That says enough for me." He shook his head. "You couldn't just say 'yes'? You have to think about it, Zoie." Silas no longer cared about the potential scene he was making. "I'm done." Turning his back to Zoie, he headed back towards the castle.

Zoie stood up, but immediately in her head, she heard Silas as if he was standing right next to her. "Don't follow me." Then one final, "I mean it."

Her heart broke, and she tried to hold a telepathic conversation with him, but he wouldn't let her in. Defeated, she sat back down on the bench.

Zhenga and Xariella were no longer focused on their own conversation, and they immediately ran over to Zoie. Zhenga asked, "What was that about?"

Zoie shook her head. "Nothing for you all to worry about. He's just struggling." She added, "It's something personal to him, so I don't feel comfortable sharing any more than that."

Xariella took Zoie's hand in hers. "I'm sure whatever it is, it's going to work itself out."

Zoie put a fake smile on her face. "I'm sure it will." She put her free hand on top of Xariella's. "So, what did you find out about your power that isn't behaving as you expected?"

She smiled. "Nothing just yet, but Zhenga is going to help me."

Zhenga nodded. "I think if we explore Xariella's past and what changed we'll be able to dig into what has led to this alteration in her power." She gently reminded Xariella, "It's an alteration, not a failure."

Xariella's eyes had a smile in them that was more prominent than Zoie had seen in ages. "I'm so thrilled that you are willing to help me." The smile behind her eyes hid away. "Especially since… well, since…"

Zhenga chuckled. "What? Since you are dating my daughter's ex-partner?" She placed her hand on Xariella's shoulder. "Cade and Stevie were not well suited for one another. It was fun for them, I am sure, but Cayden needed someone—and please don't take this the wrong way—they needed someone who needs them, and they needed to need someone." Zhenga clarified, "It's a wonderful thing, honestly, being strong enough to need someone." She admitted, "Stevie was not ready to love someone like that. I'm afraid she still isn't."

They all turned as they heard someone clear their throat. Out of the shadows came Stevie. "It's hard to find love when you're scarred the way that I am."

Accidentally out loud, Zoie responded, "That's not entirely true."

Stevie rolled her eyes. "Just because you accept Hugh's scars doesn't mean everyone else is the *saint* that you are."

"Stevie, I'm…"

Zhenga cut her off. "Stephanie, everyone here knows exactly what you did that resulted in those scars."

Stevie let out an angry sigh. "So you're excusing what he did?"

Her mother went to respond, but Zoie took her turn to cut Zhenga off. "Stevie, I am sorry for what Hugh did to you. Revenge doesn't solve anything. It provided a temporary Band-aid for him at a desperate time—and that doesn't make it right." She admitted, "I came here with Hugh on this trip because I was hoping to mend our friendship."

*Pfft.* Stevie rolled her eyes. "Sure you did."

Zoie shook her head. "Stevie, you can believe whatever you want about me and my reason for coming here. I'm not going to convince you of anything you don't want to believe." She shrugged. "But, I miss you, and that's the truth."

Stevie's healthy eye filled with tears. "How can I believe you, when you stay with him?"

"I can understand why he did something and not agree with it." Zoie hadn't wanted to have this conversation this way. She certainly didn't want to have it in front of other people.

Still in complete disbelief, Stevie added, "How could you ever trust me again? I literally led you to what was supposed to be your death. How could you forgive that?"

Sincerely, Zoie responded, "I'm not sure, but I'm willing to try." She turned to Zhenga and Xariella. "Please excuse me. I'm going to rest for a bit." She looked to Stevie. "If you change your mind, I'm ready to see how we can move forward."

She headed back towards the castle and the moment that she was in her room with her back against the door, she burst into tears.

Her face was in her hands, tears rolling down her cheeks, when she heard the bathroom door creak. She quickly sucked in a breath and wiped her tears.

It was too late; Hugh had already seen her. "Zo, is everything okay?"

He was still drying his hands when she ran into his arms, her head colliding with his chest. She buried her face in his shirt and sobbed.

The comfort of his warm arms wrapped around her. "Get it out." His hands ran up and down her back. "Get it all out."

Any willpower she had to control her crying had disappeared, and she followed his instructions and just cried until she couldn't cry anymore. Once she regained any semblance of composure, she released her grip on his shirt and made room for them to breathe.

He took her hands in his and asked, "What happened?"

Unsure if discussing what was bothering her was appropriate, she bit on her lower lip and looked at the floor. "I'm not sure that I can talk to you about it."

Hugh led her to the bed and they sat down. "You can talk to me about anything."

A residual sob-breath took control, and she pre-emptively wiped for tears that never came—her tear ducts truly were spent. She took in a deep breath and let it out, so audible that she figured that anyone in a nearby room could hear it. "I think Silas just ended things with me."

Hugh sat up straight and tightened his jaw. He asked through his teeth, "Why do you think this?"

"Because we had a difficult conversation; he said he was 'done' and walked away, asking me not to follow him. He also closed the connection between our minds." She added, "But that's not the only thing that happened."

He narrowed his eyes. "Something else happened with him? Did he hurt you?" Of course, he would automatically assume the worst of Silas. But when she shook her head, he asked, "Or some other unrelated event?"

"I tried to speak with Stevie, and she really isn't willing to budge about mending our friendship." She placed her hands gently in her lap. "I don't think that we can accomplish…"

Hugh cut her off. "Forget about our purpose for this trip for a moment." Placing his arm around her and pulling her close, he requested, "Speak your truth about why it really hurts. It might help."

"I miss my friend." She moved even more impossibly close to him and balled up his shirt in one of her fists.

Hugh's chest raised as he took in a long, drawn-out breath. "Zoie, I need you to listen to me." When she unglued her body from his and looked in his eyes, he continued. "Even now, there are days that I miss Alvin; he was my first friend when I became a part of this world. But, on those days when I missed him and wanted to reconnect, sometimes it took reminding myself that our friendship wasn't really healthy for me to stop me from reaching out." He continued, "I think you need to search within yourself and decide if your friendship with Stevie is truly worth rekindling." She felt his warm hand push a strand of hair behind her ear and then rest on her cheek. "Sometimes people come into our lives and are temporary. That's okay."

"But…"

His hand moved from her cheek to his finger on her lips, shushing her. "We will find another way."

"I don't know if there is another way to accomplish this." She looked up and caught a glimpse of herself in the mirror. Her puffy eyes were surrounded with smudged eyeliner and a dried-up stream of black made it looked as if she cried tears of tar.

Shrugging and shaking her head, Zoie stated, "I cannot go to supper when it looks like I've just got done crying my way through a My Chemical Romance concert." She grabbed a towel and headed into the bathroom.

# HUGH

While waiting for the shower to turn on and to hear the sound of the running water get displaced by Zoie actually getting in, Hugh contemplated whether he needed to stay in the room. Regardless of what the rules were—whether he was on the Council or not; whether or not Zoie was granted protection by proxy—Hugh didn't trust Reon.

He still wasn't over losing Zoie—even though she was back. Glancing towards the bathroom door, he decided that Reon wouldn't dare hurt Zoie in his own home, especially with all of her friends around. So he quickly left the room, seemingly on a mission.

He wasn't sure which mission he was actually headed for—he had so many at this point. Was it going to find the pendant that Reon had? Alvin? No, maybe he was going to strangle Silas for breaking Zoie's heart. Perhaps he was going to remind Stevie of who she was dealing with. Perhaps he would just deal with these battles as they came to him.

Hugh walked through the palace quickly, with tunnel vision leading him towards—he wasn't sure where, but it didn't matter. Out of the corner of his eye, he saw a small building in the distance, beyond the hedge maze around the pond in the back garden of the palace. He stopped dead in his tracks.

Purposefully, he made his way out the back of the palace and towards the building. Before he could even get to the entrance of the hedge maze, he was intercepted.

"Where are you going?" Stevie asked, looking him up and down, disgusted.

He decided not to lie. "The mausoleum." He began walking again.

Stevie's hand grabbed his bicep and tried to stop him, but he kept walking. "What business do you have in the mausoleum?"

He continued on his way, turning around and throwing his hands in the air. "I just feel like it's the place to be." He turned around to face the direction he was going and continued on.

Her heels clicked on the sea glass path as she worked to catch up with him. "Tell me what you are doing. No one goes to the mausoleum."

Hugh stopped and glared at her. "Leave me alone, Stevie."

"No. Not until you tell me what's going on." Even as he kept walking, she kept nagging at him. It wasn't as if it was bothering him enough to break his concentration for getting through the maze; he and Cade had worked out the fastest way through during a trip there once before—and he had a picture of it in his head from when he had looked at it from the third-floor balcony. Plus, it wasn't designed to be impossible.

Suddenly, a wall of water was blocking his way. Rolling his eyes, he turned around. "Fine, Stevie, do you want to know what's going on?"

"Yes."

"Why?" He quickly added, "Besides the fact that you just need to be a thorn in my side?"

She groaned. "Then I suppose I don't have another reason."

He stared at her for a moment and then glanced at the water and back at her. "Then just let me through."

"I don't believe that your visit here is really a diplomatic meeting with my father. I think that you have another plan." She stated, "I recognize that Silas from the night at the beach when I…" she trailed off.

Hugh didn't let her off the hook. "When you what? Say it, Stevie. The night you tried to kill Zoie—*again*." He felt the heat in his body start to raise.

She frowned. "Yes, that night."

"What night was that again, Stevie? Say. It." His eyes started to glow.

She yelled at him. "The night I tried to kill Zoie again! Yes! There! I fucking said it."

He took a step towards her, and his claws started to grow. "She's come here to reconcile all of that with you. Her kind heart has forgiven you, Stevie, and you hold what *I* did to you against her."

She stepped backwards. "She might forgive me, but I can't forgive myself," she admitted.

His claws retracted, and a deep breath settled his body temperature and calmed his eyes. "Just talk to her."

Stevie sighed. "Fine, I will." As he turned to leave, she quickly added, "…IF you tell me what you're going to the mausoleum for."

Extending an olive branch of trust to Stevie, Hugh admitted, "Isn't that where Alvin is likely resting? I think he was buried with something of mine, and I want it back." Half-truth—but he couldn't possibly show all of his cards right away.

Her jaw dropped. "You plan to open his burial chamber?"

Hugh shrugged. "If that's what I've gotta do." He turned towards the wall of water. "I didn't want to get wet, but I'll walk right through this, if I have to."

He could practically hear her roll her eyes as the water came down. "Fine. But I'm going with you."

"Whatever."

They continued on towards the mausoleum in silence. Hugh would have liked for it to at least have been an awkward silence so that they could laugh about it later, but it wasn't. It was a comfortable silence. Like two old friends just enjoying each other's company, not having to say a word.

And that, for Hugh, actually made it painful.

He tried to be cold towards Stevie, but in reality he felt many things towards her. Rage; distrust; hatred; and longing for their old friendship, just to name a few.

Hearing something squelch under Stevie's shoe, Hugh turned to see her hopping on one foot because the other was bare. The creature she had happened to step on actually held onto her shoe, and Hugh couldn't help but laugh.

She shot him a dagger-filled glare. "You know, you could be a gentleman and help."

He took his time walking over. "Why would I do that when I know you have basically flawless balance from years of yoga? You could easily retrieve it yourself."

Reaching over, he thought it would be as simple as just picking it up, but he was wrong. Hugh actually had to yank on the shoe, and the creature—a form of jellyfish with cephalopod-like suction abilities—went flying. As it cut through the air, Hugh could have sworn he heard a "wheeeeeee", but he wasn't going to inquire as to whether the creature could speak or not.

Reaching for the shoe, Stevie tried to say thank you, but it came out as a laugh instead. And as she balanced to put her shoe back on, she shook her head, still chuckling. "That thing probably is going to end up on the other side of the Abyss with no hope of ever getting back to its family."

Hugh smiled. "Well, it shouldn't try to take things that don't belong to it." Hypocritical Hugh, once again.

They started to walk again, and, this time, when it fell silent for just a little too long, Stevie admitted, "I shouldn't have tried to take Zoie away from you."

This was the one topic that Hugh just struggled to be forgiving about. "You're right. You shouldn't."

Stevie sadly said, "I shouldn't have cared about getting back in with my parents. My mother…" She paused. "My mother loves me endlessly. I mean, she's a ruthless bitch when it comes to getting what she wants, but, in most cases, she's really kind-hearted." As she continued, she shook her head, "My father still wants nothing to do with me."

Hugh's head about snapped off of his shoulders. "You mean because you wouldn't give us up at first?"

She shook her head. "No, he's over that. I more than made up for that by helping Miles with Zoie. But when I came back after…" She pointed to her face. "…this. Well, he says that I'm not fit to be in public, and, suddenly, he wasn't sure that I was the right person to take over after him…" She admitted, "I hate him. He was always looking for an excuse for me to not be good enough, and now he is taking the most superficial reason and citing it as a sign of political weakness."

"Stevie, I don't know what to say."

"I'm not asking for you to say anything."

He sighed. "No, I know about that stuff, you aren't. But for my part in it…" Again, Hugh went with honesty, but this time it was full honesty. "I want to say that I am sorry for what I did to you, and a part of me is. But, Stevie, if I said that I was deeply sorry or that even that the part of me that *is* sorry is even a medium-sized part, I would be lying." He frowned. "It's a small part. A *very* small part. And that part of me that is sorry is only able to be there because Zoie is alive."

"I understand that."

As they approached the door to the mausoleum, Hugh asked, "How can I trust you again?" He raised his hand to touch the doorknob and then put it back down. "I want to trust you, *for* Zoie. But how can I trust you *with* Zoie?"

Stevie nodded, understanding his apprehension. "I think it will take time, and we may have to give it that time." She added, "But I think maybe working together on whatever it is that you're really working on may help speed along the process."

Hugh smiled. "So you'll help me open up Alvin's resting chamber and get what belongs to me? And then clean up the mess?" She nodded, and he added, "And not tell anyone?"

She nodded again. Then Stevie added, "And maybe, after that, you can tell me what's really going on."

Hugh reached up and opened the door. The air in the mausoleum was still. Dry. Silent. Even Stevie's shoes barely made a sound on the seashell floor.

Not really knowing where to begin looking for Alvin, Hugh started on the wall closest to the door.

Stevie, however walked straight over to the opposite corner. "He's over here, unless you want to pay respects to someone else before defiling his resting place."

Hugh nodded. "Thanks. You just saved me some time." The engraving with Alvin's name on it was flush with the wall. There was no way to grab it and open it like a drawer. "Look, I'm going to admit it. I didn't think this plan through very well. How do I get in here?"

Stevie looked at him and her eyes went wide. "You didn't have a plan? For fuck's sake, Hugh, you were walking down here like you had a mission from the Gods."

He shrugged. "I saw the mausoleum out of the corner of my eye, and I just made a snap decision."

Looking at the spaces around Alvin's, Stevie smiled. "Well, I think that it is designed to open, so we just need to look for a way to do it."

"Why do you think that?"

She pointed to the right of Alvin's space, labeled "Edythe of the Woodland Realm". "That's Edie, right? And this," she pointed to the space below Alvin with "Miles, son of Alvin" etched in the granite. "This is his son." There was an empty space. "This is part of the family tomb."

"There's only three of them, though." He pressed on the blank space and the paw symbol on his arm began to glow. The sound of a lock releasing filled the room and the door to the four chambers opened.

A piece of sheet metal blocked the three filled chambers, but the empty one was open. Hugh looked in and saw an envelope. It only took him a half of a second to decide to be nosy and see if it was addressed to anyone.

He reached in and grabbed it, laughing the moment that he saw who it was for. He showed Stevie. "Should I open it?"

She chuckled. "It says it's for Mr. Hugh Davies. It may be considered rude for you to not."

He tore open the envelope, not concerned that someone would know that it was read if they saw it. He laughed even harder once he read the note and then handed it to Stevie.

**Saved you a spot!**

**You can't even escape me in death.**

**-Alvin**

Stevie laughed loudly. "He's such a jackass, even in Hell."

Hugh threw the note and the envelop back into the open space, haphazardly. "Okay, looks like we're going to have to tear this sheet metal away and then pull him out. I'll see if the item is there…"

"Maybe you should tell me what *the item* is, so I can help look?"

He hesitated. "I'll know if it's there." He found the edge of the metal and peeled it back. Sliding back the cover, Hugh was shocked to see, instead of a casket, an urn. He was immediately furious, because this could mean that the pendant was turned to ash along with him. He reached in and grabbed the urn, twisting the top off. "Just ash. Fuck." He groaned. "Fuck. Fuck. Fuck." He angrily placed the urn back in the chamber and slammed the metal back into place. "Fuck!"

Narrowing her eyes, Stevie suggested, "What about Edie? Could the item have been placed with her?"

Hugh didn't hesitate. He ripped the sheet metal back, and there it was—fixed on a ribbon around the narrowest part of the urn. He quickly untied the ribbon and shoved it and the pendant in his pocket. Again, he used all of his force to put the metal back into place—and it was far from perfect.

He grabbed the granite door and shut it and then looked at Stevie. "Let's go."

As they made their way back into the hedge maze, Stevie asked, "Why is that necklace so important?"

A half truth. "It's the pendant. This pendant and the rest of the set that goes with it can help Zoie see her father again."

Stevie stopped walking. "Why didn't you say so before?"

Hugh turned to her. "Because, let's face it, I just don't know if I can trust you."

She folded her arms across her chest. "Let me see it." She put her hand out in a gimme-gimme motion.

Reluctantly, Hugh pulled the pendant out of his pocket and showed it to her.

She looked at it for a second, slightly puzzled, and then said, "I've seen one of these before."

Hugh knew exactly where she had seen it before. Testing her loyalty, he asked, "Oh? Do you remember where?"

"My dad has something similar to this." She looked up at Hugh. "I think that it could be part of the set. You said that if we collect them all we can help Zoie see her father?" Obviously not trusting him, she stated, "I've never heard of a spell that brings someone back from the dead."

He loosely admitted a piece of the truth. "It's not like that. She will get to speak with him if we can find all four of these. Zoie and Silas have one each. This is the third. We're looking for the fourth." Hugh requested, "If you know where your father's is, please, help us acquire it."

She didn't hesitate. "Daddy has it locked in a vault in his office. He keeps it in a little box that is locked. The key is on a necklace that my mother wears." She added, sadly, "She never takes it off."

Hugh sighed, defeated. "So not only do we need to get the key from your mother, but also, we need to figure out how to get into this vault, when your father isn't in his office—which he keeps locked by magic."

She reached over and touched his shoulder. "We'll figure out a way."

# ZOIE

Toweling her hair, Zoie walked out of the bathroom. "So, do you want to match our…" She looked up and saw that the room was empty. "Okay…"

She sat down in front of the mirror and continued to scrunch her curls with a cotton t-shirt. Curly hair—wild and natural looking—took several steps and lots of product. It wasn't just letting it air dry. For Zoie, this actually took quite a bit of concentration. Otherwise, her hair would do whatever it felt—and sometimes that wasn't good, so when there was a knock at the door, she was mildly annoyed.

After a small sigh, she opened the door.

Standing in front of her, Silas looked as if he regretted every decision that he had made in his entire life. "Can I come in?"

She stepped back from the doorway and motioned for him to come in.

He stood quietly in front of the door once it closed.

That, plus his display out in the garden, was not only heartbreaking to her but annoying. "If you have something to say, then say it." She glanced over at him. When he stood in silence for a few more seconds she went back over to the mirror. "You're welcome to sit here and watch me get ready, or you can speak. Whichever makes you happy." She wasn't going to deal with any passive-aggressiveness from him—from anyone. She had stopped dealing with that when she made the decision to move to Birmingham.

He pressed his lips together into a thin line and then let out an angry breath through his nose. "I know what I signed up for when I agreed to being your secondary partner. I just didn't realize how much it would hurt when I actually came face to face with it."

Zoie turned in her chair, still scrunching her hair. "Silas, I'm going to be honest with you that I never expected you—or anyone in a secondary role—to stick around forever." She admitted, "I always assumed you would find your forever-person and just move on." She added, "Or you'd tire of me and the situation and call it quits. Or," she added after a deep breath, "…or you'd realize that you don't deserve to be second to someone that you put first and move forward with your life and someone who would treat you as first."

Silas admitted, "I just have to really think about what I want."

"I understand that." She turned back towards the mirror and continued to get ready. "Silas, I wouldn't blame you if you ran away right now and never looked back." She made eye contact with him through the reflection. "I don't want you to go. I want you in my life, but you have to do what is best for you."

He shook his head. "No, I made a commitment." Cutting her off before she could even take in the air to speak, Silas explained, "A commitment to our mission. I will help with that and then… then I will decide." He was resolute with it.

He sat in silence with his arms folded across his chest, as Zoie finished her hair and any makeup that she was going to wear.

She very strangely didn't feel the need to beg for him to stay with her in their relationship. She wanted him to stay, of course, but she didn't feel the clingy need that she would have felt in previous relationships. Zoie was beyond the point in her life where she worked hard to gain the affection of those that would reject her. As if it mattered, anyways—she had rejected Silas first, with her inability to tell Silas that she saw a future for them.

When Zoie was a little girl, she had always felt infinite. She assumed that most people had a feeling that they would someday die—a realization. But she always felt as if she could see the future, and, for her, that future did not include death. As an adult—and, now, knowing that she was a Sun Witch—Zoie could even better see that future of hers, and it included Hugh. Her future was focused on having a life with him. She could see it as clearly as a movie at the theater.

She had felt her future with Hugh, effortlessly, since the moment that she met him. Since the moment their hands touched when she handed him the apple. She initially thought it was merely a crush, but the more she learned about her powers and connected incidents from her past, the more she realized that there was a gentle ability to know some seemingly inconsequential things about her own future.

And while Zoie could sense a future with Hugh, she never saw—or even felt—that future with Silas. Perhaps that was why she felt comfortable letting him make the decision. Maybe she was finally at the point in her life where she wasn't going to force things into a box they just weren't going to fit into.

She stood up. "I'm going to get dressed now."

"I should go, then." He stood up and left, without another word.

Instead of getting dressed, Zoie sat on the corner of the bed. She didn't cry. She didn't even think; instead she closed her eyes and attempted to meditate for a few minutes.

She wanted to clear her mind of what she had just realized about herself, but no amount of repeating the word "pause" or visualizing her placing the thought in a brown leaf and setting it to sail down a river could get it out of her mind.

She wanted Silas, but she didn't need him. He wasn't the air that she breathed or the blood in her veins. What was even more shocking to her, as she spent this time reflecting, was that Hugh wasn't these things either. She was these very things to herself.

And while Hugh was a factor that would ignite the fire within her soul, he was not what kept it going. She was. Her desire to be able to be herself—her full self—without having to be something else for everyone else—afforded her the peace that she had never known before. She did owe a small part of that to Silas, for guiding her to her powers and letting them become a part of her, but she really wanted to give credit to Hugh, for being the first person to ever truly make her feel safe. For never making her feel like she had to hide anything about herself, even in the moments that he didn't agree with her.

So, when the door opened without a knock, and she felt the heat in her stomach rise, she knew it was Hugh that had come into her orbit. She smiled and opened her eyes.

He walked immediately over to her and dropped the pendant into her palm. "Only one more to go."

Astonished, she asked, "Where did you find this?"

He recounted how he and Stevie had ventured to the mausoleum and defiled a couple resting places.

Placing it in the hidden lockbox with the others, Zoie asked, "Do you think that we can trust her?"

"I don't think that we have a choice at this point." He was right. She knew a little bit about their goal, and it was up to Stevie to decide if she wanted to keep their secret or not. He explained, "I didn't give her the entire story. Just that finding them could give you a few moments with your father." He added, "She knows where her father keeps his."

Zoie frowned. "It's not his. It's Mitzi's." She knew that stealing from a thief still made her a thief, and she was quite aware that it was not their intention to give these pendants back to Mitzi, but their reason to have them was much more pure—in Zoie's opinion—than why the less than savory members of the Council were holding onto them.

"I have to be honest with you, Zoie," he admitted. "I don't have a plan yet on how to get that pendant from him." He continued, "I don't know how to get into that room alone."

Zoie sighed. "Stevie's really our only option at this point."

Hugh began changing for supper. "I'll think about it over supper and meet with Cade afterwards. If anyone is going to know how to get her on our side, it will be them."

"I think that Stevie still loves Cade, and having Xariella here… I don't know." Zoie was concerned that, no matter what, Stevie would be so bitter about Cade moving on with their life—not to mention Hugh's scarring her—that there was no chance to salvage the friendship and get her on their side. But she wouldn't lose all hope. "Maybe…" Forcing a small smile onto her face, Zoie tried to fake the hope until she could really feel it. "Maybe she will just do the right thing."

Hugh, who had started to get ready for the ridiculously over-complicated dinners that they had at this ridiculous palace, tried to support her hope into existence. He placed his hand on hers. "I think she's leaning that way."

# HUGH

Because the party was larger than the last time they'd visited, Hugh was seated between Xariella and Stevie at supper, instead of next to Zoie. He knew that this was to encourage conversation outside of usual pairings. Still, he wasn't any less disappointed to see Zoie as far away from him as possible—and next to Reon.

He didn't trust that guy.

Subconsciously—or maybe even consciously, really—he kept one eye on Zoie and Reon while holding a conversation with Xariella and Stevie. Well, attempting. The two women were talking over each other.

It was the most unusual pissing contest Hugh had ever witnessed. They weren't trying to impress anyone—just speak over each other. Perhaps to gain attention or maybe to just shut the other one up.

Whatever the reason, Hugh was over it. He was getting a headache from the sheer volume of the two of them. Still, manners prevented him from slamming his hand on the table and telling them to both shut it.

Zhenga must have been over the noise because she put her soup spoon down with a little more ferocity than usual. She dabbed the corners of her mouth with her napkin and then turned to Xariella. "You really should tell your friends what you discovered today in the garden."

Zoie's face lit up with excitement. "What did you find?" Her curiosity over things in the magical world never wavered. A new item for her to study was always welcomed with open arms.

A kindred spirit in that aspect, Zhenga smiled softly. "Unfortunately, m'dear, it wasn't an object." She said, "Though it would be a joy to find something new down here in the Abyss after all these years. We've not had a new discovery in ages." She encouraged Xariella. "Tell them."

Xariella smiled brightly. "My power—it's not quite what we had thought." Her smile briefly was veiled in sadness. "The reason that my power—my singing power where I sing what I want—well, it wasn't working."

Cade moved to reach across the table, but they realized that the distance was too great.

Xariella met their eyes and smiled. "But through talking things out with Zhenga, we believe that the reason for this was because I am truly happy, so I don't really want for anything."

"Oh, how sweet!" Zoie exclaimed happily, clapping a little.

"Gag me," Stevie murmured, rolling her eyes.

Silas, who had been silent the entire meal thus far, finally spoke. "So, what does this mean? To get your power to work, we need to make you miserable again?" He looked at Stevie and smirked. "Like you were when Stevie was your boss?" Silas had nearly as much trouble as Hugh did with trusting Stevie—likely because he watched what Stevie had orchestrated in order to kill Zoie.

Stevie let out a small scoff, and Xariella took her turn rolling her eyes. "Ugh. No, that's in the past."

Getting the conversation back on track, Zoie asked, "So tell us—what did you discover?"

She smiled. "When I scream, I send waves through the air—I knock things over!" She was so thrilled with this.

"Ooooh! That's neat!" Zoie clapped with excitement again.

Xariella nodded excitedly. "And the more I pull it from my chest, the more powerful it is. I even stopped one of the guards in his tracks. He was frozen. Not icy, but… you get it."

"I love magic," Zoie spoke from her heart. Hugh felt a small electrical spark shoot through him as he watched her.

Reon motioned toward Hugh. "Zoie, you had best watch those declarations of admiration or your betrothed may get jealous."

Hugh did his best not to roll his eyes, but he wasn't sure if he truly succeeded. "Zoie is still new to the magical world, and, if you recall, a large chunk of that time was stolen from her because *someone* decided to try and end her life." He looked back and forth between Reon and Stevie. He was never sure how much Zhenga had to do with that little plan, especially since she seemed to genuinely enjoy Zoie's company. Still, she was from a world of secrets and lies—and it wasn't just that she was a mermaid. Her entire life was in society, and Zhenga was a master at playing all sides.

Reon put his fork down. "Are you ever going to just let that little misunderstanding go?"

Hugh's fork hit the table with more force. "Little? Little misunderstanding? Zoie was nearly killed, and, let's be frank, the entirety of our world believed she was. Not to mention her mother, her friends, anyone that knew her. We all thought that she was dead." He picked up his fork and put it back down. "For months."

Reon glared at him. "You got your revenge. You didn't stop

at disfiguring my once-beautiful daughter. You killed Alvin's son, his father."

Hugh interjected, "I didn't kill Jack."

The King didn't even stop talking. "You saved Alvin for last. We all know he didn't die of *natural* causes in that prison."

"Prison? That was a fucking spa." Hugh let an angry breath out of his nose.

Reon still didn't stop talking. "We put you on the Council, despite my best judgment." He stabbed a piece of food with his fork but didn't lift it. "We have to be able to work together. Now, I have forgiven you for ruining any chance my daughter would have at a life of worth, and Zoie is no worse for wear. In fact, I think she's better off now than she was before that little misunderstanding."

Not even giving Hugh a chance to speak, it was Stevie's turn to put her silverware down with some force. "I don't have a chance at a 'life of worth'? What's that supposed to mean?"

"Now isn't the time." Reon finally took that bite of food.

Stevie blinked her eyes quickly and then squared her shoulders. "No. You felt that it was the right time to declare it, so I think that it is the perfect time to discuss what you meant."

He put his silverware down, and then Zhenga opened her mouth to speak, but Reon motioned for her to be quiet. "Stephanie, you had always been very beautiful. Popular and loved because of the way you looked. But, let's be honest that you weren't the brightest bioluminescent algae in the sea. You didn't magically gain wit when this dog scratched the beauty out of you."

"How. Dare. You." That didn't come from Stevie. Shockingly, it was Cade who spoke up on her behalf. "Do you know your daughter at all? What she is capable of?"

Reon laughed heartily. "You? You're going to stick up for her?

When you are exhibit A. You didn't want her the moment that she was maimed." He reminded them, "You literally discarded her as soon as possible after it was done."

"That wasn't why—" Cade and Stevie said in unison.

"Allow me," Stevie requested. "I betrayed them, father. Of course, they didn't want me around. They couldn't trust me." She stood up and put her napkin on her plate. "I've had enough of this. I'll excuse myself."

Reon waved her off. "Of course. Run away from your problems, just like you always do."

She paused only for a moment. It was such a brief break in her stride that most wouldn't even notice the change.

Cade went to move, but a look from Xariella put their butt back in the chair. Hugh made eye contact with Zoie and then made the decision to follow Stevie. "I'll go check on her. The whole thing was brought up because of me."

"Best let her cool off," Reon suggested, taking another bite. Then he motioned towards Zoie with his fork. "Plus, isn't she the one you love?"

Zoie looked at Hugh. "Go check on your friend." She smiled gently. "Stevie would appreciate that you care."

Hugh followed Stevie, catching up to her as she neared Reon's office.

"What are you doing?" she whispered harshly.

Annoyed, he replied with an angry whisper. "I don't know, just checking on you." He softened. "That was really rough of Reon. Even for him."

She shrugged. "That's just exactly what I had expected once I challenged him." She pressed her lips together. "It's nothing that I haven't heard before."

Stevie waved her hand over the water in a decorative pool nearby and the water traveled with her.

"What are you doing?" Hugh asked.

She shushed him. "I'm unlocking the door to my dad's office." The water surrounded the doorknob and then it got sucked into the lock. A few clicks from the tumblers and then the door creaked open just enough to be ajar.

Stevie waved Hugh in after her. "Quickly, before he has some weird sense that someone's in here."

"…Or a more realistic idea that perhaps someone sees us and tells him?" Hugh chuckled.

Stevie laughed. "We are in a palace below what is believed to be the bottom of the ocean, and you want to talk in terms of what's realistic?" She let out a *pfft*. Then they both started rummaging around the room looking for a special key or lever.

"Do we have any idea what this key or lever looks like?"

Stevie pointed to a ridiculously ornate door at the other side of the room. "I've never seen it, but it goes to that."

Hugh walked over to the door and looked at it for a few moments. There wasn't anywhere to put a key and there was no spot for a numerical combination. "Stevie, what if it's biometric?"

She paused for a moment and considered it. "It's not—we're at the bottom of the ocean, and in a palace. He wouldn't even think that someone could get in here, let alone break into his safe." Stevie cautiously approached the door. "It's maybe not even locked."

The door was wood, covered in barnacles and coral. Stevie didn't even know where to touch it.

As she reached out to place her hand on it, Hugh grabbed her forearm and stopped her. "It looks really delicate. What if when you touch it, it breaks and leaves… crumbs?"

They both laughed at "crumbs," and then Stevie said, "I think that there's going to be evidence that someone was in here without that." She put her hand on some of the coral and started sliding it around, feeling every bit of texture that was available to her hand.

Hugh went to start the search as well, but she stopped him. "No. With the way that you manhandled that metal in the mausoleum, I don't really want you touching anything." She laughed. "You are kind of like a bull in a china shop."

He chuckled. "I'll just stand guard then. Keep people out." Hugh watched the door.

"You always were a pretty good wall." She shifted her hands throughout the brightly colored coral and nearly cut herself on the dark barnacles, until she felt a smooth part. "Hmmm…"

His head snapped towards her. "What?"

"Interesting." She slid her hand further into the smooth crevice until she felt her hand hit the end of the crevice. Seemingly looking at nothing, but still concentrating, Stevie felt her hand around in the space. "I wonder…" She looked around almost frantically. "Hugh, is there some alcohol on the drink cart?"

"There's wine in the decanter," he responded, walking over to the other side of the desk. "Thirsty?"

She chuckled. "No—I just needed some fluid." She ordered, "Take the stopper off."

As soon as he did as she instructed, she waved her hand and beckoned the wine towards her. Then she directed it into the smooth area that she had found in the door.

Hugh didn't like that she wasn't really letting him know what was going on. He still had such little faith in her. This entire thing could have been a trap. "Stevie…"

"Hush." The wine filled the cavity, and, for a moment, Stevie was disappointed. Nothing was happening. And then she heard a glug-glug sound—the door was drinking the wine. She smiled as if she had discovered something great. "It's working."

Within the door itself, the mechanisms started to click and gears started to move. The barnacles and coral started to shift around on the door, and then tiny fish swam out from behind the coral into the air—disintegrating after a few seconds.

The door opened just a crack with a loud click.

It was so loud that both Hugh and Stevie looked towards the main entrance to the room to verify that no one was entering—as if they could even tell if someone was outside.

Stevie slid her hand in the small space between the door and the jamb and pulled it open. It led to a small room, about the size of a walk-in closet in an apartment. There were only three items in the room—three wooden chests.

Hugh went to follow Stevie in, but paused. He turned and grabbed a small side table and stuck it against the jamb of the door. "If this door slams shut, I don't want to be stuck in here."

"Smart."

He stood next to her in the small space and looked at the little treasure chests. "Soooo… which one is it that we want?"

Stevie pulled a small conch shell out of her pocket. It was on a delicate gold chain. "I got this off of my mother's vanity just before supper." She started to compare it to the locking mechanisms on the boxes. "I noticed that she wasn't wearing it when I encountered her after you and I paid Alvin a visit." She shrugged. "I figured this was the most opportune time to get my hands on it, since she rarely takes it off." She held out the chain. "Looks like the clasp broke, so she was probably planning on getting it repaired this evening."

She tried to fit it in the locks many different ways but none of them were working.

Hugh was starting to get anxious. All of this was taking too long, and his trust was starting to wane again. Her mother not wearing the necklace that evening was just too serendipitous for his liking. And, in this moment, it wasn't fitting in any of the locks? What if she was just stalling?

He ran his hand along a shelf above his head, thinking about how dusty it was in this secret room. It was then that his finger caught on a groove. Not just any groove, but one that had an odd shape. "Give it here." Hugh was certain that it would fit.

She handed it to him, cautiously. "Remember, you aren't the most graceful and it's delicate…"

Fumbling with it a little bit, since he couldn't exactly see where it was fitting, Hugh thought about how he didn't care if Stevie got into trouble for breaking her mother's necklace. But just as it clicked into place, one of the little wooden chests clicked open.

The lid flew open, revealing a key.

Hugh laughed and shook his head. "I swear to everything that is holy *and* unholy, Stevie, if that key unlocks another one of these chests and it has another key in it, I'm going to personally kill your father."

Stevie couldn't help but laugh. "I wouldn't put it past him." She reached into the chest and took the ancient-looking key. Holding it in her hand as if she were trying to guess its precise weight, Stevie contemplated which chest it unlocked. "It looks like it fits both."

"What if choosing the wrong one triggers some sort of trap?"

Stevie paused only for a moment to ponder that. "We really don't have much more time. How long until they send someone for us or finish supper?" She committed, pushing the key into the lock of the center chest and turned it.

Both of them held their breath, anticipating the worst. However, they received what they had hoped for: the chest opened. No tricks or traps.

Within the chest was another box, and Hugh rolled his eyes as he snatched it from its spot. "It's always one thing after another. How deep does he need to hide it?"

He was surprised when he opened the box and the pendant was just inside of it. Closing it back up, he shoved the box in a pocket on the inside of his jacket. "Let's go."

The pair of them quickly put everything back in its place, even remembering to grab the conch shell necklace for Stevie to replace in her mother's room later.

Making their way back to the dining room, they were just in time for dessert.

And more of Reon's commentary.

He looked up from his bowl and made eye contact with Stevie. "Ah, has our little temper tantrum ended?" He glanced over at Hugh. "Was it the calming effects of the dog?"

Stevie took her seat and with all the politeness she could muster and responded, "I see your spirit cannot be dampened."

# ZOIE

"Do we have to go down the well again?" Zoie asked, as they were preparing to depart the next morning. While this time she was prepared for what awaited her when they took the portal through the well—the tube of torture—Zoie still didn't want to experience it again.

As Hugh packed his last item into his bag, he shook his head. "No, there's another passage near the palace. Do you think that the King and Queen drop into the water every time they want to go to NightBrooke?"

Zoie was relieved. The pressure that came with taking the portal through the well was unbearable. "Where are we going to go, now that we have…"

He cut her off. "We'll talk about that once we're out of here." He explained, "It's just not safe to discuss anything within these walls."

She understood and continued to pack her things, carefully ensuring that the pendants were all safely tucked in her purse, which would be kept closed and near to her at all times. She placed the strap so that it was a cross-body bag, which was awkward but necessary to ensure the safety of the precious items inside.

"Do you think we should separate them?" she asked, intentionally not specifying what she was talking about.

Hugh shook his head. He got close to her and whispered in her ear, "More for us to keep track of." Taking the opportunity to kiss her cheek, he followed up by gently ordering, "Now don't say another word about it until we are out of the Abyss."

They gathered their things and headed towards the front of the palace to meet Cade, Xariella, and Silas. They were surprised to see Stevie there with a small bag.

"You joining us?" Zoie asked, hopeful. She wanted to repair the friendship that they once had, and they could use all of the help that they could get.

Reon and Zhenga entered the room, and Reon, of course, couldn't keep his thoughts to himself. "I don't see why you feel it necessary to leave your loving home."

Stevie rolled her eyes. "*Loving* home? Whatever."

Reon ignored her comments and asked, "I don't suppose this means that you're going back to *it?* Where will that leave the little vampire girl? Especially since it would be so terribly heartbreaking for someone so disfigured to be chosen over her…"

"They!" Stevie yelled. "I don't know how many times I have to remind you of a simple pronoun! Ugh!" She raked her hands down her face. "And no, I am not back with Cade. They obviously love Xariella—by the way, that's her name. Could you bother to learn that?" She threw her hands in the air. "Let's go!" She walked out the door and started down a path to the left of the palace.

The others followed, giving their quick goodbyes, but Cade took it one step further. They smirked and turned towards Reon and Zhenga, giving their salutations a little of their own flavor. "Stay fresh, Cheese bags." They flitted their hand in the air as they walked away.

Everyone followed Stevie on the dark path, illuminated only by blue bioluminescent algae. The large, strange sea trees didn't even sway, as there was no wind. The air smelled salty, but it was still.

Zoie, against all advice that she had received ever since finding out about the magical world, reached up and touched one of the limbs and pulled some leaves off. "Ouch!" Her index fingertip had a small cut from one of the leaves—which were actually sharp seashells.

Stevie stopped walking and immediately turned around to check on Zoie. As she grabbed her hand, she reminded Zoie, "How many times has Hugh told you not to touch anything?" She laughed. Then she called upon some water to wash the cut and heal it.

"Thank you." Zoie hoped that this was a sign that their friendship was on their way to being mended.

Still, she knew that she couldn't fix the wounds that Stevie sustained from Hugh. There was no amount of magic that could heal them or reverse them. Zoie truly wished that she could reverse the damage, but it was mostly because it was symbolic of the damage caused to all of their relationships—a constant reminder of Zoie's death, Stevie's part in it, and Hugh's reaction and revenge. Stevie, no matter how many scars she had, would always be the most beautiful person in the room. The bravest woman she knew. A genuine badass. Nothing could change any of that.

Stevie turned back around and led them further down the path. "We're almost there."

They approached an area where the algae no longer illuminated their path. The sea trees started to look even more sick than they did a few yards prior, and they got more and more evil looking until they couldn't even be seen anymore in the darkness.

Then a large stone door, rounded at the top, appeared in front of them. Water, illuminated with tiny little sea creatures similar to the land's lightning bugs, flowed on the stone wall around the door. Near the doorknob, which was a metal octopus with one of the tentacles as a lever, were the markings for the different beings to use the portal.

One by one, they each placed their hand over the appropriate marking and went through the portal. What was in one instance walking into the unknown dark suddenly became a cobblestone street, with a gentle partly cloudy sky, and the familiar sent of a recent rain and moss growing on anything it could latch onto.

They were back in Nightbrooke, which was much more appealing to Zoie than being in the Abyss. While the Abyss was beautiful, its leader wasn't very welcoming—no matter how much he pretended to be for appearances—and Zoie just never truly felt comfortable there.

"Okay, so where are we off to now?"

Hugh turned to Zoie and said, "There's only one place that I think is safe. One place in the mortal world where magical secrets seem to stay."

Zoie knew where he was thinking, and she sighed. "No. She isn't going to want to be involved in this at all."

"She's kept these secrets for decades—to the point that you didn't know what you were. That even after she thought you were dead, she still kept them," Hugh explained. "I feel like that house is the best place for us to regroup."

"Where?" Xariella asked.

"My mother's house." Zoie shook her head. "She's a trip. I don't know if this is a good idea." She looked at Hugh. "It's one thing for us to go there, but now… Now there's six of us. That's a lot." And, surprised that she truly did care, she added, "That's a lot of a risk to put on her. A lot of knowledge."

Silas interjected, "I agree…" after a brief pause, he completed his thought, "…with Hugh." He looked at Zoie. "Your mom has known many secrets, and she had to learn them before you were born because of your dad—and Lettie." He continued, "She tried to end all of this with your dad, and not let you be a part of it." He softly said, "She knew about me. My deal with your dad to protect you."

Zoie took a step back. "She knew you?" This was getting to be a bit much. How deep did the secrets go in this family? How long would Silas keep secrets? She didn't mind that he had things that were for only his knowledge, but when it had to do with her, she felt that these secrets were lies of omission.

"Not exactly." He explained, "She knew that your dad had set something up to protect you, but he kept her in the dark about who or what. The less she knew, the better."

That last sentence hit her. "Exactly—the less my mother knows, the better. It's for her safety. The Council…"

Hugh interjected. "I am on the Council. I'll protect your mother if it comes to that. And," he paused for a moment and looked at Stevie, "and I'm sorry to say this, but when we're done with this, I hope to change the power dynamic of the Council, and that includes removing Reon from power."

Stevie nodded. "I understand." She looked at the ground and softly said, "and… I agree."

Cade looked at Xariella, and they nodded at each other. Then they said, "Zoie, I think everyone agrees that your mother's is the safest place to rest and get organized."

Zoie looked at everyone and each nodded gently at her. "Okay. Let's find that Pittsburgh portal."

Silas put a finger in the air. "I don't think we need the portal." He reached his hand out to Zoie. "I've been to your mother's, many times. I can transport us there.”

Stevie paused for a moment. “Wait—I thought that you were new to the magical world? But you have protected Zoie—knew her father? He died nearly twenty years ago.” She continued to question him. “You can teleport?” It was clear that the lack of trust wasn’t limited to Hugh and Stevie.

Before anyone could speak, Hugh suggested, “Let’s talk about this elsewhere.” He turned to Silas. “Can you take all of us at once?”

He nodded. “As long as no one breaks the chain.”

Everyone joined hands, and then Silas sucked them all into the darkness of not existing in either time or space for a few moments, and then they reappeared in Zoie’s mom’s backyard.

Carol just so happened to be sitting on the back deck, drinking some hot tea and reading a book.

When everyone appeared, Carol nearly spilled her tea out of shock. She was able to regain her composure quickly, though, and stood up, smoothing out her pants with her hands, to invite her guests in.

She hugged her daughter and then led them all into the dining room. “What brings you here?” Carol also hugged Stevie. “So glad you have returned, m’dear.”

Zoie explained, “We need a place to…”

Carol shook her head in disappointment. “Your father used to bring his friends here to come up with plans to overthrow that tyrannical government of yours.” She sighed. “Sure, whatever, make it into your little headquarters.” She added quickly, “Just know that if I get caught by your people, I’m going to act as if I was clueless as to what was going on.”

“Proclaiming ignorance won’t spare you,” Cade noted flatly.

Carol ignored what Cade had to say and then started rummaging through the fridge. “Alabama to Pennsylvania is a long trip, Zoie.

Are you and your friends hungry?"

Everyone laughed awkwardly at once, unsure if Carol was being serious or not. She had watched them appear right in front of her eyes. Perhaps she wasn't aware of how things like teleportation worked. Maybe she thought it did take a while. On the other hand, maybe she was just joking or, it could be that she just was defaulting to hostess mode. Zoie decided it was best to just let it go.

Carol got into the refrigerator and began pulling out some cheese and meats, and tiny pickles, among other little foods that the group of them could pick at.

Zoie, while her mother was preparing their snacks as if they were a group of junior high students working on a class project, pulled out the spell book and the pendants. She opened the book to the very first page, and all of the pendants started to glow.

Zoie could feel the vibration, but not just on the table. They were vibrating in her heart. She closed her eyes and let the magic travel through her chest and down her arms. As it reached her fingertips, she placed her palms together and rubbed her hands together. As she parted them, she felt the power travel from one hand to another.

"Whoa!" Stevie exclaimed, snapping Zoie out of her little trance.

"What's all this?" Carol asked, as she slide a wooden charcuterie board onto the table.

Cade, Xariella, and Stevie all looked Zoie as she flatly said, "We're working on a spell." She wanted to shield her mother from as much knowledge as possible. Even though she knew that everyone was right—this was the safest place for them to work— she didn't agree with it.

Her mother reached over and touched the book. "You figured out how to open it, hmm?" She flipped through a few pages.

"Anything in here to bring your father back?" She walked over to the kitchen and reached for some iced tea.

An awkward silence fell over the group and everyone just looked back and forth at each other.

Hugh shrugged at Zoie and then admitted, "That's actually what we're kind of working on." He apparently didn't fully agree with Zoie's belief on keeping her mother out of things.

She took her hand off of the bottle and slowly shut the fridge and turned. "What?" When Hugh didn't immediately respond, she repeated herself. "What. Did. You. Just. Say?"

Zoie turned to her mother and explained, "Well, we're not really working on that specifically—we don't know how what we're doing will affect him. But…"

She marched over to the table and slammed the book shut. The pendants stopped glowing and vibrating; Zoie couldn't feel them anymore. "Zoie Seavers—you listen to me right now. You don't mess with this shit. This is some dark magic, and you need to leave that kind of shit alone."

When she reached over to take the book, Hugh slammed his hand over it. "Carol, I—we all—respect how you feel about this, but you need to let us work."

Carol was not afraid of Hugh. She never had been. Werewolf or not. "You promised me that you wouldn't let my daughter get hurt, and you are walking her right into Hell with this sort of thing." She looked at Zoie. "I was teasing about bringing your father back. There's no need for that. We've done just fine on our own." She shook her head and started to walk away. Turning around, she reiterated, "You really should leave this stuff alone."

Zoie got up quickly and ran over to her mother, hugging her. Carol was stiff as a board at first, surprised that her daughter would even want to touch her after all these years of animosity between them. Then, however, she relaxed and hugged Zoie tightly.

"It's going to be okay, Mom." She hugged more tightly. "I know you're just concerned for my safety, and I love you, too."

Carol's eyes welled up with tears. "It's been you and me for so long." She stepped back and put her arms on her daughter's shoulders and asked, "Do you know why you are named Zoie?"

Zoie teased, "Because you were hopped up on pain meds when they brought the birth certificate paperwork and couldn't remember how to spell it properly?"

Laughing, Carol playfully hit Zoie's shoulder. "No, smart ass." She explained, "The strange spelling is because you are one of a kind—I had known what your father was, and I assumed that there weren't others like you. Half witch and half mortal." She looked around at Zoie's friends. "The more I learned about your world, the more I realized I was wrong about that." She felt it bore repeating, "Still, there is no one quite like you." She added, "But the reason I chose the name overall is its meaning." She continued, "It means 'life', and you are my entire life. My entire purpose." She wiped a stray tear from her cheek. "I know it didn't always seem like it… I know I made mistakes…"

Zoie looked in her mother's eyes. "I know you did your best." She reiterated, "Everything is going to be okay." She took her mother's hands in hers and explained, "We have to do this. I can't tell you everything right now, but it's the right thing to do." She added, "On a really large scale, it's the right thing to do."

Her mother sighed, and then nodded slowly. "What can I do to help?" She was genuine in her offer.

Zoie smiled. "Oh, Mom, besides letting us work here, I don't know if there's—"

Cade cut her off. "Can Bradshaw get us tickets to another one of those baseball games? We're going to need something fun like that after all of this is over."

Hugh let out a very full laugh. "It's post-season and the Pirates haven't made it to the playoffs in years, and before that one fluke of a year, it was decades." Shocked at his knowledge of the sport-specifically the Pittsburgh team, Zoie stared at him in confusion.

"Baseball is such a drag." Xariella rolled her eyes. She was never shy about her distaste of sports. In her mortal life, she had once worked as a waitress in a sports bar, and the behavior of some of the patrons was, in a few words, less than savory.

Zoie respected how much Xariella still maintained her sense of self and her own opinions and hobbies, despite the mating bond. Zoie worked hard on that herself, but Hugh and she had already had a lot in common prior to meeting each other. Still, Zoie had suffered from being a people pleaser before moving to Alabama, so she made it a point to avoid that dynamic in her relationship with Hugh.

To get back at Xariella a little bit for—as she believed—stealing her boyfriend, Stevie looked at Cade and smirked. "It can be a lot of fun. Just depends on who's playing." She raised an eyebrow.

Cade's cheeks warmed and they looked down at the book. Attempting to change the subject, they started to say, "So about the Oracle cards…"

Xariella growled at Stevie. "Why are you even here?"

Not giving Xariella the time of day, Stevie continued with Cade's attempt to change the subject. "It just doesn't seem to give any indication of what card to choose…" She opened the book and started flipping through the pages.

Zoie felt the vibration from the pendants in her chest begin as quickly as they ended.

Reaching over the table and slamming the book shut, Xariella let out a loud scream—something deep from her chest and almost like a roar—knocking over cups and blowing petals off of flowers in the vase. Some of the cheese on the charcuterie board flew into the kitchen. Even Carol was pushed back by the vibration of the sound waves.

Everyone stared at Xariella.

"Are you here to help or are you here to flirt with *my* partner?" She glared at Stevie.

Carol steadied herself. "Ladies…"

Stevie stood up and smoothed out her blouse with her hands. "No, Carol, let her say her peace. We aren't going to be able to work together until she gets it out." She continued, confidently. "This has been a long time coming." She motioned with her hand. "Let out your high school jealousy." She added, "I mean you are just out of high school, right? So are you actually ready to face your emotions?"

Xariella shrugged. "Whatever."

"No, Xariella, it's not *whatever*." Stevie moved closer to her. "You just about gave Carol a heart attack, and you ruined the flowers that she had in that vase. So it's not *whatever*."

She let an angry breath out of her nose. "Look, I don't trust you whatsoever. You had me turned into a vampire but left me to die—thankfully Zoie was there to mend me and to get Hugh to step back. You betrayed everyone in this room by being part of the plot to have Zoie killed." When Carol gasped, Xariella turned to her. "Yeah, you heard that right, Carol. Stevie—who you were soooo happy to see today—was an integral part of the plot to have your daughter killed." She turned back to Stevie. "When you found out that Cade had the mating bond with me, you threatened me and walked away in tears, probably to plot some other great plan that won't work. So, forgive me if I find it hard to believe that there is any reason that you are here besides winning Cade back. Forgive me if I don't trust you."

Stevie nodded and looked at the floor. "All fair points."

"What do you have to say for yourself?" Xariella asked. "Why, oh why, should anyone in this room trust you?"

Stevie sat back down and admitted, "I wouldn't be shocked if no one trusted me." She frowned. "I did some horrible things." She continued, "When I had Tafari make you into a vampire, it was because I wanted revenge and I knew that your power would help me get it. I left you to die because I didn't care about you. You had played your part and got me what I needed. And yeah, still, I wanted revenge." She looked at Zoie. "And I am truly sorry for the part I played in your drowning. I was wrong." She continued, "The longer I spent with my father after…" She looked at Hugh, and then said, "…after I was scarred, the more I realized that he didn't actually care about me. He doesn't want me to take over for him because…" She motioned to her face. "I don't look the part. He barely speaks to me beyond the insults like the ones that you witnessed last night. He's embarrassed by me."

Zoie moved to comfort Stevie, but Stevie waved her off.

"I betrayed you, Zoie, because I wanted to gain my father's approval, but he doesn't care about me. It didn't work." She folded her hands. "He just wanted to acquire more power." She looked over at Hugh. "You were wise to kill Alvin and Jack." Before he or Zoie could deny her statement she continued, "I don't care what story you want the world to believe. You may not have done it, but you were involved. Somehow. And it was smart." Stevie admitted, "I heard him and my father one night after Zoie was gone. They were going to kill you while you grieved." She looked Hugh directly in the eyes. "You terrify my father."

"So are you just here to be on the winning side?" Xariella folded her arms across her chest, not buying any of this.

Stevie looked over at her and replied, "No, I'm here because it's the right thing to do." She added, "I also made a promise to Tafari that I would free him for his part in my plans—which have always been to free the innocents that have been wrongly imprisoned in those torture chambers disguised as gargoyles."

Carol cautiously asked, "Zoie, is your father stuck in gargoyle form?" She moved towards her daughter, hoping to get the truth from her.

Shocked that Carol knew even remotely what this meant, Hugh actually responded. "No, Carol. But he is being forced to guard them. He has been since the accident."

More emotional than usual, she grabbed Hugh's hand. "Can I see him?" She begged, and Hugh saw a side of Carol that he didn't know existed—not from his previous experiences with her or from the stories and anecdotes that Zoie had told about her.

As much as he wanted to reunite Carol with Victor, he knew that it wasn't truly possible. Hugh sadly shook his head. "Carol, you… you can't go there as a mortal." The forest was able to take the strongest immortals and drive them to madness or kill them. A mortal stood no chance.

Seeing this vulnerable side of Carol changed Hugh's relationship with her. "…And…" He placed his hand on hers. "And, I wouldn't want you to see him as he is." He didn't even want Zoie to see him, decaying into nothingness. The image of Victor's skin falling off the bones and turning to ash was imprinted into Hugh's brain for the rest of eternity.

"Take me to him and I swear to never call you Webster again," Carol pleaded, showing just how desperately she still loved her husband.

Hugh chuckled. "Carol, you can call me Webster. It's our thing, and I really don't mind." He then responded to her real request. "I wouldn't take you there even if I could. It is not a safe place for you."

She dropped her hand from his and then turned and put her arm around Zoie. "But he will take my daughter to a place that isn't safe."

Zoie smiled softly at her mother. "He can't stop me." She was thinking of bringing up how her mother regularly called her "difficult," but she stopped herself. Seeing this vulnerable side of Carol was foreign to Zoie, but she didn't want to make it go away just to make a joke or a jab. Deep down, she hoped that this moment would be the catalyst to a new era in their relationship. A different chapter.

Hugh admitted to Carol and the group, "We *need* Zoie to be there." He proudly smiled at his mate. "Only her abilities can make everything work." She was the only witch that any of them knew and trusted. Even more, she was one of the few witches that could alter time, and with all of these prisoners seemingly frozen in time, that had to be significant.

Carol moved to clean up the flower petals and said, "Well, then don't let me disturb you." She was obviously going to stick around and try to be involved, though. It made Zoie wonder if her mother was more into magic than she let on—if the anti-magic crusade that she put on for decades was merely bitterness from losing her husband.

Zoie and Hugh moved to look in the book again, but Xariella interrupted them. "I'm sorry, but are we still just going to trust Stevie? Blindly?"

Whether they just wanted this conversation to end or whether they knew through the mating bond exactly what Xariella needed to hear, Cade spoke. "Xari, it doesn't matter what reason brought Stevie to the group for this mission. She has helped us get two of the pendants, and she seems committed to the cause." They continued, "It doesn't matter if she's here to flirt with me; I'm not interested."

Silas interjected, "We need to work together, and then, if we can't get along, we'll go our separate ways." It hurt Zoie's heart a little that he was still feeling this way. She knew that someday he would move on, but she wanted it to be more amicable than it had been since the visit to the Abyss.

"Fine." Xariella glared at Stevie. "Let's get to this." She obviously wasn't convinced, but she was going to work with Stevie as required. She probably would make any contact or partnership with Stevie max out at the bare minimum.

Going through the book again, they worked out the pattern that the pendants needed to be placed in, surprised that it was different from the comments that Meadow had made about wielding them.

"I think that the spell was intended for Mitzi to be able to complete it alone." Zoie scanned over the pages again. "She probably didn't want many people to know that she froze Thomas as a gargoyle."

"Then why did she give the pendants away?" Stevie asked.

Silas responded. "Because she wanted them separated so that she couldn't bring Thomas back early when she missed him. She wanted a cure for his illness first." He continued, "Sometimes things are done for love that reason would never understand."

Zoie continued to scan the pages, ignoring Silas's little comments that were disguised as for the group but really little side comments and metaphors for their relationship. "I'm just not finding any clues as to what the correct Oracle card is." She read it aloud. "Place the Death card in reverse to the left of the Oracle card." She trailed off and muttered as she flipped through the pages, "but it never says what Oracle card."

"Maybe she kept that piece of info to herself," Stevie suggested. It was a valid point, and based on experience with Mitzi and Meadow, Zoie wouldn't have been shocked if that was the case.

Silas shook his head. "Then why separate the pendants *and* hide the book, if she knows the vital info?"

"Better to separate as much info as possible. She had never actually performed the spell," Hugh suggested, "so perhaps she didn't know it. So if she remembered one key piece of info, but not the rest..."

A throat clear from the kitchen got all of their attention. Carol suggested, "Maybe it's not vital info. Maybe it's just a random oracle card." She continued to speak as she walked to another room and then came back. "...I mean, she specifically called out the Death card and its orientation." She handed Zoie a deck of Enchanted Forest Oracle cards. "So maybe it's just whatever card calls to you in the moment."

Zoie took the deck of cards and placed her hand on the book. She closed her eyes and took a deep breath. "That's a possibility." She nodded. "Yes, that feels right."

"Then why have it at all?" Cade asked, annoyed.

As the only witch in the group, Zoie explained, "Sometimes objects in spells are just to conduct things. Sometimes, while some things work better than others, they just need something to be there to hold the power and direct it. There are times that it just needs to be something special to the one casting the spell."

"Witches are weird," Cade mumbled. "There are like no rules

for where you draw your power."

Silas scoffed. "Where do wolves get their power from? Hmm?"

"At least we can only use it when we are in wolf form."

"Bullshit," Silas responded. "Hugh has nearly leveled me in his human form many times." Then he added, "And there are limits. I can only draw from the shadows. When there are no shadows, I have to get creative. Pull from something dark or black." He continued, "Zoie's powers are drawn from the sun, and without it…" Silas shook his head. "Zoie, I don't know how you're going to be powerful enough at the graveyard. There's no sunlight."

Cade said, with some sass, "I guess she'll have to get creative."

Zoie asked, "It's not pitch black there, is it?"

Hugh shook his head. "No. It's just overcast."

Without missing a beat, she replied, "Then there's some light. I should be fine." She went back to studying the book. Looking for more clues to ensure that she would be doing the spell correctly. Sometimes there were specific motions to conduct the energy. Other times, there would be runes that she would need to draw in the air and push in the direction of the spell—among other things that could make the spell unique. If she missed a single tiny step, the spell could be completely unsuccessful.

# HUGH

"How long do you think that it will take you to memorize the incantation?" Hugh asked Zoie.

Zoie shook her head. "It doesn't rhyme; there's no rhythm to it." She admitted, "I think I'm going to need to just take the book with me." She added, "There's the setup of the pendants and the cards—Hell, the entire altar." She shook her head again. "I need to take the book with me." She frowned.

"Zoie, that's nothing to be ashamed of," Silas said, touching her shoulder. "Even the most experienced witch or warlock wouldn't be able to."

Hugh grabbed a piece of the parchment that Meadow had given them. "Then I say we rest up tonight and tomorrow, we do this." He began to write a note to Meadow, requesting that she assist them with getting through the enchanted forest in NightBrooke.

"Tomorrow?" Zoie asked, with a hint of panic in her voice.

"Hell, yeah!" Cade responded. "Don't give anyone time to get in the way."

"I'm… I'm not ready…" Zoie protested, feeling cowardly.

Silas sat in the chair beside her and took her hands. "You aren't going to be any more ready if we wait. You can do this." He reminded her, "I've seen what you can do. You, Zoie, can invade people's memories. Bend light. Reverse time." He squeezed her hands. "You can set up an altar and say a silly little incantation. No problem."

Hugh felt a light tap on his arm. He turned to see Carol, who had a frown on her face and was shaking her head.

She asked him quietly, "Webster, are you okay with that?" She pointed back and forth between Silas and Zoie.

He nodded. "Zoie and I have an agreement." He was never going to actually be okay with it, but he wasn't going to let anyone know that. Not Carol. Certainly not Silas. Not even Zoie. His heart ached at the thought of her ever being with someone else.

"Hmmm." Carol nodded. "Like Bradshaw and I have?" She nudged him a little with her elbow.

He chuckled a little. "I don't know what agreement you have with Bradshaw and the not-Bradshaws, but I suppose that Zoie and I have more of an *understanding*." And, while Hugh could only love Zoie, he would never truly understand her feelings for Silas. All he understood was that she loved big.

"That still doesn't answer my question, Webster." She asked again, raising an eyebrow. "Are you okay with it?"

He looked over at Carol. "I care only about Zoie's happiness."

She swatted him. "Forever the diplomat. Just say it—you hate the idea." Carol knew him better than he would like to admit, even after the few meetings that they had.

Hugh chuckled again. "Carol, Carol, Carol." He shook his head. "I'm not going to discuss this with you. It's between Zoie and me." He walked away and back over to the group. He started speaking so that Carol couldn't try to continue their conversation—though he wasn't sure that it would actually stop her if she was adamant enough. "I was thinking—we need to make plans beyond freeing all of the gargoyles."

"You mean like combating the battalion that Reon will likely assemble once he gets wind of what we're doing?" Cade asked.

Hugh acknowledged their idea. "That too, but I'm talking about even beyond that. After we free all of these people, they are going to need food, water, clothes."

"How do we know that all of them are innocent or can be rehabilitated?" Stevie asked. "Let's be real—I don't want murderers running around." Hugh did his best to not roll his eyes—he considered Stevie a murderer. Hell, he considered himself a murderer, even though every time that he did it, he did it for a good reason—or so he convinced himself.

Hugh rubbed his temples and then lamented, "I think that's a risk we are going to have to take." He sighed, "We don't know if this is an all-or-nothing sort of thing. I mean, Zoie, did the book give any indication as to if this frees all of them or just the one? Will you have to go one by one through the field?"

Zoie shook her head, not truly knowing the answer. "This spell was written with the intention to only freeze one person as a gargoyle. I am not sure that Mitzi intended for it to even be needed for more than one." She frowned. "Though, I'm sure, with some practice, it could be extended beyond one."

"We don't have time for you to practice." Hugh explained, "I mean, it's only a matter of time before Reon figures out that the pendant is missing, and I think that's going to happen sooner rather than later." He suggested, "Tomorrow. We have to do it tomorrow."

"Zoie, I think you need to work to free just one gargoyle before we make this decision," Silas insisted.

Cade let out a loud, annoyed breath. "Where is she going to get a gargoyle to release?"

Without hesitation, Silas offered, "Me."

"How?" Xariella asked. "You aren't exactly made of stone right now."

Silas pushed the other spell book over to Zoie. "Turn me into a gargoyle and then bring me back."

"No! Absolutely not!" Zoie refused.

Hugh cringed as Silas took Zoie's hands. "You can do this," he insisted. "I trust you." Silas looked into her eyes and reiterated, "I have faith in you and your abilities."

Feeling a golden opportunity coming to fruition, Hugh smiled. He walked over to where Zoie was sitting and started flipping through the grimoire with the spell to create the gargoyles. "You got this, Zoie." This was perfect. A win-win for Hugh. If Zoie could successfully turn him into a gargoyle and then free him, then they would be able to take steps to free the gargoyles. If she got him into gargoyle form and couldn't release him—oh well!

He found the page, put the book down in front of her and firmly pressed his finger to the page. "Let's try it, why don't we?" He was practically grinning at this point, not even trying to hide it.

Zoie, still focused on Silas, cautiously took the book, in preparation to study the spell. Silas took her hand, and once again reiterated, "I know you are going to be able to do this." The statement was so full of love that Hugh could feel it affect Zoie's mood, shielding her from some of the fear that had been clouding her confidence.

She read over the spell a few times and then, even as reckless as she thought this was, she said, "Okay. Let's do this."

"Zoie, are you sure that you're ready?" The concern in Xariella's eyes was deep. She didn't want one of her friends to fail, and she didn't want the other stuck in Purgatory for however long it would eventually take for them to figure this all out.

Zoie shook her head. "No, I'm not sure. But I have to try or we'll never know." She added, "I'd rather try now and fail than go all the way there and find out I can't even free one." She took Silas's hand. "Are you sure that you want to do this?"

Hugh felt the sorrow and fear in Zoie's heart. As Silas nodded, Hugh encouraged Zoie. "He trusts you. I believe in you."

Zoie nodded cautiously. "Okay." She rubbed her hands together to start to feel her power.

"Wait!" Carol interrupted things before they could even really get started. "Take this somewhere else." She turned to Zoie. "No offense intended, but if you can get him into gargoyle form but not out, I don't want him displayed in the middle of my dining room."

Cade chuckled. "Carol, you are always caring about the things that really matter."

She threw a cube of cheese at them, and they caught it and popped it in their mouth. She very plainly stated, "I'm nothing if not brutally honest about my feelings."

They headed out to the backyard—surrounded by the trees that kept everyone else's prying eyes out of Carol's business (despite the fact that she craved attention and told everyone everything). "Where should we do this?"

Hugh pointed towards the greenhouse. "How about between the greenhouse and that thicker group of trees?"

Unsure about doing this outside, despite the seclusion of the many, many acres of trees, Zoie started to walk over to the spot. Shaking her head, she asked, "What if I do the spell wrong and it releases a huge puff of smoke or a blast of light?"

Silas laughed, "Then it's a good thing that your mom moved

this outside."

She frowned. "What if a breaking news helicopter goes overhead?"

"What if you didn't have crippling anxiety?" Cade asked, nudging her with their elbow.

Zoie chuckled. "Fair."

Silas nodded and smiled at Cade, thankful that someone had the guts to tell Zoie very bluntly that she needed to calm down. He took his place in the grass. "Should I make a scary face or pose or something? Since I'm going to be a gargoyle and all…"

As Hugh opened the spell book and held it in front of Zoie. Not looking in Silas's direction, Hugh answered his question with an insult. "Your face is plenty scary without any effort."

Zoie smacked his arm but answered Silas. "Please don't. I need to concentrate, and I fear that you would just make me laugh if you tried to pose."

She reread the spell as she rubbed her hands together. As she separated her hands, Hugh saw tiny bits of light vibrate and jump back and forth between her fingertips—something that, perhaps, only he and Cade could see. Her eyelids closed and she took a deep breath in.

Her eyelids flipped open, and she turned her palms to face Silas. The spell specifically stated that she say the incantation in her mind only, as she moved her hands.

As she thought the words, "frozen like the ground after a winter's storm," she slowly pushed her hands downwards through the air, and then she turned them over and lifted the air she had pushed down, thinking, "Light stripped away." After that she made her hands into fists, crossed her forearms like an X and quickly pulled them into a fighting stance, breaking the X as she thought, "the clock stops ticking."

It was as if all of the sound had been sucked out of the world—no birds were chirping, no wind whistling through the grass or the trees, and not even the buzzing of electricity or the sound of tires on the roads nearby. Hugh couldn't even hear anyone breathing.

His eyes had been locked on Zoie, so he decided to look over at Silas, whom Zoie's eyes were fixed upon.

Hugh slowly turned, locking his view on the statue that stood before them. Admittedly, even he wasn't sure that Zoie could successfully do the spell on the first try. He expected that, perhaps, Silas would still be standing there, only with perhaps a stone shoe or glove.

He put his arm around her and then pulled her into a hug. "You did it!" Celebrating, he kissed her head through her hair. "Fantastic!"

She didn't thank him for his congratulatory comments, but instead went straight to the other grimoire and began to study it. She placed the pendants in formation, pausing only to take a drink of water.

"Zoie, are you not excited?" Xariella asked.

She continued setting up the altar. "I want to get him out of there before I lose concentration or skills or in case this is all a fluke."

Hugh put his hand on her shoulder. "My love, this was not a fluke. You are skilled." He could feel her nerves pulsing through his skin.

"Still…" She looked up at Hugh. "As much as you may like that he's stuck in there," she half-teased, "I really do want to get him out."

"Zoie…" He wanted to pretend that she was wrong about how he felt, but she knew him too well.

She worked quickly to get everything set. "Hugh?"

He decided to push aside his feelings about Silas and get back on task. "Do you need any help? Can I get you anything?"

Zoie shook her head. "No, I'm almost ready." She reached over for this hand. "Actually, I need your support and courage." She looked up at him. "Please."

He squeezed her hand. "Anything that you need, my love."

She stood up and rubbed her hands together, igniting her power as she had before. She closed her eyes once again, but was interrupted by her own anxiety. "What if I can't do this? What if I've locked him in there? Like Thomas?"

Hugh stood between her and Stone Silas. He put his hands on her arms and ran them up and down to comfort her. "You *can* do this. I believe in you, and so does Silas." He added, "Silas would have never let you do this if he didn't."

He stepped out of the way and then nodded to encourage her to start the spell again.

Zoie began her preparations again and then spoke the incantation, but nothing happened. The fear and failure in her eyes was accompanied by tears.

Hugh stood between her and Stone Silas again, in the same manner that he had before. "Again, with confidence, Zoie. With. Confidence."

She nodded and wiped her tears from her cheeks. "I can do this." She repeated with more emphasis, "I can do this."

"Damn right you can." Hugh stepped out of the way again. "You got this."

Zoie prepared again, and that time, when she spoke the incantation, the light poured onto the stone, melting it away.

Silas shook the dirt out of his hair and then looked up at the group. "What took so long?" He seemed a little bit annoyed.

"You were only in there for about 15 minutes," Cade responded, in protection of Zoie and out of loyalty to Hugh.

He scoffed, "It felt like days."

"What was it like?" Xariella asked, excitedly.

This made Silas laugh. "Fucking awesome!"

"Really?" She asked.

"No!" He replied, laughing. "It was dark and silent. I tried to teleport out but since it was nowhere and time stood still, I couldn't." He added, "We need to get those people out of there."

"Well," Hugh replied, gathering up Zoie's supplies and the books, "Now that we know that Zoie can complete the spell, we will do it tomorrow."

"And how do you expect us to secure the necessities—food, water, clothing—for all of these people in such a short period of time?" Xariella asked.

"Hugh, we don't even have a plan. We don't know that Zoie— no offense—can even do the spell on a large group of gargoyles. We don't have any way to get these people the essentials. Fuck, how will we get through the forest? Not to mention, how in the *Hell* will we fight an army if it comes for us?" Cade made various good points.

Zoie responded, "First of all, I'm not offended, Cade, because I agree. We aren't sure that I can do the spell successfully on the scale that we need to. My skills just may not be there yet." She continued, "But I don't know that Reon will bring an army because… Well, I don't know that he thinks it would be more than the six of us at most."

"He'll still pad his ranks," Stevie interjected.

"True, but with how many?" Zoie brought up another good point, though. "The more people that he enlists for this, the more who will know about the Gargoyles…"

Xariella interjected, "Everyone already knows. He puts on performances in the middle of Nightbrooke."

Zoie continued. "Yes, but what I was going to say is that they would know that he's creating more than are being given a so-called fair trial." She explained, "The more people who know, the harder the secret will be to keep."

Stevie shook her head. "Zoie, my dad has a way of convincing people to keep their thoughts to themselves."

"Maybe he won't have time to assemble an army?" Zoie suggested, embarrassed by the naivety of the statement.

"Zoie, c'mon, he has an army at his disposal." Silas rolled his eyes at her. It was a ridiculous statement for to have even let come out of her mouth.

Hugh interjected, "Look, we don't have the time to assemble a battalion ourselves. So we're just going to have to do our best with what we've got, and, well, that's each other." He knew that it sounded grim, but they knew that this wasn't going to be easy when they set out to do it.

In the background, Carol muttered, "Great plan." She ushered them back in the house so that their voices didn't carry with the wind to the neighbors—especially Hugh's, which was louder than anyone else's.

Silas turned to Carol. "Do you have a better one?" He said it very harshly, but Silas was not a fan of Carol's. He had been witness to some of the awful things that she had done to Zoie—not just through Zoie's retelling of instances. He had watched Zoie live through them. He continued to feel a tinge of regret that he never stepped in to protect her, but he couldn't have—Silas had been tasked with protecting her from other villains, not her mother.

Carol wasn't a fan of Silas, either, though. "Yeah, I do. It's to not do this until you are ready." She quickly added, "Or maybe trash the entire thing all together and stick to the status quo." Then she called Silas a "jagoff" under her breath and took a sip of her wine.

Zoie couldn't help but laugh. "Enough—both of you." She looked at the rest of the group and replied, seriously, "I think that

Hugh's right—Reon is going to come after one or both of those pendants—and soon—and we have all four." She continued, "If Reon gets all four of them, we're done. Even if he gets one, we're in trouble. But, like I said, if he gets all four—we're entirely fucked."

Hugh stated what no one wanted to hear. "If Reon gets all of those pendants, we're all going to be stuck in gargoyle form for eternity." He drove it home. "No one will come to save us. No one could."

Cade took Xariella's hand in theirs. "I think that if anyone wants out, now is the time to say." They turned to their partner. "Xari, I understand if this is too much to ask of you. But, I'm behind Hugh on this one. I'm going to do this because I believe that…"

Xariella cut them off. "I believe that it's the right thing to do, as well." She confirmed, "I'm in. I'm with you on this."

Hugh looked at Silas and Stevie, basically staring them down until they agreed that they were in as well. Then he said, "Okay, now that we are all in agreement…"

He was cut off by Xariella. "I would like to make one suggestion, though." She didn't wait for the okay to continue. In true Xariella fashion, she just kept talking. "I think that a couple of us should stay as lookout on the outside of the graveyard." She then volunteered, "And I think that I should be one of the people that stays out because of my scream."

Nodding, Hugh replied, "I agree, and Cade needs to be the one that stays with you." Before Cade could interject or anyone could negate his idea, Hugh explained, "Their head and heart would be with you anyways, as your mate. It's just smart."

He then waited for anyone to argue, and when they didn't he suggested, "I think it's time to figure out what we are going to do about food and water for the people who have been in gargoyle form."

As they all discussed different options, knowing that there could be a wide range of how many people they would need to assist, they realized that they couldn't just bring enough water bottles, for example. Silas and Zoie were offering suggestions for spells, while Stevie was asking clarifying questions about bodies of water near the graveyard.

Meanwhile, Hugh grabbed the parchment that Meadow had provided to them during their visit to her and Mitzi's cottage. He pondered what to write so that if the letter was somehow intercepted, it wouldn't be obvious as to what was happening.

He wrote one word on the page: *Tomorrow.*

Then he grabbed a lighter that was next to a candle in the kitchen and headed outside. The wind was soft, but there was a breeze. He lit the page on fire and watched as the ash blew away, disappearing.

# ZOIE

Beagan emerged from the darkness between the trees. "We must leave now, under the cover of the darkness that Meadow has placed on the forest. It won't last forever."

Xariella took a deep breath in, obviously anxious since her last attempt at navigating beyond the edge of the forest nearly killed her.

Zoie squeezed her friends' hand. "Meadow obviously got our message—since Beagan's here—so everything should be fine."

Forcing a smile onto her face, Xariella replied, "It *should* be." She squeezed back.

They broke into pairs, following Beagan through the trees. It was darker than before, causing the trees to look even more evil and alive than they had before.

Hugh and Zoie stepped into the front, as Beagan led them down a dark path. It took until they reached the fork in the path that led either to Mitzi and Meadow's cottage or farther into the forest that Zoie began to recognize where they were.

Beagan turned to Hugh. "I must leave you at this point." She pointed down the path that led away from Mitzi and Meadow's. "Go that way. I must visit the witches."

"Why?"

She reached up and touched Hugh's hand. "I sense there is danger for the witches, and I must check on them." Beagan looked at Zoie. "They have assisted me in the past…"

Zoie nodded. "I understand." She looked at Hugh and Cade. "They can see very well in the dark and can lead us from here."

Hugh put his hand over the little faerie's. "Be safe, Beagan." Moments later, she was gone into the forest, not wanting to take the direct path and get caught.

Zoie swallowed nervously. "Once we take a few more steps, we're going to be deeper into this forest than I've ever been." She took Hugh's hand. "This makes me anxious. It's darker than before…"

She felt her body heat up—Hugh was sending her energy through their bond, trying to calm her. "The darkness is likely just part of Meadow's magic. This forest is typically alive, and she turned that off for us."

Cade and Xariella were behind them. Cade looked at their partner and asked, "Is everything okay so far?"

Xariella nodded. "No breathing issues so far." This was a relief for the entire group. It meant that Meadow's assistance was working.

Silas and Stevie were bringing up the rear of the line. He looked behind them to check if they were being followed and decided to blanket the forest with some dark fog. Anything to keep their secret.

They weaved in and out of the trees until they reached the grey clearing. Hugh took Zoie's hand. "It's just on the other side— through this mist."

As the fog seemed to break apart, the graveyard appeared. Zoie felt her heart start to pound. She was about to see her father for the first time in nearly twenty years, and she truly didn't know what to expect or what she was going to say. She even wondered how she would feel.

When she locked eyes with her father, Zoie stopped in her tracks.

Hugh put his hand on her back. "You don't have to do this if you don't want to."

Shaking her head, she replied, "No, I want to. I have to." She stepped forward. "Dad?"

Victor turned quickly, still floating in the air above the ground. "Zoie?" He came forward towards her and then stopped abruptly, as if he couldn't move any further. "What are you doing here? You should leave this place."

She excitedly walked towards him. "We're here to set you free." The deterioration in his features was beyond what Hugh had described to her. She was unsure if this was his trying to protect her or if the Graveyard had taken so much from her father since the last Hugh had seen him. Still, she wanted to reach out and take his hand—to hug him tightly.

He floated back sharply. "There is no freedom from this place."

"There can be." She held out the pendant. "We are here to…"

Cutting her off, in a booming, angry voice, and anger in his black eyes, Victor exclaimed, "You fools! You brought them right to them!" Mist lifted from the ground and surrounded them. Victor glared at Zoie. "I made a vow to my friend that I would protect the antidote to this spell from those that wanted to abuse it, and you've brought it to them."

Silas pulled power from the darkness and pushed the mist back. "We will free these innocent people."

He flew towards him, getting inches from his face. "And, if you do, fine, but what if the pendants all fall into the hands of evil— then there is nothing to protect more innocents."

"Then we will fight to get them back," Hugh responded. "To

the death if that's what it takes."

Victor lowered the mist, and Silas followed with his shadows. Victor looked at his daughter with gentle eyes. "I have been waiting for peace for many years." He reached his hand out—bones and rotting flesh—to touch her cheek but stopped short.

Without fear, she grabbed the deteriorating hand and placed it to her face. "I know. And we hope that this brings you that peace."

The pendant bearers all stepped forward. Zoie nodded at each of them. "Let's do this…" They started to approach the entrance when the mist lifted again.

"If you cross that threshold, you will age at an accelerated rate," Victor warned. "You need to find the center of the Graveyard…"

Zoie turned to her father. "Then tell us the coordinates so that we can find it most efficiently." She looked him in the eyes. "I know you know it."

He nodded slowly. "Row 350. Between columns M and N." He added, "There is some sort of pillar or table there. I believe it is for this purpose."

Zoie smiled at her father. "Thank you." She looked at Hugh. "Ready?"

Hugh nodded, and before he could say anything, Cade stated, "Xari and I will guard the door and alert you if there's any need to rush."

The wolves looked at each other and their eyes started to glow. Their bodies stretched and contorted and their hair grew—all the while tearing the clothes they had been wearing.

Xariella looked Zoie in the eyes. "Whatever you do, do not say his name."

Nodding with understanding, Zoie replied, "And not you, theirs."

Zoie turned and she and the other three pendant bearers walked through the threshold of the gate. The moment that Zoie's feet were through, the doors slammed shut with a loud clang. The mechanized sound of a heavy lock echoed around them.

One would think that the center of the graveyard would be directly in front of the gate, with it growing and building around the center, but this was not the case.

Zoie looked to her right. There was nothing but mist and grey grass and weeds for as far as she could see. "H—" she cut herself off. "Do you see anything in that direction?"

He let out a loud breath through his nose and shook his head. In a low grumble, he replied. "Just mist and grass and dirt."

"Then left it is." Silas pulled some power from the shadows. "Perhaps we should split into two groups…"

Stevie declined his suggestion. "We need Zoie and all of the pendants together for the spell to work, and if she's in a different group, it delays that."

Fixated on a gargoyle that was almost standing proudly—with its horns pushing through a large mess of curly hair, Zoie still agreed. "It wouldn't help us if two arrived first and the others couldn't find it." She reached out and touched the large wings. She slid her hand gently to the gargoyle's shoulder and then along the outline of the many necklaces that the prisoner had been wearing at the time of imprisonment. "This is Lettie."

Silas approached Zoie and said, "Row 679, Column Z. This is her spot."

"Then we need to go 13 gargoyles that way." She motioned further inside the graveyard. She sighed, "And more than 340 that way." She nodded forward.

Stevie looked at Zoie. "There's about 50 feet between each of these rows." She did the math in her head. "It's miles…"

Zoie looked at Silas. "Could you…?"

He shook his head. "This place is everywhere and nowhere all at once. I cannot transport here." He pointed to Hugh. "He could get there faster than all of us, but it would wear him out carrying us along."

Hugh took Zoie's hand and led her away from Lettie's gargoyle prison cell. "Let's keep moving."

They walked for hours, and the further that they got into the graveyard, the more worn and weathered the gargoyles became. Some were missing limbs or covered in black mold or moss. Wings broken from storms. Discolored from the sun that they never saw.

Zoie looked down at the row and column number for a nearby gargoyle. "685." We've been walking for hours and are getting nowhere." She was exhausted—so exhausted that she wanted to curl up and cry. "We should have gotten there by now. How did we not realize…"

Suddenly they heard a "pssst" from a nearby gargoyle.

Stevie's head about snapped on her neck. "If that thing is talking to us, I'm, like, done."

"Psssst." A small blonde-haired faerie peeked out from behind a gnarly looking gargoyle.

Hugh's eyes smiled. "Beagan. What are you doing here?"

She crept out into the open. "I've come to help. There isn't much time." Beagan explained, "The rest of the Council has met with the Sisters…"

"Mitzi and Meadow?" Silas clarified.

She nodded. "They are on their way here. They intend to stop you." She added, proudly, "I bit one of the guards. He thought it was a mosquito, but in a few hours, my venom will kill him." She continued, "There is still time, however, for him to get to you."

Zoie's eyes grew, alarmed. "We are never going to make it to the center of this place in time."

Beagan agreed. "You won't make it walking. All of you have aged years already." She pointed to Stevie. "You have gained grey hair, and you," she motioned to Zoie, "are going white instead of your red. You have earned lines around your smile."

Silas interjected, "Beagan, I cannot teleport here. But you can." He requested, "Can you take us to where we need to go?"

She nodded cautiously. "I can only take one at a time, and I will need rest between."

"Zoie first," Stevie insisted, handing her pendant over. "She can start to set up the space. She's the most important in this entire thing."

Silas and Hugh each gave theirs to Zoie. Silas gently reminded her, "You can do this."

Beagan reached out her tiny hand. "Just place your hand in mine, and I will take you where you need to go."

Zoie expected to be sucked inside out, just like when Silas would transport her. Instead, she felt herself lifted into the air and the world spun beneath them, stopping abruptly at their destination.

Beagan sat next to a gargoyle and caught her breath. Labored, she asked, "Is there anything additional that I can do?"

Shaking her head, Zoie replied, "Rest. You need to regain your strength." She went over to Beagan and touched her shoulder. "Your help is more appreciated than you know." The lines on the tiny faerie's face were more pronounced than moments before.

Zoie approached the stone table in the center or the graveyard that her father had described and started laying out the altar. Starting with the small purple and gold cloth, she then opened the book to the page with the spell. There was no way to rehearse the spell at this scale, and, after completing it properly only one time to release Silas, there was no chance that she was going to have it memorized.

She laid out tarot card—Death, reversed—and the Oracle card

that called to her earlier that morning. It was from her Green Witch Oracle. She hadn't looked at what she had chosen yet; it was tucked in the spell book. That morning, she had shuffled the deck with her eyes closed and then picked a card from the middle. She flipped it over and laid it next to the tarot card. Card number 30-Tomato, for Love.

"Perfect." She smiled. Zoie figured that the love was the best way to get the gargoyles free—to shower them with love. Besides, the original purpose of the spell was due to the love that Mitzi had for Thomas. It was fitting that a love Oracle card would present itself for the spell.

Then she placed the glowing pendants on the altar cloth. Earth and Light above the cards, and Water and Love below. Next, she placed the clear quartz tower to the left of the cards and the rose quartz to the right.

"Who do you want next?" Beagan asked, slowly standing.

Fueled with anxiety, Zoie quickly responded, "It doesn't matter. I just need them here to help me set up and complete the spell. And to protect me when the Council comes to stop me."

With a light chime, Beagan was gone and returned with Stevie. Heading back to the gargoyle she had leaned on before, Beagan placed her hand to her forehead, closing her eyes.

Stevie knelt down next to Zoie. "The rose petals in a circle around the candle, right?"

Zoie nodded, checking the book. She then handed over the bag of dried rose petals and white candle. "Yes. Use them all if you need to."

Stevie leaned in closer. "Is she going to be okay?" She motioned her head quickly towards the tiny faerie who was struggling to get enough air.

Glancing over at Beagan, Zoie's heart dropped. "I don't know. This is probably a lot on her." Beagan had aged even more since she delivered Stevie. Her hair was thinning, and her skin was acquiring discoloration.

A quick chime, and Beagan was gone and returned with Silas. He helped Beagan over to the gargoyle. "Do you need something to drink? I have a bottle of water…" He pulled it out of the backpack that had some extra supplies in it. He wasn't worried about not having enough water—or anything else—because he had enchanted the darkness inside the bag. It would duplicate anything that he removed from it for as long as the spell was in place.

Reaching out, the faerie nodded. The bottle of water was oversized in her small hands. She choked a bit, drinking too much at first. She handed the water back to Silas and then, with a chime that wasn't as lively as the previous ones, Beagan was gone and returned with Hugh.

This time, when she leaned on the gargoyle, the sparkle that was a part of her was nearly gone. There was barely a twinkle left in her eyes—barely, but still there.

"They are here," she stated, between struggled breaths. "The Council… Mit… Mitzi."

Hugh, in his human form, got on his knees on the grey grass and reached out his hand to his friend. "Beagan…"

She shook her head. "There's no time. You… the spell." Her sparkle flashed a few times and she coughed.

A tear escaping his eye and running down the scar on his cheek, Hugh let out a soft, "No…"

Zoie turned just in time to watch Beagan's sparkle turn to dust and let out a light chime as she disappeared. She ran over to Hugh and put her hand on his shoulder, as he wiped his tears away.

There was no time to grieve—Cade let out a loud howl, and they all felt Xariella's powerful scream rock the entire graveyard. Some of the gargoyles shifted out of their place; grass and dirt split as if there had been a small earthquake.

"It's now or never, Zoie." Silas touched her forearm. "They're here."

Taking in a deep breath, Zoie tried to calm her anxiety. She was shaking, and if she didn't get control of herself, she would never be able to complete the spell.

Hugh walked up next to her. "You can do this. Believe in yourself, and you can make this spell work." He took her hand in his. "Four deep breaths."

She turned to him and smiled just as his eyes began to glow yellow. His hand grew in hers, and she felt his palm heat up. She didn't have time to wonder if she would ever get used to his phasing in front of her.

His hand released hers, and Zoie took a deep, calming breath. The vulnerability that Hugh had about his fear that his power would hurt Zoie or drive her away—the fact that he phased while touching her, putting that fear aside, helped her push her anxiety to a place that she could use it.

She put it in a tiny box in her mind, and then she swallowed and it sank down to her stomach. She pushed it down. She pushed it down further. Further again.

Zoie closed her eyes. Another deep breath. Her eyes flew open, and she locked in on the altar. After rubbing her hands together to ignite her power, she extended her arms out, palms facing the altar. Confidently, without even referencing the book, she called out the spell.

*Terminate the frozen moment of darkness*
*Liberate those detained in monument*

The pendants lifted, glowing even more brightly than before, and then light shot up to the sky—if that was what was above this strange place.

The wind picked up and spun the rose petals around them as if they were being carried through a storm.

Afraid to let go of the spell, Zoie held her hands out, even as the light started to rain down all around them.

The light drops fell with a ferocity of a hail storm. They sparkled and illuminated the grey graveyard like a prism. As the light touched the stone of the gargoyles, it splashed and the stone changed from grey to brown, like wet sand just touched by a wave.

She decided to focus on one gargoyle to see if the spell would work. She looked off to the right and zeroed in on the gargoyle that had its hands folded over the place that its heart would be.

The stone melted away, revealing aquamarine waves of hair. The large stone horns that had been affixed to the top of the gargoyle fell away as the woman shook her head. She stretched her arms out, as the stone fell away, and let out a squeak. Blinking her eyes, her face lit up in a smile, and tears streamed down her face. "Light. There's light!" Her hands went to her face, and she leaned over to sob. "I'm not in the echoing darkness anymore." She tried to move her legs, but they were still in stone. However, they were slowly gaining their freedom with each drop of light hitting them.

Zoie's heart lifted with joy, and she decided to expand the spell further. The prism raindrops started falling further away and faster, and the rose petals expanded their circle further, encompassing more and more gargoyles, but Zoie knew that time was of the essence. She searched her mind for her ability to manipulate time.

She tapped into all of her knowledge about time related magic, but nothing that she tried worked. She concentrated harder. *Maybe I'm not doing enough*, she thought.

Then she remembered something that Silas had said—that this place was everywhere and nowhere all at once. She wondered if it was all time and no time all at once, too. *Every-when and no-when*, she thought. That could have been why the gargoyles stayed in place without weathering too much, and, from the looks of the aquamarine-haired girl, none of the prisoners aged, but everyone else did. Her father decayed. Zoie greyed. The constant cycle of faeries for carrying the gargoyles.

She pushed the dome of her magic further. She needed to free as many as she could. She especially needed to reach Lettie—her auntie could help. Lettie was a wealth of knowledge about magic and could help spread the spell farther into the graveyard. More than that, and selfishly, Zoie missed her.

The spell was taking its toll on Zoie, though. Her energy was waning. While the energy that was vibrating from her fingertips was still going strong, the strength of her shoulders was giving out.

As the stone melted away from the gargoyles near them, and Zoie let her hands drop. The light shower stopped.

A prisoner shook the sand off of them, but their feet were still encased in stone. They were still stuck because the spell just wasn't complete. Learning an important lesson, Zoie knew she needed to follow through—but she was worried that she didn't have enough energy or confidence.

"Keep going, Zoie," Silas encouraged.

Zoie lifted her hands and began concentrating again, and the spell started up again.

Suddenly, they heard a ruckus and turned around to see Cade

and Xariella with their hands tied—and Xariella's mouth covered—and two large members of the Council's guard pulling them along. Reon, Mitzi and Meadow, and the three Shrews from the Council were leading them.

"Davies!" Reon called out. "Stop this nonsense now!" His voice was loud, like a huge wave crashing against the beach in a storm.

# HUGH

Hugh turned to Zoie. "Whatever you do, don't stop." Still in his wolf form, he approached Reon. "You have these people unjustly imprisoned. We will not stop until all of them are released."

Stevie and Silas followed Hugh, prepared to fight if they had to. Zoie had to stay focused on the spell and the prisoners. While some witches could cast a spell with one hand and fight with the other, Zoie's skills weren't there yet, and this wasn't the environment for them to find out if they were even close to being there.

"Stephanie," Reon stated firmly. "Come, join us—join me, your father—on the right side." He reached his hand out to his daughter and did his very best fake smile.

Stevie glanced at the bottle of water that was lying next to the gargoyle Beagan died on. She pulled energy from the water. "No. You are on the wrong side of this." She brought the water forward. "I will fight you if I have to."

Meadow took a few steps towards them, and Silas pulled energy from the shadows and shot it towards her. A wall of darkness cast around her, blocking her from taking any more steps. "No, please!" she begged. "I'm with you on this." She walked slowly, as Silas drew back the wall, her long black hair dragging through the grey grass.

"Meadow!" Mitzi shrilled. "You can't possibly…" The betrayal in her heart was more than Mitzi could bare.

Meadow turned to her sister and looked gently into her eyes. "Mitzi, it is time to let go." She walked back over to Mitzi and took her hands. "Sister, it's been centuries, and he wants to rest. He didn't even come to you when Pluto changed signs." Her eyes were full of genuine concern.

The gargoyles surrounding them broke free one-by-one. Most of them were confused, and as much as Hugh and the others wanted to explain to them what was going on, they couldn't break concentration from the task at hand. Even when some of them would disintegrate into bits of grey ash and float into air.

Mitzi let go of her sister's hands and ran to a gargoyle that was releasing its prisoner. "Thomas!" she cried.

They embraced, and she kissed him. Her hands went into his grey hair, twisting her fingers in his curls.

She ran her hands down his brown sweater and stopped at his chest, letting one hand linger over his heartbeat. Tears welled up in her eyes as she felt the beat of his heart for the first time in centuries—the spirits that traveled in the forest did not have heartbeats. They didn't have a need to breath, so when she held him tightly again, she closed her eyes and listened to the sound of the air traveling in and out of his nose. She felt the slight buzz of his skin under her fingertips as she held his hand.

Still, Thomas wasn't paying attention to the same things about Mitzi. He stepped back from her. "It is time for me to rest, Mitzi."

Her chin wobbled as she tried to not cry. "But I love you. I wanted to save you."

Thomas took her hand in his and kissed her knuckles. "You did what you could, but it's too late for me. What I've gone through for the past…however long it's been. It's been torture." He admitted, "I know that what you did was out of love, but…"

"…it's time for you to rest." She sobbed and put her arms around him as he turned into dust, nearly causing herself to trip as she fell forward into her arms from squeezing him so tightly.

Meadow went to her sister to comfort her. "The right thing to do is to let him go now, Mitz."

Heartless as usual, Reon didn't give them time to mourn. "All of these people—you think you are freeing them, Davies, but you are just turning them to ash." He added, with a smirk, "And none of them will be around to fight with you, so if that's what you're waiting for…" He shrugged.

Hugh shook his head. "Reon, just because they are choosing to rest doesn't mean that we aren't freeing them."

One of the Shrews shot some magic out of her hand, surrounding Cade and Xariella with thorn-covered vines.

Cade called out to Hugh, "Don't let them intimidate you with this bullshit." Just then, one of the guards fell to his knees, choking. Beagan's venom had finally taken him out.

Another witch sent out some electricity from her hand, striking Zoie in the back, knocking her down. Somehow, still, she held onto the magic, even if she did drop it for a millisecond. Her commitment to the cause remained unwavering.

The instinct to protect Zoie kicked in. In his mind, all of the possibilities of what could happen flashed in an instant. He could take many routes, but most of them ended poorly for him and his friends. Above all, most of them ended poorly for Zoie—and he absolutely couldn't have that.

Hugh knew that if he turned to help her, Reon and his guards would attack, and they would all lose. Instead, he locked eyes with the king of the Abyss. "Reon, in a matter of minutes, Zoie will have freed everyone." Continuing to challenge the king was the best move at this time. It would keep his focus on Hugh, taking away even a bit of Reon's attention from directing the others. Additionally, it would confuse Reon and his crew, as they would have been prepared for Hugh to protect Zoie with his own body at all costs.

*This* was the best way to protect Zoie. The unexpected path of choices. Trusting Zoie to make the best choices for herself. Letting Silas protect her if it was needed. Confusing the opposition.

The witch who had sent out the electricity did it again, but this time it wasn't just a quick spark. She created a cloud above the graveyard and thunder rumbled, shaking the ground and knocking the gargoyles that were only partly freed around. Lightning struck—it struck Zoie repeatedly.

She fell to the ground, and Hugh's stomach sank and his heart stuttered. His mating bond with Zoie was going to take over. He had no choice. He wasn't able to take the unexpected path, no matter how hard he tried. He began to turn.

"Hugh! No!" Silas yelled at him, and Hugh believed that Zoie was about to be safe without his assistance—he could focus on Reon again. Silas pulled darkness from the shadows and surrounded Zoie with a blanket of darkness as she lay on the ground. While this shielded her, Silas was completely vulnerable. All of his power was focused on Zoie—a choice that he was making jointly for the mission and his entire heart.

And the other witches knew this. Drawing power from the grey grass and black dirt, the Earth witch twisted the blades of grass around Silas's legs and torso.

Once the giant blades of grass made its way around Silas's neck, Reon spoke. "They will take the life out of you." He added, "They don't even need to wait for my signal."

Silas went to speak but the blade of grass tightened around his throat, choking him. He couldn't even let out a groan.

Hugh wanted to act, but he felt frozen in place, not knowing if Zoie was okay. He was failing her. His friends. The mission.

It was then that he saw the opportunity. Behind their adversaries were several ropes of black water. Hugh knew that this wasn't Silas—in his peripheral, Hugh could see that Silas was still holding the shadow blanket over Zoie. This was Stevie, drawing on the dark water of the open field outside of the graveyard. That was quite the reach, but Stevie was more powerful than she let on to anyone. Even her own family.

Hugh had a momentary lapse of trust—what if Stevie was going to use this power on them and change sides on them again? Could he risk Zoie with misplaced trust in Stevie again? Still, he made the conscious choice to rely on her in the moment. It was the only choice he really could make. Any move against her, even the slightest appearance of distrust, and everything would fall apart for them. They would lose.

"Reon, you have been falsely imprisoning people for the Gods know only how long. You've been doing this to gain power." He stepped forward. "You have completely abused the essence of what Mitzi created this spell for, emotionally imprisoning her in a dark, sick forest." Another step. "You will let us fix this."

Reon scoffed. "And if I don't? So what? Are you going to tell everyone?"

Hugh answered honestly. "I am going to tell everyone in our world, regardless." He took another step. "I do not care if we get stopped. I will remove you from your place on the Council because of this, and our world will know about your corruption."

Reon laughed. "Hugh, you would have to win a vote to remove me. The Witches are with me. The vampires usually are." He chuckled again. "You would have to forcibly remove me, and that kind of coup would get you removed yourself." He smirked. "No matter what you do, all of this will end with you, in this graveyard, encased in stone, for the rest of eternity, and once you and your friends here are imprisoned in your own personal gargoyles, who is going to help you?"

It was that moment that the dark ropes of water wrapped around his arms and legs and one hovered just near his head. "Daddy, if you do not call your team off and let go of my friends, I swear to you, I will fill your lungs and gills with this dark, evil, poisoned water."

He locked eyes with his daughter. "You will side with the man who took all of the beauty you had in this world and tore it from you? You will have nothing if you lose me. No one will protect you."

She tightened the water around his limbs. "I don't always have to be pretty," she declared. "Pretty is not the price that I pay to exist in this world." She continued, "My scars do not have to be a symbol of my strength or that I continued to exist after a battle. Sometimes they just are scars." She stood up straighter—more confident than ever before in her life. "I am more than just the pretty face that you thought I was. I am more than my scars, and I am more than my title." Stevie added, "And, Daddy, I don't need your protection. I wouldn't want it anyways." She shook her head. "Not if it involves this sort of injustice." She tightened the streams of water around him.

Reon scoffed. "Foolish child." He turned to the remaining witch. "Place them in stone. I've had—". He choked on his words.

The very last thing that he would ever choke on.

Stevie screamed from her chest as she willed the foul water down his throat and into his nose. She even released some of the water from his limbs to flood his body, drowning him. Her tears did not touch her cheeks, but instead joined the water to complete her task. As she released the rest of the water, his limp body fell to the ground with a thud.

For a few moments, he lay on the ground, motionless. Then, the image of his body flickered, as if he was becoming a ghost. After that, as he faded, his body turned into sea foam and the ground soaked up his spirit, leaving behind a golden seashell and trident pendant that he wore to signify that he was the king.

Stevie turned to the witches and the remaining guard. "If you think I won't do that to you, after I did that to my own father, you are fooling yourselves." They all froze but did not release anyone. She turned the water on them. "Release my friends, now." Just ordering them wasn't working. She added, confidently, "By order of the Queen of the Abyss." The pendant faded from where it had been lying on the ground and appeared around Stevie's neck on a gold chain.

Even though she was the natural heir, it didn't matter if she didn't truly believe in herself. Even though the healing process—if it could be called that—for her scars was long and painful, it did have one positive result for Stevie: she found out she was more than her looks. She had skills and abilities that had always been hidden because she didn't need them. Her beauty had gotten her everywhere.

The remaining guard, who was a gift to the Council from the Abyss, released Cade and Xariella, and the Earth witch released Silas, and, reluctantly, the Sun witch stopped her lightning storm. Silas released his shield from Zoie, who was lying there, hair now streaked with thick white pieces in addition to her red strands of hair, tried to get up, but couldn't.

Hugh turned to Zoie, but hesitated. Stevie said, "Go to her. They aren't going to fuck with me." She glared at everyone facing them.

Silas and Hugh arrived at Zoie at the same time. She was curled into a little ball, holding her ribs. "Hugh…"

"It's okay. It's going to be okay." Hugh turned to the guard and ordered, "Arrest all three of them."

He looked to Stevie for direction. "Don't look at me. You heard him." He put the shrews in chains, but it was almost reluctant. Hugh didn't even have the energy to wonder if they could break free of the chains with their own magic.

Silas grabbed his rope and lassoed it around them and pulled. "That will hold them."

Meadow and Mitzi—who was still in tears—came over to the group. "You need to leave."

Hugh shook his head. "We need to finish this." He knew that, for Zoie's sake, he did need to leave, so without even thinking, and going against what he said, he leaned over to pick her up, cradling her in his arms. Things appeared so dire for Zoie that his mating bond wasn't going to let him do anything other than get her somewhere else.

Meadow rubbed Mitzi's back. "It's okay, Mitz." She nodded, guiding her sister to speak.

Not even attempting to fight her tears, Mitzi said, "I'll finish it for you." She had lost everything that the spell was holding for her, so it no longer mattered to her if everyone else was freed.

Silas and Stevie said, in unison, "I'll stay to make sure."

"Me, too," Xariella added, still not fully trusting Stevie or Mitzi. "Cade, you go with them. They may need your protection, and you're the only one that can keep up with Hugh."

Mitzi started on the spell but paused. "Meadow, go with them. You will need to heal her."

"Sister, are you sure?" Mitzi's curt nod was enough for Meadow. She turned and floated alongside Hugh as he carried Zoie in his arms.

She started chanting some stuff in Latin—but Hugh's Latin language skills had been weak due to lack of use, so he had no clue what she was saying. She could be killing Zoie at this point. Still, Hugh just had to trust. He knew that the best thing for Zoie at this point was to let Meadow take care of her. He was playing it fast and loose with trust this day, and it was taking a toll on him, if he was honest with himself about it. Still, with the mating bond, his job was to do what was best for Zoie, no matter the cost to himself.

They continued to run through the graveyard, as the drops of light began to fall again, releasing the gargoyles—all of them. Hugh looked up, letting the light drops hit his face. Even though they were part of the spell that was intended to free the gargoyles from their prison, Hugh could have sworn that they were giving him hope that everything was going to work out—and that Zoie was going to be okay.

While the vast majority of them faded away into dust and ash, some of the prisoners stuck around, trying to adjust to the light and being able to really move. The more that Hugh observed them, that more it seemed that they were able to mentally move around in gargoyle form—they were awake—but they weren't able to physically move. They had been frozen. Prisoners in their own minds.

When they finally got to the gate, Zoie's father was leaning against the wall, struggling. Hugh placed Zoie on a bench while Meadow continued to heal her, and then he went to Victor. "What can I do?"

He shook his head—what was left of it. His skin was falling

away at an alarming rate at this point. "My punishment was to guard this place. Without it, there is no magic to tie me to this world." He reached his hand—just bones, though some of those were even missing at this point—to Hugh. "Take me to my daughter."

Helping Victor up, Hugh carefully guided him to the bench where Zoie was now, slowly, beginning to sit up. Hugh wanted to run to her and hold her, but Victor's time was running out, and not even Zoie could slow things down. They'd passed the point of no return for him.

# ZOIE

Groaning and touching her ribs lightly, Zoie stated, "It feels like I did core workouts for a week straight."

Meadow laughed lightly. "That's how five crunches would feel to me." She touched Zoie's hand. "You are lucky you survived that attack. It has to be because you also wield sun and light powers." She stroked her hair. "It's such a beautiful white mixed in with a beautiful red."

Zoie looked up to see Hugh and her father making their way over. Hugh placed Victor gingerly on the bench next to his daughter. He and Meadow stepped over towards the gate, to help those who were able to escape.

"I am sorry that I left you," Victor said. "I wanted to be there to teach you about magic."

Zoie nodded, not knowing what to say. She honestly didn't know if Victor was sorry to have left her; he planned for it. He found and hired Silas. He put Lettie into place. He could have given up the pendant, but instead stayed tied to this awful place. Still, she had missed him and wished he would have been there to see her grow up.

After an awkward silence, Victor asked, "Your mother… is she…?"

Zoie smiled. "She's mostly happy. She misses you, and she did her best. She's very independent."

He laughed, but it sounded more like a cough. "She was always different. Sometimes a bit difficult. Always chose the harder path." The walls of the graveyard shook. Some bricks crumbled to the ground within the walls.

Zoie ignored the deterioration of the prison. Spending these moments with her father meant more to her—they were all she was ever going to get. Thinking back to what her mother always had said about her being difficult, it was Zoie's turn to laugh. "That's a bit ironic, to be honest."

"She hoped you wouldn't have powers. She wanted all of this to end." His bony hand reached out for Zoie's, but he stopped short of touching her, yet again. His thumb fell off and turned to ash, blowing away in the wind.

To let him know that she wasn't afraid or uncomfortable, Zoie took his hand. "She just wanted to protect us." She turned towards him and placed her free hand on top of their clasped hands. "I can take you to see her. She still lives in our home."

The part of his face that still had skin and muscle smiled. "Zoie." He let out a small chuckle. "I wish we had time for that, but…"

She frowned. "No. Please, no." Her chin started to shake. "I have to take you back with me." Zoie knew, without question, that he was never going to even get up from the bench they were sitting on. "I need you."

He squeezed her hand. "You've never needed me, Zoie. You were always stronger, wiser, braver…" Victor looked in his daughter's eyes, as one of his own faded away from existence. "You became greater than I ever imagined for you, and you did it on your own." What was left of his skin disintegrated in the air, and then his bones followed suit, leaving his clothes in a pile on the bench.

Balling the clothes up and holding them, Zoie sobbed. "No! No! This isn't fair!" His clothes smelled like nothing—not death, not rot, not his aftershave that she remembered from when she was a child—nothing. She continued to sob into them as she rocked back and forth on the bench. "I just got you back. I just…"

She felt a gentle hand on her shoulder and, she instinctively wrapped her arms around the person who had come to her. She had expected Hugh's warmth, but instead, she was met with someone else. Her face was buried in a mess of red hair and gems and stones. "Auntie Lettie?" She paused for a moment and then went back to sobbing into her shoulder.

"It's me. I'm here." Lettie sat down next to Zoie and held her, running her hand through the now much lighter red hair on Zoie's head.

"I thought I would get a little more time." She sat up, rubbing the tears away from her cheeks. "I'm so exhausted, and I didn't get to say anything that I wanted to say to him."

"Hmmm." Lettie smiled gently at Zoie. "Look, we don't know what happens when we really die, but I believe that Victor—your dad—he can hear you. You can say whatever you want to him, at any time." She added, "You just have to believe."

Zoie sighed. "This whole time… I could have been down here, talking to him, getting to know him…" There was just so many regrets running through her mind. "I was really hoping that when we freed everyone, he would become whole again and… and be there to do things that dads do. Like walk me down the aisle and stuff like that." She wiped her cheeks.

Lettie hugged her tightly. "I'm sorry." She repeated softly, "I'm sorry."

Zoie looked up to see dozens of people pouring out of the gates of the graveyard. Many of them looked terrified and confused. Dirty. Exhausted.

She stood up slowly. "We need to help. We need to get these people to a safe place."

"Take it easy, Zoie." Lettie reached out for her, but missed.

Zoie turned to her aunt and nodded. "I will. I promise." She held her ribs while she walked. "But these people need help, and part of why they need that help is because we freed them unexpectedly." She shook her head. "They may not even know what year it is."

Zoie started leading people to places to sit and when she got a group together, she would explain what had happened and how they were going to help them.

They had so many questions—many of which they were not prepared for. Zoie had thought they had prepared, but they weren't even close. There were so many holes in their plans.

One woman asked, "What year is it?", and once Zoie told her, she replied, "I've been locked in there for thirty years. Certainly, my family thinks I'm dead—I have no papers. No home." She took Zoie's hand. "I swear that I didn't do what I was accused of! I didn't make an immortal child."

"I believe you." Zoie paused. "About your other concerns: I'm certain we can get you documents for whatever country is appropriate. And, for housing, we are going to assess what the needs are and we'll develop a plan from there."

She walked towards Hugh because she wanted to discuss the housing crisis—this was a definite crisis—with him. It was something that they hadn't thought of, no matter how many times they talked about this plan. Each step, however, aggravated her injuries. She had to stop and rest regularly.

However, as she walked towards him, someone stopped her and asked how they were going to get through the dark forest. "We're going to work together. We have some people in our group that are knowledgeable of the way through the forest. We'll make sure that everyone gets through." They thanked her; someone else shook her hand; and another gave her a hug. She winced at the touch but did her best not to make anyone feel bad. They had been through enough.

She started back towards Hugh, but another large group came through the gates. Zoie assumed that this would be the last group because Mitzi was with them, and that meant the spell was complete.

As Xariella, Silas, and Stevie came out of the gates, Zoie started to run to them, but she couldn't breathe, so she stopped. Silas ran to her and put his arms around her, causing her to whimper in pain.

He released her. "I'm so sorry."

She out her arms around him and hugged him. "I'll take the pain. I'm so happy you are okay."

He stepped back and smiled at her, laughing. "*You're* happy that *I'm* okay? You are the one that took lightning bolts to your body. Repeatedly."

"You saved me. Even though…" She frowned, remembering that they had broken up. Even though she knew that her future was with Hugh, she was ready to admit that she still wanted one with Silas—if he was willing, of course.

He put his finger over her mouth. "Of course I saved you. I love you." He kissed her gently. "I should never have even pretended that I could walk away from you. From us." He took her hand and put it over his heart. "Commitment to the contract with your father or not—it's always been you for me."

Zoie heard excited clapping from behind her. "I knew you two would eventually admit your feelings for each other," smiled Lettie. She then asked, "How does that all work with Hugh being your bonded mate?" She walked up and linked her arm with Zoie's. "I need to know everything."

It struck Zoie that Lettie was captured and imprisoned before Zoie had returned to Hugh. She patted Lettie's hand. "I promise to tell you everything, but we have hundreds of people to help right now." She turned to Meadow and asked, "Do you think that you could help us lead them through the forest?"

She nodded and smiled. "I would be honored to." Meadow clarified, "But first, I am going to take my sister home so that she can mourn." She reached over and took her sister's hand, pulling her close. She held Mitzi close.

Zoie nodded, sadly. "I understand." She turned to Mitzi, offering her sincere condolences about Thomas. "I am so sorry…"

Mitzi turned away from Zoie and spoke directly to Meadow. She would never acknowledge Zoie's presence again after this day. "I may have helped them release the curse, but I will never forgive that one for taking my Thomas from me forever."

"I know," Meadow replied sadly, and looked at Zoie and mouthed, "I'm sorry." Zoie nodded, understanding that Mitzi had every right to be upset. Zoie had, in fact, been the one to release Thomas.

# HUGH

Feeling the electricity begin to spark within him, Hugh turned around to find Zoie approaching him. He excused himself from the conversation that he was having and took five large steps towards her. "Zo." He gently hugged her, feeling her pain—physical and emotional—before she could even tell him about it. "I am so sorry you didn't have more time with your dad."

"Thank you," she replied, touching his cheek. Her face was full of pain with every movement that she made. "I will mourn about that later. Right now, we have a problem."

He interjected, "Housing."

"Yes. How did we miss that?" She sighed.

Hugh shook his head. "I think it's that I'm privileged to own many homes, and so is Cade. You and Xari are too new into this life to have to move around to different places. Stevie has a palace in the Abyss, where no humans can go." He shrugged and repeated, "It's privilege." He felt horrible about this error in planning. Still, it made him aware of a need, and he wondered if there were more immortal beings who were home insecure. He wanted to do something to make an impact in the supernatural world, and working on solving the housing crisis in their world could make a real impact.

Zoie took his hand. "We'll figure it out." He knew that she was right—they would. They could do anything as long as they were together in it. They had proven that time and time again.

Stevie approached them, with the Guards and the Shrews in tow. "Sorry to interrupt, but I need to get back to the Abyss; lock these ladies up while we decide what to do with them; and tell my mom that my father is dead by my doing and, oh by the way, I'm in charge of the kingdom now." She let out a deep sigh. Delivering that level of news wasn't going to be easy, even with her newly found confidence and sense of purpose.

Hugh asked if there was anything that Stevie needed from him, but the only thing that she could think of was that someone needed to find the vampire from the Council. Hugh suggested that they send a messenger, but be vague in the messaging, and Stevie agreed. He remembered that he had the petition from the vampire who had approached him in NightBrooke. "We will need to discuss this once we get you settled into your new role."

She took the petition from Hugh's hand and read it quickly. "I think we can discuss this change—once we also discuss getting a faerie representative…"

Hugh smiled. "Yes, we need someone to represent all of the beings. It's only fair."

Stevie returned the smile, saying a farewell-for-now to Hugh. "I'm looking forward to mending things in our world with you."

It took them hours to get everyone together and figure out what the needs were, and Meadow returned with a basket of food and water. Hugh wasn't sure how one basket was going to help 214 starving and dehydrated people, but his negative attitude was proven wrong yet again. The basket was enchanted, and as

Meadow emptied it, she would reach in for more and it would appear. Everyone was provided a large reusable bottle of water (that would fill when they reached the bottom), some sandwich that miraculously they would enjoy, fruit, trail mix, and a granola bar. Between that and Silas' bag that replicated things, they were able to take care of everyone.

After everyone was fed, Meadow began to lead them all through the forest, towards Nightbrooke, and almost everyone made quick work of it, wanting to get back to the world that they had been isolated from—some for decades.

Meadow's hair was only stepped on three times, and only one person had begun to deviate from the path. That person was guided back by Hugh, who acted more like a sheepdog than a wolf, as they led everyone through the dark, sick-looking trees.

Nightbrooke was crowded and chaotic, people running everywhere. It was no surprise to Hugh that some headed directly to the tavern. He couldn't help but chuckle to himself—but where were some of them going to get the funds to pay for a drink? Did they have secret hiding places for their coin under a floorboard in one of the old buildings?

He looked around to make sure that his friends were all safe, when he saw Cade standing alone, arms folded across their chest. "What's going on?"

Cade nodded his head towards Xariella and one of the vampires that they had freed from the Gargoyle Graveyard. "Tafari."

Hugh smiled and nudged Cade. "You don't have anything to worry about. She isn't going to choose him over you."

Cade grinned. "Of course not. But I still don't like the guy. He… he tricked her into this world, and…" They paused. "Oh my fucking god, I'm starting to sound like you. 'Let her have a choice' and all that shit you spouted when you met Zoie." Cade's eyes got huge and then they rolled them. "What does this mating bond do to us?" The two of them laughed together.

Hugh responded, "I'm glad you finally understand it."

Cade put their hands up. "I'm not saying that I understand it at all." They laughed and then continued, "I just know how I feel about Xari, but that doesn't mean I have an understanding about it at all."

"I'm honestly not sure that there's more to understand than that—those feelings." He admitted, "There were points today that I was so terrified that I was going to lose Zoie again. Points that I wanted to choose to protect her, but it would have jeopardized everything." Hugh said, "I went against all of my instincts as her mate."

Cade shook their head. "No, you didn't. It's amazing how fast you can think about all of the different timelines that could occur based on the decisions you need to make to protect your mate."

Hugh nodded. "I saw myself choosing her and still failing. So many times, all in a fraction of a second." He admitted, "It was terrifying."

"That's what I mean, though—I don't understand how we could do that now, but couldn't ever before." They asked, still keeping one eye on Xariella, "Like, where did that skill come from?"

Hugh chuckled. "The mating bond." He continued, "It comes with the mating bond. The moment we touch our mate, it's ignited."

Cade shook their head. "So it's in us, all this time—for you, nearly 200 years—but it takes someone else to bring it out? I just don't get that."

"Well, we have time to figure it out." Hugh started to think about what he wanted to do now that they'd completed this mission and all of his powerful enemies were silenced. He figured that he would have to discuss it with Zoie, but it had been a while since he had done research on werewolves and their genetic makeup. Maybe it was time to find out more about the mating bond.

Still, he had to put that to the back of his mind. Hugh knew that he had a lot of work to do with getting these victims taken care of. There was getting them documents, for starters. Then there was finding housing for them—that was the big job.

"We have eternity to figure out—or, more likely for me, *not* figure out—this mating bond." They laughed, still never losing focus on Xariella and Tafari. Changing the subject, Cade asked, "Do you think all of them will even want our help?"

Hugh shook his head. "No. Some of them, like Lettie, haven't been gone that long. Some of them have immortal family. Others have already set themselves up for success."

"Some of them may not trust us."

"Some saw me standing on that stage when they became gargoyles." Hugh admitted, "I wouldn't blame them for not trusting me."

Cade put their hand on Hugh's shoulder to comfort him. "We'll get them all taken care of."

He hoped that Cade was right. He wanted to take a moment, though, in all of the chaos, to not think about it. "Once we get all of these people settled, what is your plan?" Hugh asked, hoping that Cade wouldn't want to be away from him long. He needed his best friend more than he was willing to admit.

Cade shrugged. "Xari and I haven't talked about that much yet. She told me that she's always wanted to go to Bermuda but…"

"Don't we risk ourselves enough, without going to the places that humans have legends about—for good reason?" Hugh nudged them. "I don't want to hear news of your ship getting lost in the Bermuda Triangle."

Cade chuckled. "You won't." They shoved their hands in their pockets, glancing back at Xariella and Tafari. "Oh, I almost forgot." Cade held out their hands, waiting for Hugh to react. "I need to give you something." Hugh finally held his hand out and Cade dropped the pendants in it. "I think you and Zoie should decide what to do with these. You being on the Council and all." Explaining why there were only three pendants, they said, "Mitzi took hers back."

Hugh reluctantly took them and shoved them in his pocket. "I don't know that we should decide unilaterally what is done with them, but…" He nodded. "We'll figure it out." Since Thomas was resting properly, there was no reason to keep them separated anymore. Hugh was more concerned with the grimoires, which were protected by magic and couldn't be destroyed. Still, there was no place that was safe—in the entire world—from the supernatural. There wasn't anywhere that someone couldn't get to. Still, Hugh felt that it was a matter for the new Council.

# Epilogue

It took months for Hugh and Zoie to find housing for everyone that they released from the Gargoyle Graveyard, but eventually they were down to less than a handful that still needed steady work and housing, and Hugh knew the perfect place for them.

He led them through Nightbrooke to a portal that was a large unicorn statue on a standing stone. It wasn't easy to get to, though. They had to cross a loch by first taking a rickety old wooden bridge to a small island and then hopping from one moss covered rock to another, all while the mist hung heavy over the water. Finally, as they reached the other side of the loch, they could hear the sound of bagpipes playing.

The stone pulled Hugh towards it, as if there was a rope connecting him to it and he had no choice but to let it take him. The pull seemed natural. Effortless.

He placed his hand to the stone and then was sucked through into the darkness, only to find himself moments later in a green field, breathing in the cool, crisp air. Hugh looked up to the sky, mostly covered in a blanket of white clouds, and smiled. He turned to see the mountains and then looked to his other side and felt his heart lift at the sight of the purple heather, growing in random clumps as far as his eyes—enhanced by his wolf abilities—could see.

Reaching behind him instinctively, he took Zoie's hand in his. With her free hand, she removed her headphones and then pressed pause on her cassette player—"Man Eater" by Hall & Oates stopped abruptly.

Hugh let out a deep breath that he had been unknowingly holding, and he felt his entire body relax—truly relax—for the first time in decades. "Scotland."

Zoie reached over and placed her hand on his forearm. "How does it feel to be home?"

The wind picked up and flung Zoie's hair into her face, stinging her with each whip against her skin. In fact, one bit nearly went down her throat due to the force behind the wind.

Hugh took an extra hair tie that was on his wrist and handed it to Zoie. "It was always a joke that I put my hair up in battle, but it all started because I was battling the winds here in the Highlands."

She pulled her hair into a messy bun on the top of her head and then turned to the group behind them. "Hugh's going to lead us. It shouldn't be long now." She looked at him. "About how long?"

He pointed. "Do you see that castle way down there?"

Zoie squinted. "No…"

He laughed. "We have a long way to go." He turned to the group. "How many of you have the gift of speed?" Two motioned. "Could you carry others?" There were only four of them, so if they could, Hugh could carry Zoie and the other two could each carry someone. Still, he didn't know their speed or skill level, so it could end up being a disaster.

A small faerie stepped forward. "Forgive me sir, but I don't have great speed, but I can take someone with me via transport. I just have to have been that place first."

Hugh shook his head, refusing the offer. After what happened to Beagan, he would never risk that again, possibly even if it was absolutely required for survival. "No, Shayleigh. That won't be necessary."

Hugh decided that it would be better to walk. While Zoie could heal someone's sprained ankle, she couldn't bring someone back from the dead if they would twist their ankle and go spiraling down the mountain and crack their head on a rock. He didn't want to risk the lives of four people that just got out of a decades long dark purgatory.

The group of them worked their way through the rocky hills and green fields. It took them hours to get to a place where the castle felt like it wasn't actually getting further away with each step.

"This castle," Zoie asked, "is this where you grew up?"

Hugh thought for a moment. "Not exactly." As they walked, he asked, "Do you see the little shack-looking thing way off to the right?" He zeroed in on it. "That the roof is no longer present on?" When she acknowledged it, he continued. "That's where I grew up. My family helped work the farmland here."

"I thought you said that the castle was yours?"

He smiled. "It is." He explained, "I purchased it. The previous owner had fallen onto rough financial times and sold it as a last resort. I bought it so that no one would lose their jobs or their land."

"When was the last time that you were here?" She asked, as they continued to walk. They would periodically check the group behind them to make sure that everyone was safe.

Hugh didn't respond. It had been decades. He wondered if the staff would even know him. He hadn't changed much in the time that he had been gone, but they certainly have. Some of them may have died and he didn't even know. He didn't take the opportunity to celebrate their lives with those close to them. He made a silent promise to never be gone so long again.

They finally arrived at the door of the castle, and the entire staff was outside, lined up, waiting for them. As head of household stood Fiona, a werewolf that Hugh had met and helped shortly after she had turned for the very first time.

She looked the same as they day they had met—except she had changed her hairstyle. Where the long black locks had been were replaced with a short bob. Otherwise, she was unchanged over the last 40 or 50 years.

"Fiona!" He smiled, walking towards her.

"Master Hugh." She nodded. "We believe that we've kept the place in top shape since you've been gone. I hope that you find everything up to standard."

He nodded in return. Fiona was always very serious about her work and the chance that Hugh had given her. She wanted as normal life as she could have, not having to move around every few years because she didn't age. When Hugh suggested that she work for him, it was a perfect opportunity for her.

She then took the time to introduce all of the new faces, and Hugh then did the same with his group, explaining the purpose of their visit—his hopes that they could restore or build homes on the property and have jobs either in the village or at the castle. They were, of course, free to go at any time.

Then, Hugh proudly introduced Zoie. "My fiancée."

Fiona clapped excitedly. "Will we be having the wedding at the castle?" She didn't wait for an answer. "Of course, you will!" She turned to Zoie. "I will be at your service any time you need me, ma'am."

"For now, though" Hugh interjected, not wanting Zoie to feel rushed into making a decision on the wedding, "will you help everyone get settled? Zoie and I have something to attend to first, though."

He took Zoie's hand and lead her behind the castle to a small graveyard.

Zoie paused. "Hugh, don't you think…"

"…that we've spent enough time in a graveyard lately?" He chuckled and then said, "I wanted to do a couple things here. Visit my parents, stuff like that." Hugh continued, "You don't have to come."

She hadn't thought about how he might miss his parents. Because they had been gone long before Zoie had even been born, they had never been a feature during her relationship with Hugh. "Ohhhhh." Zoie followed him in.

This graveyard was much different from the one that they had freed the gargoyles from. This one, while the grief that naturally hung over a graveyard was there, still had a sense of ease and calm about it. The smell of the heather. The sound of sheep disapproving of being herded in the distance. The wind rustling the leaves and branches.

Where Hugh was standing, there were three stone grave markers. She didn't remember him ever mentioning a sibling, so she was curious. Stepping closer to him to get a better look, her nosiness caused a cold to wash over her. She let out a small gasp, despite doing her best to not react.

The first two stones marked his parents, Alan and Ethel, as expected. The third, however, was not something that Zoie had ever expected to see in her entire life: Hugh's.

He touched the stone for his father, and then turned to Zoie to explain the one with his name etched into it. "I make the assumption that they put that there after they couldn't find me."

"There's no date of death." She asked, "Do you think maybe they knew?"

He shook his head. "No, but I think they just had hope I would return to them someday." He pulled a stone out of his pocket. "Just one thing before we go."

Hugh walked over to an empty space and knelt down. Placing the smooth stone on ground, he whispered, "I'll bring more to make a proper cairn for you, Beagan."

"A cairn?" Zoie asked, kneeling next to her fiancé.

He took her hand in his. "It's a pile of stones—a marker. Sometimes it's in a stack. We place them to honor our dead."

"Beagan meant a lot to you?"

He nodded. "She was brave. Courageous. She didn't even fear death; that's why she gave everything for us. Because she knew if we freed the prisoners, we could free the faeries too." Hugh shed a tear as he placed his hand on the stone again. "Your sacrifice won't be forgotten, Beagan. I promise." The wind took his tear before it could reach his chin. "I will continue to fight for the equality that you dreamed of."

He had already begun the fight. Upon Stevie's taking her place on the Council, they decided to replace the Shrews and to add the Faeries, too. They freed the faeries that had been imprisoned. When they announced all of the changes, they let the supernatural world know what had been going on, and introduced a democratic method for council members. With Hugh being elected to lead the Council, he knew that he could enact real change, and he planned to. Still, he vowed that he wouldn't overstay his welcome on the Council; when he was no longer effective or what was needed, he would step back.

He stood up and then helped Zoie back to her feet. They walked out of the graveyard, and he put his arm around her as they paused to look out over the green field and the castle. The wind whipped around them, slapping the tall grass against their jeans.

"Would you be opposed to staying here for a while?" Hugh requested.

Zoie looked up at him and smiled. "I would love to make a home here with you, Hugh Davies."

He placed a gentle kiss on the top of her head. "Home," he whispered, with a smile.

Hugh felt even more at ease than he did when he first stepped through the portal. After more than 150 years of running and reinventing himself, he was back where it all started—where he always belonged—standing on the land that was his home, holding the person that his heart called home in his arms.